THE CHRONICLES OF CAIN

THE CHRONICLES OF CAIN

Battle of Ages: Book Two

A Novel By Ken Branscum

iUniverse, Inc.
New York Lincoln Shanghai

The Chronicles of Cain
Battle of Ages: Book Two

iUniverse books may be ordered through booksellers or by contacting:

iUniverse
2021 Pine Lake Road, Suite 100
Lincoln, NE 68512
www.iuniverse.com
1-800-Authors (1-800-288-4677)

ISBN-13: 978-0-595-38255-2 (pbk)
ISBN-13: 978-0-595-67608-8 (cloth)
ISBN-13: 978-0-595-82625-4 (ebk)
ISBN-10: 0-595-38255-X (pbk)
ISBN-10: 0-595-67608-1 (cloth)
ISBN-10: 0-595-82625-3 (ebk)

Printed in the United States of America

This Book is Dedicated to,
the two most important women in my life.

To my immortal beloved,
Your delicate, pristine facade must arouse the jealousy of the angels themselves.
You are the very vision of beauty and everything that a woman should be.
And I am the luckiest man in the world to have you love me,
You will always have my mind, my heart and my soul,
I love you today tomorrow and forever.
And if I lived a forever you would always be my one and my only true love.

You are everything a man could dream of in a woman,
Even though you are stubborn and drive me crazy some days,
I can only think of two things to change about you,
One that you will always be healthy,
And two that you will always be happy.

With all my love,

Ken

For Kristen,
The heavens above are jealous! The stars feel outclassed! That shiny angel on
the Christmas tree has met her match at last!

And I can assure you that there are people green with envy too…because
none of THEM have ever brightened up my life like YOU!

Love you,

Ken

Contents

Cast of Characters and Titles

Ackilon—Title of a priest in training

Ambala—Mira's daughter

Amun—A divine being

Anander—Priest of set

Anubis—A divine being

Barinka—Vine Mother

Bendilho—Priest of Set

Blood Mother—General of the goddess' army

Bryleder—Priest of Set

Cain—Brother of Able and observer/watcher

Celeste—Blood Mother

Dalinar—Leader that replaces Schilo

Death Mother—Title of the leader of the women's order

Drum Mother—Title of the head of the drummers

Duncan—Young archeologist

Eoolos—Priest of Set

Gammaw—Storyteller

Geb—A divine being

Harvest King—Ritual title bestowed once a year

Horus—Son of Isis and Osiris

Isis/Goddess/Hag/Kali—Mother of the world/Osiris wife

Joli—Drum Mother

Joseph—In charge of the workers at the dig

Kamet—Lion sent to destroy the men in the mountains

Kerschwin—Priestess of Isis at Mohibhar

Lalton—Noble Man

Laurentilo—Set's assassin assigned to protect Rau

Leon—Noble Man who sacrifices himself

Lotara—Priestess of Isis

Lucas—Joli's Lover

Meander—slave/Schilo's son

Mira—Death Mother and leader of Thera

Mornia—priestess at Mohibhar

Osiris—Father of the world/Isis husband

Polander—Schilo's teacher

Ra—Sun god/child of Isis

Rau—Set's Chosen

Schilo—Set's Chosen/Dying Priest

Set—Brother of Osiris/God of the Men's sect

Sobec/Tristen—A cursed man who befriends Duncan

Tezable—Young priest accompanying Schilo

Zadog—Leader of the Noble Men

Zu—Brother of Set's chosen

The Word of Set

The ground shook as the god strode toward the man through the swirling incense. Heat from the god's great belly set the air to shimmering and the perspiration to rolling down Rau's muscular back as he crouched before the god. Roiling from the god's mouth, the heavy musk struck Rau like a paralyzing fog. Even so, Rau knew what it was the god intended and offered himself willingly to his demands, horrific as those might seem to an ordinary observer. Oceanic power gripped Rau's shoulders, and he found himself penetrated to the deepest foundations of his being, found himself penetrated by the wisdom which spring forth from the god. He found himself swept away as he opened himself to the god. When the god gave him back his body, Rau knew what had to be done, he saw the missing men, knew who was responsible, a chorus of voices sang within him willing him to complete his task, renewed and strengthened. About him the odor of Set seemed to come and go as a needle will turn to the magnetic north when north is sought.

In the ancient darkness of the shelf of sacrifice Rau held his ritual position as sweat poured off him. Had someone looked in on him, a lambent darkness would have been seen to fill the chamber in which he stood and his raspy breathing would have been mistaken for animal noises. With an unnatural suddenness, Rau shivered violently and stood ungracefully, as if he had just wrenched himself free of a grim encounter. No one would call Rau tall, but his lack of height was not noticeably a defect. Shuddering from the sudden cold of this subterranean room, Rau stood in the darkness.

As he collapsed the fourteen caught him and carried him to the stone of surrender. There they began the rituals of radiance. Rau was trying to make sense of this powerful possession, trying to remember indelibly, trying to make tangible the god in whose service he stood, alone, in need, and filled with power undreamed of and yet hollow as an oyster shell after the starfish has finished his meal. Seldom had the god taken him with such anger and rage. Rau's heavily muscled form trembled. His fists clenched and unclenched as he slowly assumed the posture of reception stretching his muscles languidly but with meaningful purpose.

Throwing on a mantle, he emerged from the sacred springs and the fourteen. He pushed open the heavy oak door, loped across the temple precincts, pausing only a moment in the middens. Animal needs remedied, his god's needs still unsatisfied, he walked into the courtyard like some dark predator in search of prey. Rau crossed to the training school where he knew he would find what he was looking for.

There in the combats, he found the sky clad form of his brother giving instruction to the initiates. For a while, he stood listening, watching the amazing form of his brother's body, his rippling chest, his radiant long hair of the assassin's guild, his uncut warrior, as he lectured about the skill of changing strokes.

"Remember," Zu said "you are in control of your own body. You are the only one who knows how the treasure moves in your loins. Your adversary will attempt to distract you, to amaze you, to divert your attention from this all important movement of your soul's substance. If she can distract you she can have what she wants more than anything else, your treasure. But you can frustrate her. Change your attack. Plunge in deeply knock on the very door to the bright chamber itself. And stay there. Arch your back; raise your feet off the bed. Put all your weight on the attack. Let her feel the mass of your body foisted on this one point. Then ease out slowly, when your treasure ceases to churn begin again, this time with a new pattern of thrusts, taken from the forty two. Perhaps the two shallow one deep thrust, perhaps the short stitches, perhaps the dove's wings maneuver. Your choice, vary it, never take the same stratagem twice. Keep her off balance always building towards releasing her jade flows. Breathe. Remember to breathe. Sometimes the battle moves so fast you will not remember to breathe. Alright now, let's go back to the mats." Zu noticed his brother standing in the back of the combat floor and motioned to one of the other instructors to take his place before he came to Rau. Rau looked different, Zu decided. Something had happened. What he wondered?

Rau and Zu embraced like brothers, like lovers, like twins bonded beyond mere kinship. "Tell me brother what has happened," Zu asked.

Rau hesitated. Even in ordinary embrace Rau noticed Zu's body bespoke an unnatural grace. They fit together these bodies in the easy embrace of twins as Rau hesitated to answer. There was in this moment of hesitation, love for his brother and a reluctance to risk on such a mission the joy he took in his brother's presence. But the breath of the god coiled around his ears again, and Rau knew there was no choice in the matter. Gripping Zu's shoulders and caressing them at the same time Rau pushed him away gently, reluctantly.

"Brother, I have something important for you."

"What is so important, Rau, that you could not wait until I had finished teaching?"

"I have had a disturbing and unusually powerful sending from Set. A possession unlike any I have ever known. I am charged with a task and you are a part of it, my brother."

Suddenly intrigued and fearful that he may offend the god whom they both had served since the earliest days of their youth, Zu was keenly alert now. He asked with a soft voice, "You've had encounters before, what makes this one so potent?" Then with growing curiosity he cleared his voice and asked, "What kind of task?"

"We must make our way to a city called Cassoria. You must leave soon before me. I will bring up the army behind you. Set and the other gods are assembling a company of heroes who will call themselves the 'Shadow Company.' Zu, the great Isis herself is the quarry. We are going to attack her at the source of her poison; you will be part of the advance guard. Your task is to seek out the goddess, to reconnoiter her defenses and to await my armies so we can obliterate her in her ultimate seat of power. The gods are coming to me, all of them. Only Osiris hangs back now. Even Ged has come with his earth power and longs to see Isis restored to harmony with the gods. There is such urgency in this quest that although I can not go with you now, Set has commanded that you must make all speed to depart. As soon as I have made the preparations that Set has commanded of me, I will follow you with the god's speed."

Zu groaned inwardly, but knew that there was to be no argument. There never was with the gods. He'd known they had not found the source of the Hag's power, of course, but the name Cassoria meant nothing to him. Rau moved to Zu's side as if to stroke his hair which now that he had long kept his shorn, seemed more beautiful than he remembered. Instead he playfully grabbed a handful and spun Zu about; Rau pushed him to the door and planted a foot in his backside.

"I mean now, before you literally become the father of our country, you breeder of all the world's wenches." Zu tumbled towards the door, caught himself and stretched in the cool morning air. Rau was always amazed by the radiance of Zu's body. How the gods danced in his flesh. He was almost too beautiful for manhood, but his armored warrior screamed otherwise. Zu flexed his back and made menacing but playful gestures at Rau, "I will now dress to meet the morning maidens of the outer world. Perhaps I shall leave a trail of yelping infants behind me to mark my path if you are too slow to follow. Tell me where I must go and what dangers I may encounter."

The two brothers fell to playful battery, pawing and punching as they used to do as lads playing in the new morning straw. The two were close; it was easy to tell as much. Rau clearly knew what he risked for Set as there was much about the playfulness that carried deep sorrow only a father could have seen. Rau stopped suddenly when he breathed in Set's aroma: He knew the time for sacrifice was at hand.

"When you have dressed brother, come to me, and I will equip you, instructions and such arms as will serve you well in this task." With that Rau strode out of the training ground and was gone. Zu watched him go, watched his other half go, vulnerable without him, and watched himself now vulnerable without Rau. Even so he went one last time to lay in the summer sun with one of the willing women of Set's temple. Though his public lovemaking was a private scandal, no one ever spoke of it since it was beauty itself uniting with mortality, or so they all said when they were privileged to witness it. And today Zu did not care who saw.

Tristen, Warrior of Visions

The vial looked small, harmless, yet the green gray glass sparkled with color. Tristen saw many such vials and containers in the apothecary shop, it was not for them he came. But if he were forced to tell the truth at the point of a sharp object, he'd probably tell a different story. He told himself, it was Elizabeth he was interested in. Elizabeth of the golden eyes. Elizabeth of the pungent kisses. Elizabeth of liquid dreams. Tristen prided himself on being always ready. He ate all meals as if he were training for his last battle. He dressed always as if he were going to fight to the death. He rode as if he were riding to battle. He made sure his muscles were always tight, his sinews flexible. If he had no adversary to meet, why then he spent three hours in sword practice with his father's sword master. If his father's sword master had other things to do, then he would spend three hours in hand to hand combat with his father's master of weapons. If his father's master of weapons was otherwise occupied too, he would swim across the lake and back. Always it was the brink Tristen lived for. And it showed. Not that he was a strutting braggart. But in his walk and posture in everything he said, in each gesture, there was hidden a sharp knife poised at the ready.

While Elizabeth's uncle was his father's master healer, her father had learned the healing arts from a different angle. He was a master herbalist, some said a sorcerer, and if by sorcerer was meant a man who knows how to used herbal preparations and concoctions from animal sources to heal or sooth or change people's moods. Then, yes, he was a sorcerer. His most sought after product was a particular love potion made from the venom of snakes and certain funguses only he knew. If the beloved did not respond to this drought, they died. So it was not only a love potion, it was also love's revenge. Older men also sought out Elizabeth's father, Jaccobus, because it was said he could make old men perform like young men. And so he could. But it was also said he could make young men perform like demons in battle. This is what excited Tristen's imagination. How would it be if there were a potion he could take just before battle which would give him the strength of ten men, the speed of the cobra, and the concentration of the hawk? And Jaccobus had just such a potion, he knew because he over heard Jaccobus and his brother talking about one ingredient which the potion needed, an ingredient so rare as to render the mixture impossible. This ingredient was bear gall, and not just any bear gall, but the gall of the mountain silver-back. Tristen knew that the silver-back was an awe inspiring creature, said to be responsible for more deaths in the mountains than any other save, perhaps avalanche in winter.

Tristen waited his time, and this evening before Elizabeth was to arrive he had set himself to talk to Jaccobus. Jaccobus was a quiet man around customers, but he liked Tristen, indeed he hoped Tristen might one day give him grandsons.

"Jaccobus," Tristen called out. "Jaccobus, are you back there?" The curtains which separated the workroom from the front of the apothecary shop parted to permit the entrance of a small man completely bald, but with the most gigantic mustaches in four kingdoms.

"Ah Tristen," said Jaccobus, "Elizabeth isn't here yet, she'll be along shortly, just be patient."

"Jaccobus, it is not about Elizabeth I've come, it's about bear gall."

"Good lord," said Jaccobus, "do you have ambitions to be an apothecary? Just what do you know about bear gall?"

"I know enough to know it is rare, dangerous to acquire and important for a certain potion I am interested to obtain," said Tristen.

"Just how do you know about this potion?" Jaccobus asked, his eyes narrowing as he stared at Tristen.

"I'm not a fool, Jaccobus, I have ears, and I have masters of the martial sciences who teach me what I have to learn. And I know the potion exists. I know you know how to make it. I know you haven't made any for a long time because you haven't any silver-back bear gall."

Jaccobus sucked in his breath and said quietly, "so you know the silver-back? Do you also know what this potion does? Do you also know its side effects?

"I know it makes you stronger than ten men. I know it gives you great agility. I know it gives you ferocity of purpose," said Tristen.

"All these and more, it gives. But once you start to take it you can never be without it. It is terribly addictive. Moreover, it makes you prone to murderous rages, rages that are beyond any reasoning to stop. Oh Tristen, please do not ask me more about this potion. It is a secret art I learned long ago from a forbidden source. I would not have you bitten by its venom. Look, let me confide in you. You know you love my Elizabeth, I know she loves you. I hope you two will be happy, but those hopes will be dashed if you seek this potion. You will hardly be fit for either fathering or for husbanding if you learn its bright song."

The old man had grown very quiet, a tear curled at the edge of one eye. He had no other daughters. His only son had been died in infancy a year before he found Elizabeth. Elizabeth was his only hope for an old age surrounded by grandchildren.

"What if I get you the gall, will you make me the potion?"

"First, the gall of one adult silver-back will make about a royal measure of the potion if, that is, you kill the bear in the early morning before it has eaten. Gall collected from a bear after it has eaten is very poor and low in volume. Secondly, you must kill the bear silently. If the bear gets angry or in a rage, it can flush the gall through its system. There can be no confrontation with the bear."

"So how do you kill it then?"

"Ah, you still want to collect it? What if I offer you a potion which will enable you to make love all night without failing? Or a potion which will enable you to see in the darkest night, as if it were noon? What about a potion which will cure any poison you might encounter? Or a potion which will make any person you give it to tell you the absolute truth? There is even a potion I have which can make you irresistible to any woman you wish to sample. Wouldn't these satisfy your longing for victory in battle? These are not addictive, and they have few side effects. Can't I talk you out of your longing for the Fire Cup?"

"Is that what it's called, the Fire Cup?" asked Tristen.

"So my teacher said it was called anciently," Jaccobus said without emotion. "It has one last side effect, Tristen. It will make you unable to sire children."

"It won't make me unable to perform, will it?" Tristen asked shaken.

"No, it may even improve that function, but no children will ever result from such encounters with the fair sex," sighed Jaccobus.

"Great, just what I want. Now where are these bears and how do I kill them?"

Jaccobus went to the back of his shop and came out with a razor sharp wolf's rib bone, about three inches long and a piece of pig white meat. "First, you must find where the bears are hibernating. Then you must go there in early spring just as the bears are coming out of their long sleep. This bone tucked inside pig fat must be placed in their runs. One will eat it.

Three days later, it will begin to growl with pain. Its droppings will be filled with blood. You must follow this bleeding bear until it drops dead, but it must never see you. The bile sack will be distended with bile since it cannot eat but will try to digest its own blood.

When the bear falls for the last time you must take it before it is dead, and split open its belly. The bile sac must be unbroken and placed in this horn container. If you can bring this to me I can make the potion. But what will you give me for my art?" Asked Jaccobus.

"What do you want? Tristen whispered daring to think what might be asked.

"I want a grandson," said the old man looking at Tristen with steely gray eyes.

"And I want him to have clear title to your lands and estates and your royal lineage."

"You're not asking much are you," said Tristen.

"No more than your father would want, though I doubt it is my family he would be allied with, if he had his choice."

"You shall have what you want, old man, but when she is with child and when you have the gall, you must make as much of the potion as you can, and reserve it entirely for me. Moreover, I will have the other potions too. In addition, you must mount an expedition after I have left to secure more gall, as I do not think I'll be supplying you with a second sac."

"How will your father know the child is yours," asked Jaccobus.

After a long pause in which the room grew very silent, Tristen finally gave his reply. "I will leave Elizabeth my signet, and a last will and testament declaring her my wife and the child my heir. You will have to secure three notables to witness my signature."

The two men stared at each other for a long time in complete silence. It was a silence which was only broken by the gaiety of Elizabeth as she entered the shop. What followed in those snowy months was only what they had agreed to, a quiet marriage, a legal will witnessed by the Mayor, the sword master and the weapons master, all sworn to abject secrecy, and an expedition into the wilderness as the snow pack began to breakup in early March.

Elizabeth

Soranta had been running for days the cursed bastard's of Set's chosen's had their trackers hunting her and her precious bundle that she kept close to her chest. Soranta knew there was not enough time to reach the great temple. Already the strength was leaving her legs, the pain in her chest enormous, the lesions on her back were terrifically painful as the cloth of her cloak rubbed against them with each step she took forward.

Finally, in a last desperate act she found a one of the old sacred sentinels and gave her treasure up to its protection. A silent prayer to the goddess came to her lips unbidden as she lay down her burden and fled. Soranta longed for the quiet she knew was upon her. When it took her its great black iridescent wings, talons breaking her spine as it took her, it covered her in shadow: its great red beak slashed just once as she stared into her gentle and forgiving eyes.

Soranta ran until there was no running left in her. In her arms a precious bundle was pressed close to her chest. Soranta knew there was not enough time to reach the great temple. Already the strength was leaving her legs, the pain in her chest enormous, the lesions on her back were terrifically painful as the cloth of her cloak rubbed against them with each step she took forward. Finally, in a last desperate act she found a one of the old sacred sentinels and gave her treasure up to its protection.

A silent prayer to Isis came to her lips unbidden as she lay down her burden and fled. Soranta longed for the quiet she knew was upon her. When it took her its great black iridescent wings, talons breaking her spine as it took her, it covered her in shadow. Its great red beak slashed just once as she stared into her gentle and forgiving eyes.

         *   *   *

What she was, no one knew. The young Jaccobus had found her squalling beneath a great yew tree deep in the forest where he had gone to collect medicinal plants. She was wrapped in emerald green cloth, which looked to Jaccobus as if it had been torn from a court gown. There was a lapis pin which fastened the swaddling clothes into a neat bundle, a lapis butterfly. She was a beautiful infant the bluest eyes, and wisps of brilliantly blond hair. Jaccobus who had never married knew instantly what she would become, his hope for a happy old age surrounded by family he himself could never produce.

Elizabeth had grown into a beautiful woman. She was intelligent and warm. She loved games and physical sport. But she was especially wise about men. She knew how to charm them, she knew how to please them, and she knew which ones she should avoid and which to encourage. Before she was fourteen all the men in the town loved her, as they would their own daughter. Of her father, she could not get enough. She learned his craft and especially loved going with him into the forest to collect herbs, fungus and various barks and insects. Old Jaccobus regularly thanked whatever gods had set her in his path for their great good fortune.

It may be supposed therefore, that as Tristen grew it was no accident that his eye should fall on Elizabeth. What prince would not wish such a woman at his side? But of suitors she had plenty and Tristen's marriage was already the subject of political matchmaking. It was hopeless, the young warrior knew, but not beyond possibility either. At least he could have her as his lover; at least he could make her his own regardless of his state obligations. Every prince needed a consort and an herbalist. Or so he thought.

Elizabeth had not been displeased at Tristen's advances. What young woman would not be flattered by the heir to the throne's attention? But she was determined not to fall prey to his advances without exacting something in return. So she played him like an angler plays a fish, she cast the bait; she let out plenty of line and waited. The bait had not lingered in the water long, for prince Tristen and taken it almost immediately.

The invitation to accompany her into the forest to add to the shop's stock of medicinal plants and insects and small animals, was a godsend to Tristen. He dreamt of taking her under a waterfall. He dreamt of rolling her in the fragrant grasses and ferns. He dreamt of her ivory skin next to his and the longing grew into an obsession. Their outings were always curious, as Elizabeth never went without an old serving woman to help carry their gatherings. The old woman was not someone Tristen had anticipated, but to be near Elizabeth he would accept any encumbrance.

Slowly she began to share some of her father's lore with Tristen, but only what the thought nearly everyone else already knew anyway. Once he complained of a headache and she pealed off the bark of a large white tree growing by a stream, let it steep in the water for a moment to soften it, and said "Here chew on this, it will relieve your head's ache."

Tristen was quick to pick up the line, "What does my lady have for heart ache then?"

"Well there's Rue tea, or Heart's thorn poultice. Many things can stop a man's heart from its ache. What do you think causes yours?" She asked feigning her father's professional tones.

"Ah," said Tristen "My heart aches for the caress of a beautiful woman, for the tender words of a fair maiden."

"Well that shouldn't be hard for a prince to secure. Let's see there's the Lady Melinda. She would give you both and probably a little more from beneath her skirts if you began to bleed. I imagine her skirts could make quite a nice bandage for your wounds."

"You're a cruel woman, Elizabeth. You know very well the words I want to hear, and from whose lips I want to hear them," Said Tristen.

Elizabeth looked for a diversion, and found it in an oak full of mistletoe. "Look Tristen, mistletoe. I must have some; did you think to bring your bow?"

"No bow, no arrows either, only a heart willing to serve his love."

"Well then, perhaps I could climb up there it doesn't seem too difficult. It is a big tree. The limbs look sturdy," said Elizabeth looking up as if measuring the best way up the tree.

"It will take sturdier limbs than yours, though they might be very pretty. Let me see if a prince can secure his love's delight."

With that Tristen scrambled up the trunk of the tree using the rope from his saddle as a brace thrown around the girth of the great oak. When he approached the first major limbs, he called down. "Which one shall I take, Elizabeth?" Where is the most mistletoe?

"To your left," she called back.

Up Tristen climbed, his thin acrobat's frame seemed perfect for tree climbing stressing the increasingly thin branches less than a heavier man might have. Finally, he came to the first big growth which he cut with his dagger. The branches fell into Elizabeth's out stretched skirts. "That's enough, please come down."

"Hold out your skirts and I too will fling myself into them," said the prince in jest. "Watch yourself; I have a thorn that might prick your tender skin."

Elizabeth was about to call back a merry quip when she and her maid servant were rushed by two men who had been watching from the heavy undergrowth. The old woman tried to protect her charge, but was paid for her office with a dagger thrust to the throat. As she lay bleeding out her life on the ground, Elizabeth stood stock still as if struck to stone. Somehow she knew these men. But she had never seen them in her life.

"Come my lady, we've found you at last," said the largest man fingering the lapis butterfly at her throat.

They however, had not counted on Tristen who was always ready for a fight, even when he was high in an oak tree. Seemingly from out of now where

Tristen landed squarely in the middle of the large man's back. He heard bone crush as the man's chest struck the ground and Tristen's weight pressed him down. He never stirred again. Tristen rolled and was on his feet, dagger in hand ready for the second man in a heart beat.

"You do not know what you attack, my lord," said the second man.

"I know that you have my friend there and have killed her maid. What more do I need to know, do you think?" Said Tristen.

As the man tried to answer Tristen's dagger appeared in his throat and the second man fell silent gasping out his life on the body of the old woman, his first victim.

"Who were they, Tristen? What did they want? They acted as if they knew me?" sobbed Elizabeth who had come out of her stony trance abruptly.

"I don't know. Let's see if they bear any marks of identification.

As Tristen examined their bodies one thing became very evident, they were from the Hag's guard. Their bodies were marked with the blue chevrons of her guards, and what's more they'd been unspeakably mutilated.

"How any man could allow himself to be so mutilated, I do not understand. These people are an abomination; their cult is a desecration of all that's holy."

"What do you mean, Tristen, how are they mutilated." asked Elizabeth.

"I dare not show you, it is too horrible and anyway has to do with their male parts."

"Tristen, I am studying to be an herbalist, I am not unaware of how a man is arranged. I know more than you suspect a young woman might," she said as she touched him on his neck, brushing her fingers along the curve of his ear.

He looked at her amazed, with a longing. She met his eyes directly with equal longing. Tristen drew back the man's clothing so she could see. At first there seemed nothing amiss, except the male organ had been slit along its underside from its base through its crown. Furthermore three gold bars with rounded heads pierced this flat member at equal intervals along its length.

Elizabeth remembered to faint at the sight, although she never forgot the sight of the blue chevrons on his belly and the gold barbels in his groin.

When she roused, she found herself some distance from the corpses, cradled in Tristen's arms. He was weeping. Whether from happiness or grief she could not tell. When he saw her eyes open and staring at him, a broad smile broke his tears.

"I was afraid the shock might have been too great for you, Elizabeth. There are some abominations even we men quail at. But I'm glad you've awakened, we have to get out of here lest these two have reinforcements. I'll drag the carrion out of sight, while you gather up the herbs we'd found. Then I'll put you on my horse and we'll make ourselves absent from this place."

Elizabeth put her hand on Tristen's arm and said, I only got a quick look, but were those barbels gold? Shouldn't we take them?"

"Elizabeth, if you think I'm going to salvage gold from a corpse, you're quite mistaken. Besides I have enough gold for you and your father, if ever you need it, and it will not be stolen from the bodies of dead men."

"I think you're making a mistake to leave the hag's gold in the earth. The stories my uncle tells me about her leads me to think that they may have singular properties we cannot guess at."

"If you want them you will have to get them yourself. I'm not touching them except to drag them back into the brush." Tristen was nearly disgusted with Elizabeth's demand. But when she looked at him with that look of hers' there was nothing he could do.

"Alright, alright. But only because you're the herbalist and have knowledge I may not know. I'll harvest them for you, but what you'll do with them I do not want to know" said Tristen as he stood Elizabeth on her feet and dusted himself off.

She busied herself with gathering the packets her maid had neatly made for the herbals they had gathered that day. And before she let Tristen drag her maid into the undergrowth, she tidied her up as best she could.

"I'll send someone back for her when we get home. She died trying to protect me; I can't leave her body here in the forest for the wild dogs and pigs to ravage."

Tristen ignored her still upset with the harvest of the gold barbels from the two dead men from Temple Isis. He hoisted Elizabeth on to his horse and vaulted up behind her and her packages, and rode back to town.

Cain smiled as it heard the hooves of the wild pigs approaching. The scent of fresh blood always caressed their wide nostrils from miles away. Their broad bristling backs moved through their runs in the undergrowth as Cain followed Tristen and Elizabeth.

Quinn

The spring came to the valley long before it touched the mountain tops where the silver-backs slept in their winter dens. Elizabeth had long since found her place in Tristen's bed, and her belly began to announce the presence of a new life. Jaccobus had discovered by his craft that she was indeed carrying a son, an heir. He could not have been happier. So it was that he began to teach Tristen how to survive the expedition to the silver backs. Tristen never liked jerky, but as it was all the food he was likely to get for quite some time, he set himself the task of liking it. But that was not what disturbed him, Jaccobus had begun to wear in his ear one of the barbels he and Elizabeth had harvested in the forest. He mentioned it only once, and Jaccobus had confirmed Elizabeth's suspicions. These were not mere lumps of gold.

They had magical properties, and already Jaccobus' hair was beginning to turn from the grizzled gray to jet black and his thickly creased crow's feet were thinning and smoothing back into the corners of his eyes. He seemed years younger.

Also some of the instructions Jaccobus was giving him seemed outrageous, but if the cup of fire was to be his, he had to take the herbalist's craft seriously.

Finally the day came when he would have to leave. The pack animal he would take with him was lightly packed. If it survived he would bring back not only the silver back's bile sac, but also its hide, its head, its tongue, its liver and its kidneys. Jaccobus insisted that these all had immense properties for healing and should not be left to rot on the mountain side. The animal seemed hardy enough, but Tristen could not imagine how it would survive the long climb.

Elizabeth came to him as he was completing his kit; she took him in her arms and pressed into his hand a small package. "Remember me, my love and come home safe."

Tristen looked at what she gave him, it was a small package tied in a blue ribbon.

"Look at it after you've left and whenever you think of me in the night" and with that she left him.

The road was steep once he left the valley, and he was glad he had begun his journey in the evening. He had told his father he was going hunting alone, and as always the two fought about the wisdom of his going unattended. But Jaccobus had insisted the bears must never know a human is near or they will never take the bait. So he could take no one with him. As he began the climb, he sought for the first camp which Jaccobus had told him about. Sure enough there it was, the hollow in the rocks protected from the wind and right where he'd said it be was food for his pack animal. Why he had ever let Jaccobus convince him that this dog would be a good pack animal, he did not know. But it was certainly big enough and docile enough. Hell, a boy of ten could ride the beast like a horse. So he guessed it would be able to bring back the bear's salvage.

When he settled into the cleft of the rocks and set the small fire in the hollowed out stone Jaccobus had told him would be there, he drew out Elizabeth's packet. There was a letter, and a small awl, and two of those cursed golden barbels.

"My love, I know how you hated gathering these, but they are powerful resources. They will give you strength when you most need it and they will bring you back to me. Use the awl to pierce your left ear once in the lobe and once half way up. The barbels unscrew from the posts, insert them into the punctures you make. They will heal so quickly you will hardly know you've drawn blood. Trust me my love. Elizabeth."

The revulsion he felt for these barbels was immense. Yet he resisted his first impulse to throw them into the snow down the mountain. Tristen wanted above everything else power as a warrior, he knew this whole expedition was about securing for himself special forbidden powers, and he was willing to pay a price for that power. And he could not forget what the one had done for Jaccobus. Tristen knew that when he returned, if he returned, he corrected himself; all the gray in Jaccobus' hair would be gone. What would two do, he asked.

Steeling himself for pain, Tristen did as Elizabeth asked and pierced his ear and inserted the barbels. They had been cold to touch, but as the barbels met the blood in his ear, they grew very warm, almost hot. Soon he felt nothing, neither pain nor heat. And he slept.

When he awoke he did not know where he was. He was not in his camp on the mountain side. He felt pain in his wrists and immediately discerned that even though he was totally in the dark he was tied down spread eagle. The room was warm, and he was not in danger he felt, why he was not sure, but he knew he was not in any danger. He fell back into his sleep as Cain adjusted his blankets.

When he awoke again, he saw dim light and he was still restrained, but there were people around him, there were women around him. He tried to talk but his voice was gone, his tongue was dry and still. He was a prisoner and his captors were women.

"It is time?" said one.

"Well past time," said another.

"Is he ready? Said the one.

"I think he will serve us, how can he not?" said the other.

Tristen felt the bed clothes which had kept him warm being drawn off him; the cold air struck his sky clad body like a welcome slap.

"He is a muscular one," said a third voice.

"Yes and he looks to be willing enough, look how he rises to pay his respects."

Tristen felt his manhood readying itself for battle, his battle lance stood like a thorn on a rose bush, at a sharp angle. He would puncture these women if they dared to try him, he thought.

A hand caressed his chest, curling around his nipples. Her hand was cold against his warmer flesh. He quivered at her touch, the taut muscles of his belly recoiled as the fingers traced the ridges of his waist.

"See the chevrons of our lady, how clear they point the way," said another.

Suddenly six hands began to rub warm oil over his chest, and neck and arms and chest and thighs and the sinews of his groin. Hands gripped him, kneaded him like dough ready made. Never had he felt so aroused, so powerless, so willing to do battle. Odors assailed him now, musk of women, of fern and cedar. The light was extinguished and they were on him, how he tried to fight, how he tried to keep his seed from them, how he tried to beat them at their own game, but he couldn't. Once twice, three times they broke the dam of his blood and the fish of his flesh swam into new oceans, crossed new land brides, found continents un-thought of.

Tristen fell into the abyss of unconsciousness only to be awakened by a deep dread in the pit of his belly. He was alone. He was sky clad but free of his bonds. The weight of the darkness became oppressive; it gathered in on itself somehow, coalesced. A fragrance struck him like a whack on the side of the head. More stench really, fragrance of sandalwood, stench of woman's blood, odor of death. Before him three eyes glared at him, a grinning set of teeth. He saw the palms of many hands each holding a different weapon swirling in defiance. One dimly seen brandished a severed head. A nimbus of black fire lit the inky room, Black illuminating darker black. An apparition stood before him, a female horror, the slit of her like magma, a belt of severed male members ringed her hips. He lost control of his muscles, all but one. It rose up like a lotus bud ready to open in the summer sun. He lay helpless before this terror. From his lips the word "Isis." Her name summoned inquiry.

"Who calls my name, mortal? Does my lover Sivi call me?" A black hand reached out and cuffed the left side of his head. "How is it you wear my darts in your ear? Do I know you? Speak mortal."

But Tristen's tongue died in his mouth, even as his body lay abased before her. Her black legs moved towards him, bells at her breast telling him she drew nearer. The fumes of her penetrated him lifting him to her, she dragged the bloody head across his face, the bloody meat of its severed neck leaving a wet trail as she lowered herself to meet the surging flower of his mud.

The heat of her was astonishing, it was like being sucked into a furnace, a furnace of delight and of wonder and of yes and yes and of hope across generations into the abyss. The gates of him opened to her, and she took more than he had.

When he awoke again she had levitated him to her and one of her hands gripped his maleness as if it were a sword. He was beyond rigid, he had become as metal. He was the hilt of a war sword which jutted out of massive block of stone. One foot pressed down on his chest and with a great heave she pulled out of him all that was male, a bright sword—lightning bolt for blade. Another hand gripped him by his throat and raised him to her hideous face. In his terror he saw all that was himself flash in her hand: he knew she wore a belt of such bright swords and his was to be her newest weapon.

"Did you think to approach me?" The bellow of rage sounded more like plates of the earth's crust grinding than a human voice speaking.

"Did the Set think he could send a mortal to do a god's work?" she mocked.

"Puny men, you do not know what you do. Nor will I forgive you. I will meet you, if you come, with your own sword, and neither you nor Set himself shall remain whole. You will worship me whenever I command it, as you do now."

As she spoke she waved his male sword in bright arcs around his face. A shudder came over her. A magma crack appeared in her inky chest. A beautiful white hand emerged from her chest, followed by a sleeve of green damask. It took the bright sword from Isis's hand and slid it into the cleft it had been ripped from. As he fell into night, Tristen thought he saw a lapis butterfly on this sleeve and heard Elizabeth singing a familiar tune.

He did not know how many times they came to him in that place. He did not know how many took him in that place. He did not know why they let him go. All he knew was that when he awoke he was being licked in the face by his pack dog. He was fully dressed, the skin of the silver back lay trussed up and ready for travel, as were other packages he did not remember making. He heard motion to his left and saw a young woman busying herself at the camp fire. Tristen reached for his dagger and found it exactly where it should be, drew it out silently and stood ready for battle. Something was wrong, however, he was weak, dizzy when he stood and he could only croak defiance at his companion.

"Well enough friend mine," the woman said to him "back you are with us? Some of this drink you, it will help. Nearly frozen to death were you when found you I did coming out of the mountains carrying whole Silver back. Delirious you have been for days. Lucky me it was who found you rather than travelers other. Gold and fur you have would bring a gold more than Quinn has."

Quinn spoke in the mountain dialect of her people, and Tristen understood only bits of it. But she seemed harmless, and was offering him what tasted like broth. He sucked it greedily down, and looked at her carefully as the broth cleared his head.

"Liked you that? More where that came from is there." She refilled his cup and again he drained it.

"Very good sign that, appetite. Live you may after all. Good is that. A reward maybe for help mine? Fine clothes, gold ear plugs, handsome dagger, rich you must be. Quinn help you. You help Quinn. Quinn needs help from fighting man. She thinks you just might be the one."

Tristen found his voice and said. "Do I understand you to say you found me in the mountains? Hauling out a bear, the entire carcass?

"Talk he can, talk he must. Yes, found you I did, wrapped in the silver back here. Thought a bear you were, until the blood on the snow I saw. Found you nearly dead I did. Sick you were, frozen nearly, hurt somewhat. Dragged you here, packed up your bear, and tended you Quinn did. Quinn wanted you alive, she did."

Tristen listened to her talk, and half understanding her knew she had saved his life. He pushed himself up so he could better see her, and what he saw was not unattractive. She was lean and angular. Her hair was long and braided in a very odd way; it seemed to form a crown into which a row of gilded camels had been woven. She was heavily tattooed, at least what he could see of her was, her hands and wrists, her throat and ears were all covered with strange markings, he could only guess at.

"Qu...Quinn," he croaked.

"Name mine, Quinn is," She answered.

"Name yours, what? She asked.

"Tris...Tristen," he made out.

"Tell me who you are?" He said as his voice began to serve him again.

"Questions has it? Well answers Quinn has." She had an odd way of talking to her self and to him at the same time.

"Only living member of my tribe is Quinn. Guards of the southern pass were we, Against Isis we stood long ago, came she did, her we could not stand against. Dead all my people are. Quinn was away, searching for help she was. Need companions I do."

"Don't ever say that name, Quinn, promise me. Never say that name."

"What do you know of this black one, Tris…Tristen" she said mimicking his cotton mouthed stutter.

"I don't know much, but while I was unconscious I had a nightmare beyond horror, and she was part of it. I know we must not say her name, if we wish to travel unmolested," said Tristen.

"Hardly fit for travel you are. With the silver back you were heading where?"

"Verbabanc. An apothecary asked me to secure the silver back for him."

"Pay you well he will, this big female silver back. Worth much skin is. Things in packets too valuable? Save you Quinn did. You Quinn help?"

"Yes, I will join you in your cause, if you will just help get me off this cursed mountain and back to Verbabanc and my wife.

"Take you home I will. Tristen rest. Quinn watch." Wife you have? Sad Quinn is it to learn of."

Their arrival back in Verbabanc was met with unusual rejoicing. Elizabeth had been delivered of a beautiful son, while he had been away, and Jaccobus of course, had shared his joy with Tristen's father, Lein. Lein at first had greeted the news with skepticism but when both the sword master and weapons master had confirmed the marriage, Lein accepted the idea, and was generally pleased with an heir to his throne. So when Tristen returned he was a father, and the King's heir apparent, and a hero who brought back a trophy from the mountains. Quinn was greeted with great ceremony, as her people had long been known and revered by the folk of Verbabanc.

But Elizabeth knew more than she said. When she kissed him, she caressed the two golden bolts in his ear and he knew she was holding something back from him. Later when they were alone she undressed him with great tenderness, looking for wounds, frostbite or injury from his ordeal on the mountain. Tristen was relieved to find himself unchanged and that his helmeted warrior saluted Elizabeth with as much fervor as before.

"Well beyond bruises, and loss of weight and a sore right knee, you seem remarkably unscathed," Elizabeth observed.

"The Queen's barbels seem to have done their work uncommonly well. And this fellow," she said gripping his hilt exactly as the dream Isis had done, "needs to drink at the sacred well, I think. Come my love and slake your thirst and my hunger."

"But you've just borne our son. Are you sure it is alright?"

"Listen, who is the herbalist here, you or me. If I say drink, drink! Now come to my arms and tell me about this Quinn woman to whom I owe your life."

This was a night unlike any other night in Tristen's experience. He was the tender lover, attentive to Elizabeth's needs and desires, caressing and stroking. Gone was the acrobat of pillows, the warrior of the sheets. Tristen had no need to prove anything anymore to Elizabeth, and Elizabeth knew she would soon lose Tristen to another adventure. If what Jaccobus had said was true. So it was a welcome home and a farewell of love all at the same time, and though they neither of them addressed this truth, with their every touch they said hello and goodbye.

The Quest

From between the thick grove of date trees, the golden red orb that was the Sun god Ra cast a fretwork shadow upon the old canal down which the barge sailed. It was a graceful craft, antique in design high prow, gracefully arched bow a fitting conveyance for the journey on behalf of the god Set. The silver reflections of the water were broken here and there by the swift but concealed bodies of great crocodiles as they moved beneath the shadow of the barge. The only sounds that Cain heard were the geese's honking that hinged through the bank-side brush and the gentle noises made by the water protesting the boat's passage.

Zu kept to himself and at first was difficult to see, particularly in the deep shadow cast by the ornate structure of the stern. The difficulty was not only the result of his attire; he was garbed entirely in black from his head to his soft sandals. A black linen helmet covered his long hair and held a scarf which concealed his face. A long curved sword sheathed in an ornate case hung across his back. The only glint of light came from the wicked looking silver dagger which hung from his waist. But Cain also noticed a subtle glamour cast over the traveler that made observers disregard what they saw. It was a ward he wore, like an additional cloak, a ward not of his own making. In the dark canopy of foliage, Cain might have thought this strange, but then the water road to Cassoria was no stranger to the exotic. The barge moved swiftly, but there was something studied about the traveler which suggested he was in no hurry to reach his goal, yet ready for anything that might come at him.

As he stood on the deck of the barge, he mumbled to himself, and Cain might have heard him complain: "If I had known it was this going to be far from the citadel of Set, I certainly would have brought companions. I had not thought there would be so few villages and in them such a scarcity of handsome women on this canal. This sleeping alone is not really what Set made me for. Clearly, I should have taken a company of bearers with me and traveled by road." Or again Cain might have heard, "I'm glad they never took my hair, I'd be in an agony now I've gone so long without bathing. I must be standing in a pool of odor as thick as mud. I hope there is nothing here about that thinks man stench the odor of food."

The wide old canal lead to an old city called by the sea called Cassoria. The numerous barges he passed told Zu much. They confirmed that it was a fabled traders' city, rich with produce imported from in heavy freight barges and in large ships from a great distance. Rau had said that he would find his companions in this old city, and perhaps much else. It was on the edge of the territory which Schilo had cleared of the Hag's temples, and from which is brother had made such an effort to consolidate the hold of the gods. It was to this border city that the gods were calling their heroes to search out the source of these assassinations which were the bane of all the gods and their temples.

Zu ground his teeth to think of gentle Alant and his son going down beneath all those rats. And the Ackilons he had taught in the combats. They were all gone, reduced to blood tinged gnawed bone and scraps of cloth. The kind of attack these represented could only be the work of a powerful priestess through whose body Isis was working. She had to be found. She had to be identified. She and her whole temple had to be razed. So the gods had decreed. But why Cassoria? What did the gods know about Cassoria that they had kept hidden?

Because it was a fabled traders' city, rich with produce imported from a great distance, merchants from the three oceans came there to find markets. Mercenaries from four continents came seeking a worthy cause, or companions capable of heroic deeds. Thieves who called no place home came to Cassoria in search of victims and treasure. Zu wondered how many other assassins came to Cassoria in search of prey. Months ago, it now seemed to Zu, his brother had told him a company of fighters were gathering in Cassoria assembled there by the gods. Rau said something about a "Shadow Company." But he said nothing about how Zu should find them. "Trust Set," Rau had said. Zu was not quite sure. Set will let me know when I am near, surely. Now and again he was sure Set's odor was curling around his ears, but it had been so long since he'd been in the baths, he was not sure it was not he himself who was so redolent.

Rau knew this was an opportunity to strike against chaos, he knew any priestess of such power would occupy such a seat of power and would contain treasure, at the very least ritual artifacts of great power. These Rau would have to assess and dispose of, but there should be enough treasure to attract even petty thieves. So the priestess redoubt would have to be secure against the ordinary intrusion. It would take extraordinary stealth to find her, and the assistance of the gods to escape once she had found them. Zu wondered what kind of knowledge Rau would need and how he should secure it, if, that was, he survived the encounter. All these thoughts and many others besides roiled through the young man's shrouded head as he rode his fine horse toward Cassoria.

As his barge came out of the heavy brush and date palm plantations which lined the canal, it took him across miles of gently rolling hills heavily cultivated in barley, vegetable gardens and beyond which the dark shape of a large tower began to emerge from the far horizon. As he traveled he began to occupy himself with discerning the shape and function of this edifice, until finally he was able to recognize a small but efficient keep even now under construction.

Soon, he could see carpenters and stone-masons working on the outer walls of the keep. The strong walls were surrounded by great earth works designed to disadvantage the attacker. From a distance it seemed that a small army of termites was building a fortress: Clearly someone was taking advantage of the good weather and relative peace to strengthen his defenses against future threat. *A wise man rules here*, thought Zu. As the barge entered canal which pierced the outworks of Cassoria's fortifications, he saw a lone stone-mason beside the canal hard at work on a huge slab of rose granite from which was emerging the clear outlines of a stele of remembrance.

Mumbling to himself again, the young man observed, "Someone has died here recently. Someone of power and position from the looks of that stone. Assassins are at work here too perhaps. I wonder whose. Ours or hers?" The stone-mason stopped his work and stared at the handsome barge as it maneuvered into the canal nearby. The sharp eyed artisan was a master mason and skilled in stonework such as only mages might know.

So the ward of disregarding was apparent to him as was the tattoos exposed as the stranger's cloak fell away from his hand, as he gripped the barge's rail. The eyebrows of the stone mason arched in wonder as he observed the strange tattoo which seemed to writhe with of a life of its own. The stone-mason clucked to himself that Cassoria was certainly attracting the wrong element these days and warded himself against observation as he returned to his labor.

Not much further on Zu saw a canal side black smithy where thick armed broad back smiths were hard at work hammering long swords into shape on dark anvils near the huge blackened forge which glowed red-blue in the dark interior of the smithy. "More than defense is planned here. Someone prepares for war," mumbled Zu as he tried to observe more without being too conspicuous.

As the barge swung into the dock, the stranger rocked with the jarring the craft took as it came along side of the great stone pier with its high packed walls of merchandise and cargos from afar. Rau had said that Cassoria's temple was not far from the canal, and so his heart had been gladdened when he saw the temple flags waving briskly in the sun and wind. When he disembarked he did not have to ask directions he simply headed off in the direction of the flags and before long was standing in front of the great bronze gates of Set's citadel in Cassoria.

Suddenly, Zu was very proud of what his brother had accomplished. Schilo had begun this temple, but Dalinar and Zu had made it their special purpose to strengthen it beyond most others in Set's Realm. Its thick stone walls were high and massive, sloping up at an angle which made assault doubly difficult. The thick gates opened onto a second gates which were set into walls equipped with kill holes from which archers could attack the enemy who penetrated the first gate.

The guards noticed at once that Zu was one of their own and opened the way for him. He was met abruptly by the warden of the gates who inquired only briefly of him his identity before welcoming him into Set's sanctuary. Zu was eager to find the baths and was led immediately into the elegantly appointed tile rooms of preparation.

"May I be of service to you," an Ackilon offered Zu.

"Certainly, have someone take my traveling clothes and wash them, and notify your guardian that Zu, Brother of Set's Chosen is here." The lad stiffened as he saw Zu disrobe, his long hair and beard, his body hair all screamed assassin, but the tattoos where what held his attention. As the youth hesitated to stare at the rippling health of Zu's body, Zu smiled and said, "Come back to me and teach me your name and be my guide to this citadel, if your guardian permits. What is your name?"

"Sonderval. Sacred one, my name is Sonderval. News of your coming has been with us for several days. But I did not know…"

"Enough," said Zu, "we will talk of your news when you return. Now take my greetings to the guardian." Zu felt he'd been too long from the steam as he entered the thick cloud of vapor. How wonderful it felt, how welcome. He sat on a stone bench near the great marble basin where the slaves placed stones freshly from the fires and laved them with water. Several women emerged from the steam and offered to bathe him and tend to his hair.

With a wave of his regal head he accepted their offer and reclined into their offices. Great pitchers of warm water poured over his broad shoulders and mane. He stood and allowed them to pour warmth over his back and hips. Delight filled him as their hands laved him with warm oils, and wrapped him in linen sheets to lay on the inclined stone benches nearby. The warmth and odor of the perfumed oils were intoxicating. For the first time in days he permitted himself to relax and to dream.

At first he found it odd he was dreaming, as dreams did not often come to him. This one took him swiftly, with stealth. He found himself in a forest watching a fight between three men while a beautiful woman watched. He was mesmerized by the woman. Her beauty was astonishment itself, Zu's warrior began to take armor in anticipation of combat. How he longed to hold her in his arms, to run his hands down her long back as he thrust his warrior deep into her golden well and drank deeply from the springs of her mouth. He saw the two assassins of Isis quickly laid low by their opponent and how his body moved with power and purpose. Zu marveled at his gymnast's strength and suppleness.

The short coupled body seemed made of sprung steel and emanated a radiance he saw as a corona around his body. "He would make the fourteen powerful indeed," thought Zu estimating his form and potential. When he stepped out of the brush and made his presence known to the survivors of this battle, they ignored him at first. That is until he touched the woman in praise. She fell back in alarm and distaste. Her companion came immediately to stand between Zu and the woman. Zu offered his hand in friendship and the other slapped it away and flew into him pinning him expertly on the rough ground. But a trained assassin was not to be so easily bested and within a blink of the eye the two were separated and Zu spinning to his feet.

"Who are you and what would you take from us?" His adversary asked.

"I am Zu, brother of Set's chosen and I would take from you only what you would willingly give, your friendship and your comradeship in combat. I had not known this woman was your slave. Has she given you many children?"

She is not my slave, and she is not to be assailed by the likes of you. As the two squared off for a contest of arms, Zu was shaken awake, his unbidden dream vanished as he opened his eyes to behold the guardian of the temple.

"I am sorry to disturb your rest, sacred one, but there is much to discuss. Will you not join me in the pools where we can talk as you finish your cleansing?"

Reluctantly, Zu rose to his feet with the help of the Ackilon who removed his sheet and led him to the pools. The three sky clad men entered the sacred pools heated from the volcanic springs below and watched as the Ackilon poured cold water over the head of the guardian and himself. Zu stepped from the pool and allowed the Ackilon to brush his long hair before he stepped into the long skirts provided him by the attendant women. With quick practiced movements, Zu wove his hair into combat rings and pulled a long cloak over his shoulders. He was still perspiring gently when he strode out of the baths into the audience hall of the temple where the guardian made him welcome.

"Set's Chosen gave us a sending that you were coming so we have been diligent on your behalf with inquiry and search trying to determine what it is the other gods have done. But it is hidden from us as it is from the other temples. None know of a "Shadow Company," or any attempt which is being made on the queen's citadel. We are at a loss to know why this has been hidden from us. But that it is so, is clear. Perhaps, the gods are reluctant to expose this effort to general knowledge. Whatever is the case, we have failed you in this and offer you only our apologies and whatever assistance you may need.

A chill ran down Zu's spine. That the gods had concealed this enterprise from the temple could mean only one thing, the temple of Set had been penetrated by the goddess and her agents. He knew he could not leave a compromised temple behind him. He would need it as a place of refuge at the end of his task.

"How near are the Ackilons to initiation?"

"We are preparing even now for the ceremony at the end of the week. Will you take your place among us for the singing?"

"Certainly. I would be honored. But first I must assure myself that the fourteen are ready for Set's Chosen. Have them meet me at the stone of surrender in an hour. We have much work to do." Zu turned to the guardian and asked him to take him immediately to the stone of surrender.

"As you please, sacred one," the guardian said with growing irritation. The two strode off down the corridor until they came to the chosen's chamber. There in the center of the large octagonal room was the rose granite stone with its channels cut as required.

Zu looked at the guardian, removed his cloak and long skirts to confront him. "I require a thorough examination of the temple. The silence of the gods is ominous and can only mean that the temple is compromised. I will first wash you in the waters of my life and then you will wash me in the waters of your life. We must begin with a pure source or we cannot find out the contagion," Zu said in his voice of command.

"Willingly brother of Set's chosen." The guardian was quickly sky clad and knelt before Zu on the stone of surrender as Zu washed him in the waters of his life. And then knelt as he himself was washed. The two retired to the sacred pool where they discussed how the contamination may have occurred. They found no answers ready at hand.

When the fourteen arrived, each was washed in the waters of life. The first was washed by both Zu and the guardian and each of the fourteen in turn washed the next until Zu was satisfied that they were uncontaminated.

They were all puzzled at these results. Why was there silence? Why had the gods turned away? Why had Set himself not shown himself? Zu felt as if he was wearing a shroud, so separate from the god did he feel. He began to feel unwell.

"I must get some fresh air, go with me to the ramparts, guardian." They dismissed the fourteen to the pools, and clothed in long skirts they climbed the stairs to the building's roof, and then walked the bridge to the ramparts. Zu stared over the city and felt the shroud lift from him, and turned to look at the guardian. "Can you not feel it?"

"Feel what sacred one?" The guardian asked very concerned.

Zu looked at him out of the corner of his eye, curled his eyebrow and wrinkled his nose. "When I came into this temple, everything seemed perfect. This is a beautiful, well run, well designed citadel. You are to be congratulated for the way it is kept and for the discipline you maintain. Yet, I began to feel that I was walking in side my burial shroud the longer I was inside the temple walls. Out here, I feel alive again. There is something desperately wrong here, but I cannot detect what it is. How long has it been since anyone here has been possessed by Set?

"Why, none of us possess that kind of skill. Rau himself has never been here. Schilo came, and Dalinar, but never Rau. So it has been at least ten years since someone of that level has attended our ceremonials," Said the guardian as if he did not understand the nature of the question.

Zu wrinkled his nose as the odor of Set curled around his ears, his eyes grew round, as he spoke. "I think that is about to change, though I am an untrained vessel, I am a vessel nonetheless." In that moment Zu assumed the posture and Set possessed him, but it was unlike any possession Zu had ever experienced. The god took him and yet did not take him. He was god, yet he was with god and not the god. It was an odd oscillation he experienced. His nostrils flared to his god-heightened senses sensed contamination. He looked at the guardian and found him on his knees, and adoration.

"Rise up, rise up. This is time for battle, not time for praise. I need you with me, strong, and alert. My battle companion, not my leader of prayers." Zu heard himself say from somewhere beyond himself. The guardian stood and walked behind Zu-Set, his garments in a heap at his feet. They crossed the bridge from the ramparts back to the roof of the temple, and Zu-Set began to circle the perimeter of the building. He stopped, fell to his knees and pawed the ground, like the earth-pig, red clay tiles gave way beneath his powerful hands, and a second set of tiles came into view.

"What have you found, Holy one, show me that I may serve you."

Zu-Set continued to dig, ripping away the red paving tiles exposing those beneath it. Soon a space several bodies long and several wide was exposed and clearly there was a second set of paving tiles beneath which bore strange markings, lines bending and curving, black against white. Zu-Set stood, "Quickly bring the fourteen and give them such tools as are required to expose this subpavement." Zu listened to himself speak amazed at what he had done.

Soon the roof was filled with people and red roofing tiles disappeared into stacks exposing the white and black sub-roof to the sun. When it was accomplished they all stood in amazement. On the sub roof was a labyrinth of a sort they have never seen and at its center was the Hag. She was represented as if she were seen from above as if by a bird hovering overhead. Zu-Set stepped forward, "How was this possible? Who could have done this desecration? Remove these tiles with care, the black pigment on these tiles is menstrual blood, potent in its power. They must be removed from the sacred precincts taken beyond the city, washed in the Water of life and then cast into the sea. In this way can the power of the Hag be removed from my citadel."

Zu heard himself announce before he felt his knees buckle and his spine collapse. Quickly he was in the arms of the fourteen, and the guardian was summoning priests and Ackilons for the cleansing of the temple. Zu felt the god leave him as a kind of tearing and a ripping. He went pale. It had been many years since Set had taken him and Rau had never given him any instructions that this might happen again. Indeed, Zu suspected that Rau did not know it could happen again, unless Rau himself were in difficulty. Perhaps in some way this was a stratagem launched at Rau. As Zu tried to think through the fog that enveloped his mind, he felt the warmth of the fourteen surround him, their strong arms and chests against him. He took their radiance again and again, he seemed insatiable. His dark body reeled at the intrusion of so much radiance so empty had it become in the sundering of Set. Their hands reveled in his hair as they massaged his body back into life, they washed him in the waters of their lives, and fed him until he was sated.

They lifted him from the stone of surrender then and gently lowered him into the sacred springs where their strong hands continued to stroke and massage his flesh back into health. When he came to himself, he was wrapped in linen sheets as the fourteen held him six to a side and one at head and foot as proscribed by the rituals. When he opened his eyes, they lifted him to his feet and removed the sheets drying him and offering to lead him to the couch of life where he might rest. The large ornamental bed was reserved for Set's chosen, but they had surmised that the twin of Set's Chosen would not desecrate such a sacred place.

Zu lay in total exhaustion, but felt an odd exhilaration never-the-less. He had just begun to lapse into sleep when a loud commotion roused him. Zu scrambled out of the couch of life and tugged on his long skirts. As he made for the door, two Ackilons offered him their shoulders to lean on, and together the three headed towards the sound of battle. Zu was startled to discover that the noise was coming from the roof, and so they made for the stairs and encountered wounded men blocking their way. Zu pulled himself together pushed the Ackilons away and commanded a way be made for him. Quickly he traversed the stairs and emerged onto the roof to discover the Hag herself confronting the guardian and the fourteen.

"Stop, all of you immediately. Back off. Leave her to me. Zu circled the apparition slowly as the odor of Set began to curl around his chest, but he noticed that the spicy fragrance of Anubis was there also as well as the odor of grain and blood. As the Hag turned to deal with him, Zu was possessed by Set, Anubis, Horus and Min. He trembled as the gods took him, his eyes rolled back in his head, and he spoke with an unearthly voice of command quadruple and at once one.

"Why have you come where you are not wanted? Why do you stand in the sun instead of the shadows you prefer? What does Isis want from the gods and Men?"

As from a deep within a cave where the bones of the sacred dead are stored against need, the voice of Isis echoed across time and space to trumpet in these winds. "This city is my city! This temple is built over my ancient soil, sacred to my rites. I caused these sacred tiles to be placed here, I ordered these to be hidden so the temple of Set might participate in my sacred city. Yet I find you come hither to attack me, I find your rituals put to uses hostile to me and I find you in particular abhorrent to my purposes. The apparition seemed rooted to the four great tiles on which her image was painted, but as Zu-Set-Anubis-Min-Horus watched she began to move through the maze seeking to come at him.

"Guardian, bring the water of life to the roof, bring it from the cisterns, bring it now," Zu-Set-Anubis-Min-Horus bellowed as he prepared to meet the apparition. Zu moved on the white, as Isis moved on the black, delaying her approach, stepping over channels she would have to traverse, the human vessel allowing the gods greater mobility than the blood tied apparition had. When she seemed near, Zu would step away causing her to backtrack. Suddenly the guardian appeared with a silver bucket, with four priests behind him, and Ackilons behind them, each carrying the water of life. The apparition stopped in her tracks and bellowed.

"I will have you yet, and this temple will be razed and all within it gutted like fish drying the morning sun." In the same instant the priests hurled the contents of their buckets at the center tiles, dissolving the design completely. The apparition dissolved at the same time screaming curses at Zu, swearing she would rip out his throat if he came near her citadel.

Zu stood as if one pole-axed, as the gods fled his body. The fourteen came to him but as they tried to pick him up, they noticed his skin was hot as if he were being consumed by a fever. They stripped him thinking to bathe him in the waters of life, but stopped when they noticed his chest. Above his left breast was an ice white tooth design emerging from the tan slowly as an ice crystal forms on wet soil in winter. Below a talon flared in black edged in red against the tawny skin. On his other breast Min's flail was etched and below it a flaming dagger looked like a new burn. These new tattoos were still steaming as if they were more like brands than sacred signs of power. The Guardian came to Zu and pressed his hand on his shoulder, "Sacred one, may we aid you? Will you let us lift you and give you succor?"

Zu rallied enough to open his eyes, smile oddly as if his lips did not move entirely at his command, and seemed to give ascent. Gently the fourteen picked him up as if they were carrying a sacred ark. He seemed lighter than they remembered, and yet more precious. His long hair had come undone and lay across the hairless shoulders of those who carried his upper body. His sacred body amazed the fourteen who found their warriors taking on armor even as they held him.

They took him to the stone of surrender but he made no effort to respond to their offerings. After a while, they decided merely to cradle him in their arms until he might come to. Zu slept in the radiance of their bodies, blissfully as if in his mother's arms. After a long while they wrapped him in blankets and lay him on the couch of life. The guardian began a vigil with two of the fourteen one at head and feet in constant chanting while Zu slept. Never had such things happened in Set's citadel in Cassoria. They had heard of such battles between the gods and Isis of course, who had not, but never had they come to Cassoria. They felt at once honored and defiled, sanctified and polluted as the guardian set about removing the tiles and all that had been polluted by the dissolved menstrual blood. It took nearly three weeks for the restoration, but when it was completed, the Cassorian Citadel of Set was as secure as any in Set's kingdom.

Zu had taken weeks to regain his strength. He had never been prepared for such battle, and he hoped he would never be forced to bear the weight of the gods again. He was honored that he could, and that they should consider him fit vessel, but he needed training if it were to continue. He wrote to Rau news of what had happened:

> *My brother, Sacred to Set.*
> *I write in haste and in exhaustion for I have had terrible battles here in Cassoria. I am amazed at what has happened I ask you to forgive me in advance of my telling my tale. I do not seek such attentions from the gods, they take me as they please without my consent. I know who Set's chosen is, and I will defend his choice against all rivals.*
> *When I arrived at Cassoria I was impressed at the fine ramparts of the city and of your citadel here. The Guardian is a capable fellow, but as he gave me no news of the Shadow Company, even after he had sent his ambassadors out to the other temples I began to fear that the Hag had secreted a spy amongst the priesthood. I enacted the cleansing rituals we*

learned from Dalinar. All were undefiled, but I felt as if I were wearing a shroud the longer I stayed in the temple. When the Guardian and I went to the roof to inspect the building, Set took me for the first time and rooted out an amazing structure on the roof.

I believe you should send messengers to all the temples of the gods and ask them to carry out similar roof top inspections. We found here a great maze under the paving tiles of the roof, a maze painted in menstrual blood on white tile. In the center four tiles was painted a mandala of the Hag from which she herself rose to defend her sacred maze.

When I confronted her Set, Horus, Min and Anubis all took me at once, and then I am told a terrible battle broke forth which was only stopped when Set ordered the guardian to wash her in the water of life. The silver buckets routed her but as they dissolved the menstrual blood designs caused enormous pollution of the roof which has had to be rebuilt.

Pray you protect me from such combat hence forth. I am nearly dead of the consequences. The Cassorian fourteen are peerless, but only fourteen. Without their care you surely would have lost a brother. Please forgive me for usurping your resources in this manner. I have not yet found the company of heroes. I will leave here as soon as I am well enough to continue.
Your brother,

Zu

Zu sent the letter back up the canal with a courier, and gave himself over to the task of repairing his strength. Everyday he bathed twice and he began to work the combats soaking up the spoils due the victor. He drew on the radiance of the fourteen and ate whatever he fancied. Beer such as they had in Cassoria was his. But the bread was as wondrous as the fruits which came here in great plenty from near and far.

He marveled at his new ritual markings and wondered what they might mean. If only Rau could tell him, but it was not the kind of thing one could describe in a letter, let alone tell of hidden powers. It was not long after his letter had been received that Zu received a letter from Rau telling him his warning had been well received as the mazes were turning up all over Set's kingdom. A technique had been created for cleansing them without summoning the Hag though one whole temple had been lost when the process was not taken seriously enough.

As a consequence Rau was planning an expedition to rescue that precinct and would be delayed somewhat in the coordinated attack they'd planed. Rau professed to be mystified about why the gods were visiting on him such duties, but he thought his twin had no cause to seek forgiveness, as he had always been the right arm of Set's Chosen, and Set's Chosen rested well in the strength of their friendship.

One afternoon, the guardian came to him and asked him to give a class in the arts of the Combats, as he had just learned that Zu had been master trainer of the Combats in Set's Citadel in the bright desert. Zu agreed and on the next morning appeared at the Combats as trainer. He'd been observing the training going on at Cassoria, of course, and knew it was in capable hands. But there were hidden things not known to many which might make the difference between winning and losing the treasure of radiance for which they fought.

One of these was iron shaft, a training technique so secret that Zu had first to examine the students to see who qualified for this teaching. The first requirement was length. Iron shafts could not be under seven inches. The second requirement was thickness. Iron shafts could not be under four inches in circumference at the thickest. He had given these instructions to the trainer, who had winnowed his class for the special teaching. He had specified even the special quadruple washed river clay he required and the kind of trough he needed to hold it. First, he taught the sacred postures and the ritual dance of slow motion thrusting required to bring the radiance to a fine hue. Then he showed them how to straddle the troughs and thrust their warriors into the fine wet clay again and again. At the end of the training session Zu gave them a foul smelling herbal bath of his own making to anoint their armored warriors with. The ointment stained the warriors a dark green and was not to be washed off for the week of training. Above all he taught them that during iron shaft training they were not to lose their man's milk under any consequences, as to do so might be fatal.

The resulting strength and desensitization made the prolonged battle for the well both possible and necessary. The actual training removed the iron shaft students from combat for a week. On the next week the results earned by the iron shaft warriors during the combats were amazing. None had defeated them, and they had maintained their armor for well over an hour. Zu gave all his secrets as regards the iron shaft training including the ingredients required to make the ointment to the Guardian so that in time Cassoria became famous as the repository of this fabled training technique.

The Cleansing

Rau began the gathering of men and warriors. He launched a series of lightning raids attacking each village within a ten days ride of the Temple. Obliterating all signs of the goddess. Her temples and wayside shrines were pulled down. Her sacred images were shattered when ever they were found. The men of fighting age were conscripted, pressed into training and armed. All roads radiating out from Set's Temple were cleansed of her traffic. And when this was done, Rau found himself in charge of a considerable force, some ten thousand men.

Sure of his strength, he again assaulted the ramparts of the desolated temple and this time found them defended, though neither well nor ably. The slaughter of the Hags troops was quick and once more bodies bloomed in the goddess's orchard. Now, however, Rau was determined to obliterate all signs of the temple. Teams of plow horses and experienced farmers with plows began to reduce the ramparts, filling in the great ditch and leveling the soil over the sacred precincts. The orchards were burnt, the tree stumps removed and the land plowed. The central precinct was drained, and the slabs of basalt and marble which lined it were shattered. The caldera was attacked by a thousand men with picks and shovels and it too was leveled.

Three weeks later, the sacred circle was a barley field, plowed, planted and under cultivation. The great ceremonial way was plowed under as well, and all roads leading up to the precinct. At the sacred heart of the old Temple, Rau built a training school where Ackilons would learn the martial arts of the ivory stem and the jade well. He would occupy this site permanently and in force. His garrison would see to it that the tradition of women assembling here to worship the Hag would be permanently ended. Never again would the monstrousness he had witnessed be seen here. It would be a pattern repeated over and over again wherever Rau conquered an ancient temple of Isis.

When after nearly a three month period of massive public works, the land was cleared of the ancient memory and planted with barley and construction of the new school nearly completed; Rau turned his head to his borders. He required that all men between the ages of fourteen and twenty-four serve Set. Once trained, they were subject to summons in defense of Set's temple and his laws. It was gratifying when Rau discovered that the men of his lands valued his training and his new teachings. They were fastidious about turning in women who seemed head strong, or whom they suspected of still worshiping Isis.

After several years of quick trials and hundreds of impaling's, the worship of the goddess was effectively replaced with the worship of Set and his allies. A newly revitalized cult of Set had taken root and was growing. The creation of new temples, the training of new priests, the construction of new baths near old springs, often originally sacred to the goddess, and the inauguration of the new family system began to produce a period of relative tranquility.

Rau dissolved all relationships previously bonded by Isis and required the new system of bondage to be instituted. Many women were cast off in this process, as their husbands took women in bondage. Rau brought these abandoned women into his temple compounds and under the watchful guardian of a new goddess, Howthar, the cow goddess, created new traditions for women. Women protected by Howthar could become trainers in the sexual combat schools, and those who wished could bear children for the Ackilons. For many women it was a liberating experience, as for the first time they found themselves honored for their prowess in the sexual arts rather than for their abilities as cooks and gardeners and brood bearers. Though these were also highly prized by the temple. In the temple precincts women went about with face and hands sky clad, and they were allowed to grow their hair long, and lustrous.

Indeed it was one woman in particular, Deirdre of Volun, who took this idea and created for the cult of Howthar many of its most sacred militant traditions. It was she who first saw that bearing children was itself a kind of battle, a battle with the demons of infertility. It was she who saw that women could be every bit as much of a warrior as men. Women could defeat men for control of the sacred mound and its hidden well; women could defeat those in eternity who wished to block the door between the worlds, through which new warriors came to join Set's legions. Children became not gifts from the goddess but captives snared in the bright world, lured here by display of captured treasure, and brought helpless and sky clad before Set's chosen on the stone of surrender.

Rau was so pleased with Deirdre that she became his constant companion, and together their warriors fought continually. She to seize his sacred treasure and he to drink his fill from her jade fountain without paying the toll. She and her sisters bore him many children. Indeed it was through her prowess that Deirdre was able to bring the Temple of Howthar to Set's compound. It was she who became the first high priestess of the cult of the Cow goddess, and she who Rau loved among all women.

The Warrior Priestess

Rau looked down upon the small village, as he sat in his heavy leather saddle astride his great stallion. He fingered the ivory end of his long handled ax, contemplating what would be his best avenue of approach. Volun had a reputation, it was one of the sacred seats of Isis, and held one of the central mysteries. Its Temple was small but potent. On the surface it was merely a rounded dome supported by twelve pillars of basalt. Sacred to the moon, this Temple was the gateway to a huge complex of caverns where women worshiped Isis in unspeakable rites.

It was to the Temple at Volun that many of the original priestesses of the Hag had fled after the destruction of the sacred caldera. Set's Chosen coveted the caverns and hoped to possess them in the name of Set's initiates. But that meant he would have to evict the present tenants, and they seemed prepared to defend their underworld with special fervor.

As Rau sat on his crest observing Volun, so too Lantra stood on the steps of her ancient Temple watching the tiny figure on the distant horizon. She knew that the Hag was withdrawing from them and that the ancient ways were going. But she had spent her childhood here and many of her fondest memories were to be found in the festivals to the goddess which had been held in Volun for as long as anyone could remember.

She was not a tall woman, but she was well built, strong from her work in the gardens and orchards of the Hag which lay beyond the city walls, and from her long hours spent as a midwife. She was not young, but she was at the peak of her sexual abilities. So she decided that she would personally challenge this man, this Chosen of Set. On their encounter, the fate of her Temple would depend. This way she could prevent her charges from death and her beloved Temple from utter destruction. Or so she hoped.

She spent hours in preparation; she bathed in cold waters from the subterranean fountains. She rubbed herself with bouquets of herbs, with lavender and with parsley. She tied up her hair with a garland of roses, dressed in her most gossamer silks and sent a messenger to Set, that her city would be open to him if he would join her for a feast.

No one could have been more surprised than Rau when he received her message. He had expected violent opposition, and he knew that the walls around Volun were well defended. His reply was cautious but warm.

"Yes, I'll come. What have I to fear from such a one as this?" He asked himself. Little did he know that Volun was at once more and less than it seemed.

Rau's mount picked its way carefully down the steep incline towards the main processional way leading into the city. The red earth here was rutted and heavily eroded, he noticed. It was not a particularly attractive city, he thought as he entered its heavy gates and rode past the ranks and ranks of armed men and women.

They were doing their best to look ferocious, he thought as they beat their shields with their swords when he rode by. The city center was the site of the Temple, and all roads led to it. Broad avenues, he observed, were important to move men and materials across the city quickly. It may not be pretty but it was laid out by a soldier, he thought. Standing at the top of the great staircase, stood Lantra wearing the huge golden mask of Isis and sitting on an elaborate ceremonial throne. She was in the aspect of the golden one herself, perhaps she even was possessed by Isis, Rau thought Set would come to him were that so. So he boldly marched up to her and would have halted only at her side, had her guardians not barred his way with heavy lances. He stopped and addressed her.

"Great queen, I have accepted your invitation in peace, why are your streets crowded with armed soldiers? I have come with only my personal guard to greet you, and I find myself surrounded by shield beating guardians. Is this the act of one who wishes to be at peace?"

"We are not at peace," She answered. "We are at war with the gods, as you well know. I have asked you here because I know what desolation you are capable of and I would preserve my people. I do not want to see the roads heaped with the dead and dying. I do not want to see the Hag's march again across the battle field harvesting their black fruit. Must we have war? Is there no way we can restore the harmonies?"

"The days of the Hag are finished. Her hegemony is overthrown. The gods stand with me to bring a new day when men will no longer have to acknowledge the Hag's claim that their warriors really belong to her. I have seen her desolation. I have witnessed the slaughter of the Harvest King. I have seen and heard the sacred solar drum. Do not tell me of desolation. I do not think there is any way we can go back to the old ways. But I have instituted a new order, the order of Hawthor to replace the Hag's order and if you wish to join me on the stone of surrender, I will see to it that you and your priestesses will be incorporated into that new cult."

Lantra rose up in great anger. "Who are you institute a new women's order? How do you dare to create a cult for women's mysteries? What new desecration is there to be?" We will have no more of this."

With that Rau was doused with a black liquid, hurled at him by women who had closed on him from behind the soldiers. He recognized it immediately for what it was, the black blood of the dying, the pollution from which there was no cleansing. But Lantra had not counted on Set and the Tooth of Anubis. Set came to Rau and possessed him. Anubis came to him and possessed him. All who were around him drew back in horror at what the now black blood drenched form was doing. Rau raised his arms high and turned around for the crowd to see, and from his breast a light began to glow, it radiated through his clothing.

The tooth seemed to grow larger and larger until it encountered the black pollution. At that moment a hiss of steam was heard, and a red flame burned all along the circumference of the polluting stain. Suddenly as if a torch had been set to oil, Rau exploded into a fiery conflagration. His long skirts, his traveling robe and tunic, his leather sandals all burst into a violent inferno which engulfed Rau-Set-Anubis. He stood there in the midst of flame, his body rigid. And just as suddenly the fire was extinguished. A white ash was all that remained of the death which they had hoped he'd endure.

Yet the fire he had ignited leapt to the black blood on the marble steps and it too burst into flame and was consumed. The women who had thrown the black liquid themselves burst into flame and ran through the crowds screaming. Many tried to put out their flames, and they themselves were immolated. He turned to Lantra in a black rage and said,

"So this is how you honor your guests, is it?" With that he grabbed the lance which had formerly blocked his way and hurled it into her with tremendous force. It sailed into the golden mask and split Lantra's skull with a resounding crash. There was a quiet in the temple as the enormity of what had happened settled in. It was as if the life had been drained out of the city. There seemed no purpose left, if Lantra could be so easily murdered. Where had the goddess been? Why had she not protected Lantra as Set had protected Rau? Surely, Set was mightier than the golden one. Maybe what he said was true, the time of the goddess was at an end.

Rau was quick to capitalize on his attack. With as much authority as he could muster, he walked up to the fallen priestess, and tore off her golden mask. Brandishing it over is head he turned around to address the crowd. They were awestruck not only by his physical beauty but by the brilliance of the tattoos which marked his body. The serpents of Set seemed to writhe in the sunlight, and the tooth of Animus was like a glowing lamp on a dark night in the middle of his chest.

"Citizens of Volun," Rau began, "I offer you the love of Set. We offer you membership in the League of Cities protected by Amun, Anubis, Set, Horus, Ra and Min. This is a new time. The old time is complete. Join us or fight us. There is no alternate path. I offer you my hand in victory and in peace. Oppose me and you will all die horrible deaths in agony and despair. None will be spared, neither women nor children, neither dogs nor horses. My troops will leave your city now and give you time to bury your queen with proper ceremony. But at dawn tomorrow, if your gates are still closed to me, I will destroy Volun utterly. Remember what you saw, today. Tell those who did not see it, and give me your answer with the dawn."

Rau walked in majesty, as only the powerfully muscled god girded flesh can, down the temple stairway. He mounted his horse and slowly cantered down the broad avenue to the city gates. Those who saw him marveled at his tattoos as well as at his male beauty. That as much as anything convinced many to join him. But the display of power in repelling the corruption of the goddess was ultimately unanswerable.

And during the night there was a great stream of women leaving the city. They tried to loot the temple and make away with its treasure, but this time Rau had encircled the city with troops so they were stopped and searched. Those who could, walked on, but all the carts of treasure went no further. In the dawn all the four gates of the city were open, and half the population had fled. But what they took with them was merely the clothes on their back, and sometimes not that.

Rau was amazed to see the great wagons of temple treasure and property massed at the northern edge of the valley. He was pleased, because now he would not have to do the desecration himself. But he was also saddened because many of the temple elite had fled. He gave the order to attack the fleeing refugees as soon as he saw the number trying to escape. The carnage was terrible as his heavily armed cavalry cut down the former citizens of Volun in their hundreds and in their thousands. By mid day Rau issued his order. "Bring to me the severed breasts of all the women you have slain, and tie to your horse's tails all the infants they had among them. Impale their men and mound up the dead at their feet. Pile up your harvest here in front of the northern gate and then gallop your horses around the city."

That evening the trail of blood that ringed the city was only matched by the huge mound of breasts collected at the city gate. In the distance a trail of impaled men and mounded bodies arched to the horizon. Rau ordered that the breasts of the women should be strung like fish on a stringer and hung from the temple columns. When the black job was done, the breasts hung like fleshly bells from every surface of the temple. And there they were left to rot as a grim reminder of the goddess' defeat.

The Map of Wonder

As Rau began to consolidate Set's hold on Volun he gave his old friend, Bendilho, the task of securing the Hag's temple. Bendilho was wise in the ways of the Hag. He was particularly interested in the Hag's cult and had studied the ruins of her temples Rau had found or created. Bendilho was therefore the perfect supervisor of the seizure and refitting of the temple. Rau had seen the potential for this temple to become a major sanctuary for Set's cult and so he had charged Bendilho with the survey of the temple so that rebuilding and refitting could get underway. Rau had learned never to leave a temple unoccupied. Once conquered it had to be refitted, rebuilt so that the most sacred precincts of the earlier religious cult could be part of the fabric of the new order. The old power would be forever shattered in this way.

The next morning as the sun rose Bendilho gathered his tools, his wax codex and stylus, his measuring rod and his pendulum and his assistant the Ackilon, Charlon. Charlon was young, probably seventeen years old. He was an orphan Rau had found in one of the villages early in his career, but very dark and very muscular for one so youthful. Bendilho had taken a liking to the young Charlon as he seemed of a studious nature, and like himself quietly athletic. But he especially appreciated the care Charlon took as he assisted Bendilho. There grew a special bond between the two, Ackilon and Priest. Bendilho took special pains with Charlon, determined to see that he had opportunities to learn and to explore the world of Set's Chosen. As the two rode to Volun the plain was awash with the color of a spring, such as Bendilho had not seen in a long while. The city gates lay open to them, and the city streets seemed oddly quiet, as if a great mourning had suffocated its people.

The streets were littered with household debris and the wind blew cold down them. Charlon was surprised when he first saw the Temple festooned with the black stringers of Rau's conquest, even though Bendilho had warned him what he'd see. He was even more surprised to see that the people of Volun had laid flowers and other offerings on the steps of the temple in honor of what they had lost.

"Rau is being too gentle with the citizens of Volun," Bendilho muttered, "It is probably the work of Deirdre and her cult of Howthar. If he does not take a sterner hand with them, we will have trouble I'd guess. Though you did not hear me say any such thing."

Charlon nodded his head, remembering what he had been told and watching everything Bendilho did. Once Bendilho had established his credentials among Set's guardians, as his first act he ordered that the stringers removed and burned and that the steps be watched so that all such offerings should be removed immediately upon discovery. Charlon was fascinated with the Hag's temple.

"You said this was a place of power, Bendilho. Can you show me how to know it is a place of power?

"Can you not feel the power?" Bendilho asked?

"Not really, what does it feel like?"

"It's very difficult to explain. But I can tell you that it is subtle, which is why we don't eat meat and why we don't take fermented grain. Meat is a powerful aphrodisiac and dulls us to much of the gods and their calls. I can also tell you that when you are in the presence of power, you will know. The skin on the back of your neck will begin to itch and sometimes there will be quivers chording your spine. Gooseflesh is sometimes a key. That's how Set always effects me anyway. You stick close to me and you may discover it in this assignment." The two made their way up the steep and broad stone steps into the temple.

"What do you see, Charlon?" Bendilho asked.

"A lot of stone, black stone. A large room with a raised platform at one end. No windows, very dark."

"What kind of stone?" Bendilho asked.

"Marble?" Chrlon, asked.

"Slate and some basalt. Here the floor is all slate, the walls are mostly basalt. But look here. What do you see?" Bendilho answered in his best teaching tones.

"A huge stone."

"How huge?" Bendilho prodded.

"Massive, look how the floor is smooth until you reach this area and here it is very irregular. The stone is probably sixty-two lengths long, and twenty-one wide. I wonder how thick it is?" Charlon mused imitating his teacher.

"Are there any other stones like this built into the walls or floors?" Bendilho asked? Charlon began to search the walls, and the floor.

"Here's another. And another." Charlon called. He began to run the length of the room carrying his torch as he ran. Soon he returned to where Bendilho stood in the center of the room.

"Probably twenty-eight of these big stones."

"I'd bet there's more elsewhere in the fabric of the temple, now why should these stones be here?" Bendilho asked.

"Aren't these stones like the ones I heard Rau destroyed in the great avenue to Hag's temple near Set's?" Charlon.

"Exactly," Bendilho smiled.

"Why does the Hag want such huge stones?" Charlon asked?

"None of Set's chosen are privy to the Hag's secrets, we don't even know where the Hag's chosen gets them or how they transport them to the Hag's temple. That is one of the mysteries the Hag as kept to herself. But we do know they are sources of great power, which is why when ever we find them we shatter them, bury them or on rare occasion when we find the power useful we leave them alone. I am beginning to wonder if this temple can be refitted without first shattering these stones."

"How can the Hag's stones be useful?" Asked Charlon.

"Well the two stones Rau left standing in the great way were specially for men. One was said to cure impotence and the other was said to restore fertility. There were originally some sixty such stones in the ceremonial way. They all had special powers, though many of these powers were hidden from men. When Rau overthrew the Temple he ordered all but those two to be heated in fires until they could be shattered when cold vinegar was thrown on them. Others were tipped over and buried where they stood." Bendilho lectured.

"What is the shape of the room?"

"Well," Charlon ventured, "It is longer than it is wide."

"Rectangular then?" asked Bendilho.

"No, not rectangular, it's wider at the end than at the top, and its sides are curved." answered Charlon.

"What do you suppose its function was?

"Rituals, ceremony, reception of visitors, probably like our large public hall at the Temple," Charlon guessed.

"Exactly. Now why is it dark in here, why all the black stone? Why are there no windows, no natural sources of light?"

"The Hag is a creature of the night, isn't she?" Charlon asked.

"Well to some degree, I suppose, but the reality is that darkness is the cloak of Isis, it is the source of fertility, the fountain of life. I mean listen. If you want to plant a seed, do you lay it in the sun on a white stone?"

"No. That's silly" Charlon was quick to respond.

"Of course, it is. You find some dark soil, rich soil, poke a hole in the soil and bury the seed in total darkness. If you've done it right, then a plant will grow. Where does a woman have her sacred well? On her shoulder?"

"No, that's silly too," Charlon joked.

"Of course, it is silly, the woman keeps her sacred well in the dark warmth between her legs. But that is exactly why the interior of this Temple sacred to the Hag is dark. But what conclusions can you draw by seeing these ancient stones built into the fabric of this temple?"

"I'm not sure." Charlon hesitated, "does it have something to do with the age of the temple?"

"That's what I'd guess. My guess would be that this is a very ancient place of worship and that these stones were part of an original temple which were later used to build this one. I'd guess that originally this temple looked like the one near Set's temple. The difference here is that a city grew up around this one, and perhaps over the years the people of the city in their gratitude rebuilt the temple along more modern lines which maintained the privacy of the Hag in the increasingly crowded confines of the city. At least that is how I read it."

"Would we ever have been permitted this far, when the Hag's chosen controlled this great Temple?" Charlon asked.

"Perhaps, if we were special to the temple, special visitors or supporters of the temple, or the harvest king, perhaps."

"I've heard of the Harvest King obscenity." Charlon spat.

"Pretty horrible, I'd admit," Said Bendilho.

Bendilho walked down the length of the room to the raised platform, "What do you make of this?"

"Probably, where the Hag's chosen or cultic image itself stood."

"That's what I would guess, too. There's a door here with a staircase, let's see what we find down there." Bendilho led the procession down the stair, into a series of rooms. At the bottom of the steps they were confronted by a series of walls, they could see the tops did not meet the ceiling quite.

"Rau said there was a maze here, and it looks as if we've found it." Said Bendilho with real concern in his voice. "He said he'd had it cleared however, and there was no threat left in it."

"What did he mean he'd had it cleared?" Charlon asked.

"Just that such mazes often were protected by one or more guardians whose job it was to see to it that only those who were initiated entered. We obviously, wouldn't qualify." Bendilho carefully affixed the end of a spool of thread to a bracket in the wall, and began to unwind it as they stepped into the maze. He continued. "Ok so tell me what you see here."

"More black basalt walls and pavements." Charlon said

"Any of the great stones we saw above?" They proceeded into the dark interior of the labyrinth awed by the peculiar structure of the place and the complete darkness they encountered. The walls were loath to give back light cast upon them, so their torch light seemed to be sucked into the darkness. Bendilho was comforted by the ball of twine he held as he and Charlon entered the Hag's labyrinth.

"Stop here," Bendilho said quietly drawing his breath in between his teeth. "Tell me what you feel."

Charlon stood still peering into the darkness. "Cold, I feel cold."

"That's not it. Drain yourself of all thought, stretch out your senses and try again."

Charlon handed Bendilho his torch and stretched out his hands fingers wide as if there was something to feel. "Cold, a little breeze, that's all."

"That's still not it. Take off your tunic and stand here. Close your eyes. Stretch out your senses, search. Put your hands down at your side. Imagine that from each finger a ray of light emerges from each finger, now move your hands slowly up as you slowly turn and that in this action you've spun a web of light that hangs just beyond your touch. Now feel along that web with your out stretched senses. Let every pore come alive with the task."

After a long while as Charlon did as he was ordered he whispered nearly inaudibly "Wha...what is that?"

"Describe it." Bendilho asked.

"It feels like the wings of moths brushing against my flesh, like a walking stick is crawling up my spine."

"That's it exactly. What else."

"I feel as if we're being watched."

"Ah," said Bendilho, "you aren't blind as we feared. You can see her. What you have sensed is the Hag's power which is very strong here. Put on your tunic again, take the torch, let's see why this is a place of power."

Quickly Charlon complied and together they held the torches close to the walls. At first they couldn't see anything. There were strange lines drawn in the basalt walls, spirals everywhere. Charlon quickly called to Bendilho.

"Look at the floor."

The stones of the floor were dark red, the color of blood. There was a huge stone in the floor, its surface irregular, it was warm to the touch. There were flecks of gold and glass in the stone which caught the torch light and gave off an eerie light.

"Look at the ring," Charlon whispered.

Indeed near the wall quite out of sight was a black ring which sat in a circular depression exactly its size. Without a torch, only those who knew it was there would have detected it.

"What shall we do?"

"We'll mark the thread so that when we wind it up again, we'll know we need to look more carefully."

"Are you sure we'll get back here easily."

"Good point, perhaps we should just look in. do you think you can remove the stone?"

"I can try," answered Charlon with a sense of growing excitement. The boy reached down and pried up the ring as if it were the latch to the stone, but the ring came away clean. There was no hinge here.

"What happened, Bendilho asked.

"Nothing except that this ring isn't attached to the stone as we thought. It's just a ring." Said Charlon

"Put it back immediately." Bendilho said in a near scream.

Charlon did as he was told, but felt alarmed at Bendiliho's frantic demand. "What's wrong? What is it? I don't understand, Bendilho, what could a ring possibly do?"

"The Hag's rings are not for such as us. We will mark this place and come back for what we've found when we have Set-Rau with us. It is enough that we have found her power in this place. But remember what I tell you. Such a ring is beyond us, and not to be handled casually. I thought it was a lifting ring that would allow us to bring the stone up on one edge, as if it were a door. I have heard about her rings, the ancient scrolls tell such stories about them that any who encounter them must act as if they are in the presence of the Hag herself, in the presence of the most dangerous enemy." Bendilho replied in an anxious whisper.

"Is it wise to leave such a powerful artifact behind, once it has been discovered?" Charlon asked.

"Is it preferable to leave a giant python behind once it has been sighted?" Bendilho asked. "Of course, it is. You will see more of that ring than you will ever want to see. You may already have, look at your hand," he said gripping the boy's wrist and bringing it into the light. "What have you done?" Bendilho raised Charlon's hand and showed him he was missing a finger. Charlon was shocked.

"What has happened to my hand?" Charlon held his hand up and wiggled his fingers, the middle finger was missing two joints. Where it ended was a bleeding stump. "I can't feel the wound, there is no pain at all. What happened?"

"Did you put your finger through the ring?"

"Yes but?"

"No Buts. You can't possibly understand what has happened, I'm not even sure I do. You're just very lucky you didn't lose more. Here wrap your hand with this." Bendilho tore a length of cloth from his tunic and wrapped Charlon's hand tightly. Come on let's get out of here."

Bendilho led the way forward not back the way they came. His torch blazed brightly into the gathering darkness. After a long while, he stopped again.

"What is it Bendilho?"

"I don't know, but there is something odd here, I can feel it somehow. Come forward. How's your hand?"

"I still have no pain in the hand, and the blood seems to have stopped."

"Let's have a look?…This is astonishing." Bendilho held Charlon's hand up and saw that the wound was completely healed, but the joints were still missing. "Actually, that's a relief, I've heard that sometimes such a wound can begin to grow until the victim has been entirely eaten by the ring. We were lucky, this time."

"What's here," Charlon asked, cradling his hand and looking about.

"I'm not sure exactly. But something is here. You examine that wall, and I'll begin over here."

The two began a careful scrutiny of the alcove they found themselves in. It seemed to be perfectly ordinary, like all the others it was constructed of thick basalt slabs.

"This is interesting," Charlon said.

"What have you found?"

"There seems to be a hole here in this wall."

"Careful now, show me," Said Bendilho.

"See there it is," pointing with his index finger at a slot in the wall.

"There seems to be something in there. Give me your knife. I think I can get it out." Bendilho took Charlon's blade and probed the cavity with it. Blood began to flow, Screams were heard. The cavity began to slide about on the vertical surface of the wall as if the whole wall was liquid and this cavity was the only solid part. Bendilho took his knife and slammed it into the cavity with brutal force. It sealed up and was gone as if it had never been there. But the knife was also gone.

"What in the name of Set was that," Charlon asked?

"I'm not entirely sure," answered Bendilho.

"Do you still feel what you did?"

"No, what ever it was, it is not here now."

Bendilho took his torch and swept it across the wall which was now as blank as all the others had been. Pausing for only a moment to knot his cord, he continued pushing through the maze. They went for a long while until they came to another staircase which led down. It looked entirely out of place. It was a grand ceremonial stair, more appropriate for wide open public spaces than this termination of a dark maze. Together Bendilho and Charlon walked down the stair, awed at its resplendence. It seemed to have been ripped out of some princely palace. Its rose marble and gilded carvings could not have been more out of place after that basalted labyrinth.

Bendilho stopped on a landing and turned back to look up the stairs. "Now tell me what this is, Please young sir."

"I haven't the foggiest idea. It's very odd. This grand staircase seems made for royalty. But it's all wrong. The stair should end in an equally ceremonial hall."

Bendilho said, "My guess is that another building has been incorporated into the Hag's Temple in ages past. Just what it was I don't know but I guess it was designed as an earlier ceremonial hall. That function is long lost however."

"But why maintain it so sumptuously then." Charlon asked noting the gilt work still brightly burnished and the marble clean and unblemished.

"Maybe we will learn why at the bottom," Bendilho mused.

As they came to the bottom of the stair they were confronted by a single room, queer in its layout as it seemed to have no recognizable geometrical shape. Here it was curved, there it was angled, it was the essence of irregularity. Everywhere someone had used a black tar paint to black out the designs on the walls and even on some of the floor area.

Bendilho was about to leave when he tasted the milk of life on his tongue. It was an odd sensation, to have his mouth flowing with the savor of life itself without the ritual presence. But he knew it was a sending from Set. There was something else here. Bendilho took a torch from his companion, Charlon, and held it and his own more closely to the blackened walls and watched the flames carefully. At one point, the flame acted as if it were in a breeze: to this area Bendilho gave much more attention. He looked carefully and saw in the floor scratches as if something heavy had been moved across the stones. One panel of the wall seemed poras, air seemed to move through it. Bendilho handed a torch back to Charlon who received it with anxious welcome. He touched the black paint with a third finger and then brought it to his nose.

"Ugh, I wonder…" he said thoughtfully as he touched the torch to the paint. Instantly there was a blaze which ignited the whole room, the two ran back for the stair and made it about seven steps up before the fire was gone as quickly as it had come.

"Tell me what's going on Bendilho," Charlon asked. "What was that all about?"

"Sorry, I have begun to notice that whatever we found seemed to come to you, so this time I decided to ward you and see what Isis had hidden here. I was right, this was a trap. But now look."

Charlon followed Bendilho back into the queer chamber and noticed that the walls were covered with portraits of the most beautiful woman. Five different panels all depicting the same woman, a queen, a goddess? Who? But the floor was more interesting to Bendilho.

"Look Charlon, it's the floor they were trying to hide."

A mosaic pavement which had been hastily covered over by the black tar paint was partially evident between the ash and stains of the fair. It was not just that the artist who crafted it had been gifted, but as Bendilho swept away the debris with his foot he saw that this was a map of some kind, a map that extended behind the wall, a wall that was clearly a recent addition. Bendilho want to the wall where the mosaic seemed most interrupted. He ran his hands along the crease where two panels met. He pushed. No response. He shifted his weight and pushed a second time, and the panel slowly gave way before him. He opened the separation between the panels large enough so he and Charlon could enter. What they saw was beyond them at first.

As the light began to reflect off the floor they saw an entire three dimensional map rising from the floor in front of them. Rivers were marked by actual flowing water, mountains rose up valleys lay exposed. Bendilho found it difficult to talk, he was so awed by the massive map which seemed to extend into the distance in all directions beyond the light of their torches.

Charlon moved forward toward a tall shape over which a cloth had been thrown. With a quick jerk he tore the shroud away and stood paralyzed by what he had done. Before him stood the Hag in all her horrid power. She was at least twelve feet tall, twelve arms rotated around her, eleven hands held a different weapon and one held a freshly severed human head. She was squatting over a recently slaughtered body. Her powerful night black body was magnificently arched tensed with power. Power roared from her almost as if she were a bonfire. Bendilho caught Charlon by his arm and together they eased back out the way they came. Somehow the horror followed them. She didn't move, and yet she moved. She seemed to change posture and yet it was the same posture, the muscles rippled across her back as she moved.

Bendilho and Charlon somehow found themselves at the top of the stairs and then in the main hall above. It was almost as if she had hurled them through time and space out of the sacred undercroft. Bendilho collapsed on the floor, Charlon grabbed him by the neck of his tunic and dragged him out of the main hall, and on to the stone threshold. Looking over his shoulder, Charlon saw the Hag lurching towards them. It was the last thing he saw as he fell into eternal darkness.

Bendilho found himself in the street on a bed of flowers, the offerings of a mourning city. Charlon's body, gutted lay on the top step, a black shade hovered over him, intestines hung from her teeth and then she vanished. Bendilho clawed his way upright and stared disbelieving at the ruined body of his friend before he collapsed into the arms of the fourteen and Set's Chosen himself. Rau's face was a mask of rage, his fists clenched in raw emotion.

Bendiliho's End

Rau held Charlon in his arms. He knew instantly his mistake. The temple had not been cleared, it was very much alive, she was very much here and capable of defending the sanctity of her holy places. Charlon was evidence of the virulence of her presence. Rau pledged on the body of his Ackilon that she would be banished from this place forever. After Bendilho had given his report to Rau regarding the great map and the ring he and Charlon had discovered, he was given the task of accompanying the treasure wagons to Set's Temple for examination and storage. With him were a large contingent of Ackilons and Soldiers. Enough to protect the treasure and ensure Bendiliho's comfort after his ordeal.

Bendilho was very glad the expedition against the Hag at Volun had fared so well. His entourage as a small fraction of the one he had left the temple with. Most were still in the city conducting clean up. The sight of Charlon's body beneath the hag, his intestines in her teeth, still visited Bendilho in dreams. The Hag's grinning maw still haunted him as it streamed curses upon Charlon as it held his corpse above the brutal hacking death which had descended upon the women of Volun. The armies had paused only briefly as Charlon had been honored with Set's crematory fires and his body crimsoned into night. Rau had exacted a terrible price for that death.

As Bendilho was jostled by the unevenness of the road, one question plagued him. Had it been necessary to impale all the women and enslave the rest? Had the price he paid been necessary. Were the long winter nights of loneliness which the men of Volun were going to fall heir to worth the result? How long would it take Rau to replenish their stock of women? What had the carnage accomplished? Sure the rites of the hag had been obliterated in Volun, but she was not extinguished. Sure the abomination she had called a nation was desolate for a great circumference around Set's citadel. The bright gardens of her temples lay in burned rubble. The beautiful orchards which surrounded her temple had been turned into a horror of stench and death when her priestesses had been impaled on their sharpened trunks.

He was jostled out of his reverie when the great treasure wagon he was riding in came to an abrupt halt. Rising to his feet to peer over the driver's box,

Bendilho was surprised to discover he was completely alone. He scrambled out onto the road, drawing his fabled sword given him by Schilo himself and warded by Set, Bright Revenge, from its sheath as he did so. Lines of saddled horses stood still as if paralyzed: their riders lay on the ground, their intestines in the mouths of gray shadows. Then the shadows were gone. An eerie silence had descended on the road and the emerald glade it passed through. Bendilho ran down the road, calling for his Ackilons. The young men were everywhere slain, disemboweled. Their warriors cut away. The white horse his youngest son had ridden stood stock still, the scarlet and gold tunic, the broad leather belt with the insignia of Set still gripping it, lay in the dirt at its hooves. The boy's body lay mangled in the dirt, intestines looping around his form like some grim serpent. The priest of Set fell to his knees in shock cradling the head of his son whom he had only recently acknowledged and pledged into priesthood. He held the boy's face to his, catching a last scent of his body. He looked wildly about him. An unearthly silence muffled everything.

Then in the grass and brush at roadside he heard a rustling, it grew louder until it became a torrent of susurrations, as if a million tiny feet were on the move. Bendilho saw nothing until it was too late. The boiling tide of brown-black rats surged out of the grass at the side of the road covering it, taking the long line of horses down in its forward momentum. Surging over the corpses of the soldiers and Ackilons. The war horses who had trampled the hag's soldiers into red mush, who had surged into the broad ranks of her soldiers, did not protest the attack at all. They merely crumpled like balloons which had sprung a slow leak as the rats in their millions tore to shreds what had been prancing war horses caparisoned in scarlet and gold only moments before. Now it was the scarlet of raw flesh he saw, and the white of bare bone.

Frantically, Bendilho drew in the soil a circle with his sword and uttered a warding charm he had been taught from earliest childhood. He stripped and washed in the waters of his life. He caught the scent of Set and thought the god was coming to his aid. But suddenly, Bendilho felt as if a cascade of blood had been poured over him. Its warm salty thickness blocked any hope of Set's penetration. He recognized it for the horror it was, menstrual blood. The rats came up to the circle, they seethed over each other, clawing and leaping until one such heap fell forward and broke the charmed circle, as if by accident. A flare of sacred fire blazed up. Bendilho prayed for Set's intervention. A cascade of ash replaced the first several hundred rats which fell into the charmed circle, but when the menstrual blood touched the charm it faded. In an instant Bendilho was arm deep in rat teeth and claws, and while he kept swinging his sword at invisible attackers, he drew no blood. As he fell into eternal darkness, his last thought was "The Hag is here among us. Rau, Oh Rau, I have failed to warn you."

Later that afternoon when the rear guard came upon the treasure caravan which Bendilho had headed, they were grief stricken to discover the skeletons of horses and of their friend, still holding his fabled sword in a rictus of terrible combat, his body protected only where the water of his life and touched it. The Ackilons and soldiers' bones were scattered everywhere, picked clean of flesh. Only a single rat did they find, or rather the rags of one clenched in Bendiliho's skull's bare teeth.

When Rau heard of the disaster he summoned Tezable and the two rushed to the site. They were dumfounded. Gentle Bendilho had meant a great deal to the sacred twins. Rau ordered the bones of the men to be gathered up and Bendiliho's to be treated with special care. Nothing seemed to be missing from the carts packed with ritual treasure. But Rau knew they contained something terrible, something he had to deal with carefully.

The Hag's Door

Rau had never seen such treasures, the priestesses of the Hag had pulled out their most treasured objects for transport. He was sure that had they chosen instead to hide them, he would never have found such an enormous array of sacred artifacts.

Many were clearly ancient beyond anything he had ever encountered, but there was one cart which resonated power quite outside the ordinary bronze and gilt images and implements seen in the others. Rau had it brought around to an inner courtyard and carefully unpacked. Layers of cloth, ritual garments of brilliant design, heavy with cultic significance, wands and scepters, sacrificial knives, and a carving in wood. As Rau passed his hands above the objects it was from this carving that power seemed to ripple like water over a brook full of stones. It was an odd piece, small, carved in a dark wood. It was so encrusted with black resinous material that the details in the carving could hardly be seen. When Rau reached down to touch it, Set immediately possessed him and blocked his hand.

"Quickly," Set-Rau spoke in a firm voice of command, "bring me some silver tongs, or heavy silver rods. Just make sure the metal is silver and that the objects will allow me to retrieve this artifact." His inner circle of fourteen all scrambled after tools, one soon returned with a silver blade and a long silver rod.

"That will do nicely," Rau-Set said as he pushed the rod through the hole at the base of the object. Gently he raised it up and carried it to the stone of surrender. As if he were depositing an infant in a cradle, he laid the object down with infinite care.

"Bring me water from the spring," he commanded. Quickly several of the fourteen sprinted to complete his order. They returned with several clay pots of warm water and handed them over to Set-Rau who carefully poured the contents over the image. What happened next was scarcely believable. The gray marble stone of surrender turned blood red as what had been dry and caked was revealed.

"Menstrual blood," Rau-Set screamed. Thus warned, the room emptied abruptly. The channels cut into the stone flowed red with blood far beyond what the water could have moistened. Cisterns below filled quickly and began to back up. Rau-Set moved quickly to the hallway where his fourteen waited anxiously.

"Quickly, go down to the cavern and break open the storm doors, let the cisterns drain or we'll all be fouled here."

The sound of bare feet against marble echoed in the strangely silent corridors of Set's temple. Rau-Set returned to the stone of surrender and stripped. He reached into his abdomen and withdrew the stone of reckoning. It seemed to be a black shadow circled by darkness. Carefully, Rau lay it on the image before him. Abruptly, the room was filled with memories of other days, and other places, and other people. Shadows crossed the walls, where none should have been. Those who watched from the hallway were struck blind. Their panicked screams filled the room. And just as suddenly the room emptied and fell into quiet again. The gray stone was cleansed of its ruddy hue, the image was uncovered and exposed to view.

It was a very odd thing. A bald woman, great flat dugs, squatting, her hands emerging from behind her shins gripped each side of her vulva and pulled it open into a gaping portal. Her mouth open in a scream, ivory teeth sharp jagged edges set into the wood, caught in her teeth was a black stone rat. Her three eyes made of gemstones, seemed to look both backwards and outwards and in all directions at once.

It was astonishing. An image of the Hag in what Rau through was her most primal and ancient form. Probably the most sacred image in the entire Temple complex at Volun, Rau-Set thought.

"Bring me six sheets of hammered gold," Rau-Set barked. Instantly those among the fourteen who were not still stricken with their blindness, ran to produce what was demanded.

Rau-Set took the thin sheets of gold, and using the silver rod and knife began to encase the image in gold. He worked intensely for a long while, and then barked an order for a metal worker's hammer and tongs. These too were quickly produced. Before long he had encased the ancient stone image in gold foil, so that none of the original surface could be seen. Even so, he took great care to make sure the image was preserved in all its detail and design. When he was finished Rau-Set leaned over and picked it up. He turned it over and over in his hands.

"Morantus, come to me."

The young Morantus ran to his side in willing obedience. Carry this to the artisans' shop and bid them encase this in bronze and then in clay. My guess is that we're going to find more of these objects and we'll need a place of permanent concealment. I want you to dig a deep pit inside the temple grounds, near one of the thickest walls. Over this pit I want a small out house built. Deposit this object at the bottom of the pit and close all the other latrines in the temple. No one must ever be tempted to retrieve this artifact. Remember no water of life is to be wasted in the latrine. The collectors must still be used, so that the baths may be supplied. They will never believe there is anything of value at the bottom of a cesspit. Let no one see you place this object in the bottom. I want this project completed within two days. Take whatever assistance you need. Nothing has higher priority."

Set-Rau picked up the stone of reckoning and placed it over the cobra's flared head and pushed. When anyone looked the tattoo was just as it had been although now the image of the stone was blacker than it seemed possible to achieve with mere ink and needles. Then Set-Rau took the blinded among the fourteen into the sunlight and bid they kneel before him. He anointed their eyes with his very substance as he chanted the sacred history of his cult. By the next morning they were able to see, although their sight was always thereafter impaired.

As Set left Rau, he collapsed into the expectant arms of the fourteen and the second fourteen carried him to the stone of sacrifice where they began again as they always had. As they washed him in the waters of their lives, Rau began to weep uncontrollably. The remnants of the first fourteen and the second were nonplused. Rau seemed given to an enormous grief that could not be slaked. When questioned, he could not explain his tears, except that he mourned Bendilho and the Ackilons. But there was something enormous in this grief, far beyond what they connected with Bendilho. They carried him to the darkness of the springs and there they fed him for hours. He seemed unable to get enough of their caresses or warmth. He trembled and shivered, like a man with fever.

Finally, the fourteen called for their new Ackilon Morantus. He was about fourteen and had been found at Volun during their first reconnoitering. Rau had said when he first saw him, that here was a boy in whom the god walked beyond even the beauty of Polandus. And so it seemed. He had taken to the training with skill and energy surprising all his trainers. He was tall for his age, and yet well muscled. He loved to ride the horses bareback and continually surprised everyone with his ability to juggle as he stood on the bare backs of galloping horses. He was vitality itself and inexhaustible in the combats. So they thought this marvel might add something to the efforts of the fourteen. When Morantus offered himself to Rau, it was as if a strong wind blew over the troubled sea. Rau calmed down immediately in the complete darkness.

Thereafter Morantus and Rau were never far apart. The lad became his personal valet. The fourteen's recognized that here was an energetic form in which Set walked unbidden, that a sweeter temperament and more intelligent student could not have been found. Even though the ordeal of the Hag's avatar had drained Rau enormously, the fourteen soon found him stronger than ever before. And they thanked Morantus for this transformation.

The Hag's Ring

After he saw that Bendiliho's remains where honored and that the sacrifice of Charlon had not been in vain, he began to issue orders. By the end of the day an enormous force was assembling, by the next morning the dismantling had begun in earnest. When they began with the roof, the Temple of Volun came apart like an onion. Layer after layer of rebuilding gave way. The irony was that when they got down to the main hall, they found that the great stones which had formed the original circle where still in place. Walls came down revealing the ancient order, the ancient stones themselves were mute testimony to the power of the place.

Rau was about to order the great stones toppled when Tezable came bursting into Rau's temporary audience hall across the street from the Hag's Temple.

"You must stop. There's powerful treasure about to be lost in the collapse of the great stones, Remember Bendiliho's report."

"What is it, Tezable?" Rau asked in consternation at being interrupted with out respect of the proper protocol.

"Forgive me, Set's-Chosen. But we are about to make a great mistake. Charlon and Bendilho found a ring in the maze below the audience chamber, a ring of awesome power. In the few moments of handling it Bendilho said Charlon must have put his middle finger through the ring. The finger was missing its first two joints. Although it bled profusely he felt no pain and within a few minutes it had healed completely. It was hidden in a depression exactly the shape of the ring in a blood red stone, which was both wet and warm. They apparently put it back as soon as they saw what it was capable of. Old Bendilho knew it required someone of your ability to handle it. If we do not move quickly it will be lost."

"Why do you think it should not be lost? If it is as powerful as you suggest, perhaps that is exactly what should happen to it." Rau said.

"I think an artifact that possesses that kind of power should be identified and secured, perhaps in a middens, but its whereabouts should be known. Its location guarded. The goddess is far too powerful to allow her to act through that artifact, as she surely will if we do not act," Tezable replied.

Rau stood and embraced Tezable, "I was right to put you in charge of the excavation. You have guided me correctly. Bring his report, so you can guide me, I will do as you ask."

After a short time, Rau moved quickly to the demolition site. Quiet orders issued to the right priests stopped all work. With a suddenness which struck Tezable like a hammer blow, the work-site fell silent. The workers climbed down carefully, silently and stood behind Rau. He turned to Tezable and pointing to the stairs said simply,

"Show me."

The twine Bendilho had left was still in place, so he had no difficulty in leading Rau to the stone. Rau stepped forward and instantly both Tezable and Rau knew that Set was upon them. The odor was unmistakable. Rau assumed the position and Tezable saw what few had seen, Set take possession of his chosen. Rau-Set walked carefully around the stone, he held his torch close to the floor. The red liquid covering the stone caught fire slowly and burned with a reticence unfamiliar to Tezable. It began to burn more brightly as it met the depression where the ring had been. Rau-Set looked at Tezable and handed him the torch as if to say, "Ok where is it?"

Taking the torch in his hand, Tezable knelt down and ran the middle finger through the depression now absent its treasure. His finger caught the burning liquid and came away alight. Quickly extinguishing it against his tunic, he held his hand up so Rau-Set could see. The middle finger was missing two joints and most of the third, where the bloody stump ended a small black circlet hugged the webbed flesh between Tezable's index and third finger. Rau caught Tezable's wrist and took the ring between his thumb and forefinger and eased it upward, slowly. Tezable sucked his breath in as joint by joint his finger reappeared. Rau dropped the ring into a small square of gold foil he held in the palm of the other hand.

With a smooth motion Rau-Set wrapped the hoop in the gold and dropped it into a small leather pouch. As Rau-Set completed the gesture, both of them felt an enormous power close on them. Rau-Set turned to confront the power, and instantly Tezable was astonished to see that Set was not alone, in that small alcove. The space was crowded with gods. He counted Horus, Amun, Min, and Anubis and three more he could not name. The five waited in an incandescence of the presence. Tezable saw little else as he fell into paralysis.

What happened next Rau remembered only vaguely. But as he stepped forward to confront her felt her disdain and her contempt. As she came into apparent view, he could see she was not alone. She was accompanied by a train of goddesses, hundreds gathered behind her as the Hag reached for the leather pouch containing her ring.

Set spoke, "So you would reclaim your power? Tell me why I should surrender to you what I have wrapped in the flesh of the gods? Tell me what this ring is to you that you should appear in your strength in this place."

A voice, gravelly with earthen sleep, spoke in a rasping whisper, "You have taken the ring of entry from the stone of emergence, and you have violated the well of being itself."

Set, gripped the pouch tightly in this left hand and laughed at the Hag. "Your time is over, your rule is finished. Your gate is in my power and the tears of mothers will not tempt me to give it back. You know you cannot reclaim it as long as it is locked in Set's gold." He turned his back on the Hag, and Tezable found himself running with all his ability never stopping until he was outside the Temple.

The earth moved and the Temple collapsed in on itself, the great stones of the sacred ring which had been poised to fall, were toppled on the basalt slabs forming the labyrinth crushing all the sacred precinct. Tezable looked for Rau who was collapsing into the arms of the fourteen who carried him off in a litter. He tried to remember what he had seen, but his memory was a fog.

No sooner than Rau was gone did the demolition begin anew. The great stones were dug out of the pile of debris and set upright. One after another great fires were built around them, barrels of cold vinegar were dashed on the white hot stones shattering them into shards. The shards were stacked in carts and carried off to rivers and scattered. Slowly the basalt walls of the labyrinth were exposed to the light and shattered with great hammers. The great red stone was prized out of the earth and shattered as the others had been. Only this time fragments of the threshold were taken to Set's Temple where they were set in pavements in the hall of reception.

However, Rau commanded that the fragment containing the depression in which the ring itself had lain should be reserved and positioned centrally near the stone of surrender. Slowly the temple was reduced smashed and carried away. When the demolition team came to the great stair leading into the ground, they summoned Rau again.

Rau and Tezable conferred for a long while at the head of the stairs, and then they ordered the workers to begin excavation of the square above the chamber of the Hag. This space had been a ceremonial terrace built into the Temple precincts, and now as men with digging tools bent to their task, the ancient pavements came up revealing a mass burial beneath them. An incredible thatch of human bone lay beneath the pavements. Rau had this carefully removed and burned in large stone urns around which intense fires were built. When these bones were reduced to ash, the ash was thrown into rivers and dispersed.

When the last of the bone was excavated, they digging teams came on a layer of huge stones laid in radial geometry. These Rau also ordered removed. Great ramps were cut into the earth to free the stones and ease them out of the ground. These too were subjected to the fragmentation routine and given to the rivers. Finally the diggers began to break through the vault below, exposing it to the light. Great care was taken to cut the vault away so that the mosaic Tezable had described might be as little damaged as possible.

Just as he had predicted a huge stone sculpture of the Hag squatted in the center of the mosaic. They waited until high noon flooded the cavern with light and then descended on the statue. Carefully they wrapped it in gold foil and then in sheets of bronze. The diggers extended the ramps into the cavern and the huge Hag statue was brought to the surface. When the towns' people saw her, they wept in agony; tearing their hair they rushed the workers dragging her from her ancient seat of power. Rau's soldiers made short work of them, slaughtering them all as they approached. In all, 372 died that afternoon, their bodies were cremated, their ashes were scattered. The great Hag moved on her ponderous rollers to Set's temple where a great pit had been prepared near the south wall. She was lowered into a pool of the Water of life and was soon covered over by the priestly earth. Into this new middens everyone made contributions. Her defilement and desolation was complete, Rau thought.

After the Hag-stone had been disposed of and the vault exposed to the heavens, Rau and Tezable made a tour of the ruins.

"Now that the Hag's power is broken here we can see what this trouble was really about," Rau said as he waved his hand over the great mosaic. "What do you suppose this is? It's some kind of map, obviously. But the question is what is a map of? More to the point, when is it a map of what? This is obviously more than it seems." Rau thought out-loud.

The two walked the circumference of the three dimensional map which extended far into the cavern. It was obviously very old. Suddenly Tezable pointed to a place on the map and motioned Rau over.

"Set's Chosen, I think this is this very temple we are standing in. Look, it's a different design from what we knew, but here is the mound and its stone circles. And most importantly here is the ring."

"But look at the size of the ring, it is so large the Hag is standing inside of it," Rau wondered aloud. "That ring must be a portal of some kind but how does it grow so large?"

"Do you suppose this is really the ring or something else?" Tezable asked.

"If it is the ring, then its size is variable. I think you brought Set a very powerful artifact. Just what its powers are we will have to examine. But I suspect you are right. This represents the Temple we have just overthrown. So over here is the ancient Temple near Set's own. There is the great ceremonial way. So what does that tell us?"

"Just that we have here a master plan for the Hag's dominions as they must have been thirty or forty generations ago."

Rau scratched his head thoughtfully and speculated, "I'd guess that it's more like sixty to eighty generations ago. This temple seems to have been a place of power from very ancient times. Look at the temples and cities we don't even recognize in places we should know. I had hoped to use the building relatively intact, but I didn't realize how powerful a site it was. Before we build the new public bath I have decided what to put in this ancient place, this map must be preserved. Do you think it can be done?"

Tezable was silent for a time, scratching his head looking about at the proposed task. "Yes, Sets-chosen, if you will tell me where you would like it transferred." Tezable answered pensively. "But it will slow us down immeasurably would you not be just as happy with a drawing?"

"No, indeed, this is a potent map, I do not know what we will find as we dismantle it, but it must not be left undisturbed or simply scattered. There is too much information here for a drawing to record," Rau ordered.

"The training pavilion in the old temple site just below Set's Center needs a planning pavilion. Organize the work and let's get on with it. This map will be invaluable in rooting out the Hag's empire, moreover it will allow us to replicate her map with a more modern one of our own." Rau whispered hardly hoping he would live to see Set's empire as great as this map suggested the Hag's had been or was still.

The Combat

It was during this time that Zu decided he was well enough to begin his own search for the secret shadow company. He moved out of the temple and secured rooms at an inn close to the wharfs. It was not a very savory place yet it would do for a traveler in search of other travelers. He adopted the long robes of a merchant as disguise along with the appropriate leather shoes and belt complete with knife and money pouch. He rolled his hair up under a turban and went about the wharfs making inquiry after ships which might take him to castle Isis on a pilgrimage.

One evening after a fruitless day of searching, he ambled up the stairs to his room. Inside in the moonlight, Zu could discern that he had company. At first he thought some traders might have communicated with the shadow company who had come to test him. But when the maid stepped out of the shadows into the moonlight streaming in the window, Zu saw that this was welcome company.

"I've been watching you for a week she said. You look like someone who enjoys the company of women, though I never see you with any. So I've come to share your bed and see if you are what I think you are."

"What might that be, little one?" Zu said easily.

"A man who likes combat and has a capable warrior."

The use of the cult phrases surprised Zu and intrigued him. "What do you know of the combats? What temple did you train at?" He asked.

"I know very little. Only what women whisper behind closed doors. So, I've come to see what it is all about, to see if it is what I've been told it might be," she whispered bravely. "You won't kill me with your sacred dart will you?"

"Hardly, little one. But if it is a sacred challenge you offer, then I am for you." He shed his cloak, and unbuckled his belt as he moved toward her. She was not coy this one. She slipped into his arms with an eager warmth, and Zu was surprised to discover her garments slip away at a slight tug. Her long tresses cascaded down over her bare breasts, upturned nipples hardening as they rubbed against his silk under gown. Anxious hands pulled this gown over his head and caressed the warm muscled chest beneath it, sliding beneath his hips undoing his leather boots and pushing downward. He soon found himself shucked like an oyster, fingers moving quickly to free his ankles of his boots. As this delight busied herself with his boots, he gestured the two sacred asps free and with the flick of a wrist hurled them onto the bed. He watched them as they took up station along one of the bed's great pillows. He knew they would guard him during his passion. Set would not lose his servant so easily.

They stood there before the casement, like Isis and Osiris in a warm exploratory embrace. Quickly, Zu swept her up in his arms and carried her to the bed where he deposited her in a tangle of arms and hips. He chuckled with surprise.

"You're not new at this, are you little one? How shall we begin this fracas?" She gave no answer. Her smile spoke all he needed to hear. Her silken legs were white in the lunar glow as he positioned himself between them, her belly was taut and the peaks of her bosoms were luxuriant. Zu kissed these latter wonders by way of establishing his right to the territory and held them firmly in each hand. He felt the arch of his warrior crimson with need, aching to drink deeply from this sacred well, to dive into it in search of treasure. But he restrained himself, as his fingers began to explore this exquisite battle ground, luxuriantly furred and wet to touch as it was.

She writhed beneath his hands as his fingers stroked her thighs and caressed the small of her back pulling her off the bed and mashing the length of his warrior horizontal into her bright furrow like a plow about to cut turf. At last his fingers of one hand found the sacred well and began to slide deeply in and out while the fingers of the other hand pulled gently at her short hair. One finger, two fingers, three fingers.

Zu's other hand searched for the small guardian of the well head and seized it. Her hands began to pull him down to her, but he resisted. She sought his well armored warrior, and finding it, ran her nails down its rigid body gently, until she found the eggs he kept in his heavily furred pouch. Then she began a careful massage of these mysterious globes and a stroking the long length entire until Zu found he could not restrain his attack further. He let loose the dog of war and plunged into her, slowly, as the tight wetness of her gripped him as a wrestler might. He retreated outward and attacked again, taking more territory this time. She opened before him like a well trained army will sometimes feint before a foe drawing him into her strength before she springs her attack.

Suddenly, her legs wrapped around his waist, heels digging into his hips; her hands stroked his back, nails telling him the weakness of the fortress he was about to breach. Soon Zu had committed the full force of his sapper within her burrowing into her fortress, laying charges of explosive passion beneath her high walls and parapets. His main force began to assault the door of her temple with steady pummeling. Floods of amber liquor met the purpling helmet of his warrior as she arched her back to meet his thrusts, thrust for thrust.

Surprisingly, Zu found himself losing the battle, so he plunged in deeply and pinned her against the bed for a time drawing upon stores of resistance, curling his tongue back into his mouth. Then his mouth sought hers, and he drank deeply of her, his hands gripped hers, finger for finger, as two wrestlers might. He began again, withdrawing his heavy thatch from hers until his warrior paused nearly at the lip of her spring. He toyed with her then pressing himself into her gently, caressing her with the ridges of his helmet only, as if his warrior were to sip from the flood of her passion, taking his time collecting himself.

Without warning then he plunged half way in and out again, nearly withdrawing. She drew breath in shock, her hands found his buttocks and she forced him down upon her, as if desperate to keep her attacker in the fight. She forced him into her deeply, aiming his thrusts where she needed, wanted, demanded they go. Zu was surprised. He had been in many combats but never had anyone managed him so expertly.

But Zu was not ready to surrender himself to her just yet. He wrested control of himself again and suddenly withdrew completely, his iron shaft glistening in the moonlight, corded with throbbing veins along its massive form. Zu knew his warrior was bigger than most men, and the sight of himself in the moonlight made him proud, too proud perhaps. His powerful hands found her legs and slid them up so her ankles were on his shoulders, as he began to massage her wet harbor with the crimson barb of his champion. Without warning he found the trail he sought and sent home his scrappy harrier, turning her up on her shoulders slightly so he could sink in completely to her temple gates.

The walls of her burrow gripped him more tightly now, the new pressures sent cascades of pleasure up Zu's spine. She felt the difference too, and soon she was spending again, biting her hand to keep from screaming with delight. Zu had beaten her, twice she had let loose her radiance, and twice he had taken her treasure. Zu rammed her with fast strokes so that his heavy bag slammed into the ruby cleft of her velvet citadel, sending shivers of bliss deep into his pavement hard stomach. Again he approached the edge of no return, and he slowed toying with the lips of her second mouth, first delicately then roughly with his steeled combatant, until he regained control. She was his a third time. Victory! Zu screamed silently. She is well and truly breeched.

If that was effective, Zu thought, another position might be better. Already the radiance had poured from her temple three times and he felt refreshed, renewed. Quickly he grabbed her legs and turned her over on her chest. The valley of her spine glistened in the pearling light. Her hair stuck to her shoulders, so moist had the battle made them. She looked over those beautiful shoulders at him through a veil of hair, a look of fear and amazement in her eyes.

He pulled her rump up to him and began to caress her hips and belly, feeling for the stiff little warrior who stood guard at the wellhead. Rolling him between two fingers, Zu awakened the little man until the maid was squirming for relief. Happy to oblige, Zu guided his blood hungry berserker into her once more and began to attack her treasure house for a fourth time. Slowly, in deep, in shallow, deep, shallow. She began to moan and work her battlements upon him, as his hands gripped her back and shoulders. When Zu felt a powerful surging in his loins, he pinched his hips to stop the flood before it began. Seizing control of the motion, Zu began to send his trooper into the fastness of her fortress with irregular patterns, Deep, Deep, shallow. Shallow, deep shallow, shallow.

Each time his hips struck hers, a wave would ripple through her woman's flesh until it crashed against the shore of her waist. Soon the pounding surf once more had the ancient herds within his blood racing for the gates. She began subtlety to seize the rhythm until it was hers, not his. A roaring came to Zu's ears. The maid sensed she was winning an important battle so she added a swaying motion to his, seizing Zu's glittering opponent with muscles she only discovered she had in this position. In shock, an explosion of muscle and seed shook Zu to the very root of his being, as his control broke and he flooded her with the spoils of her conquest. The exquisite pleasure of distended organs became wondrous pain, as she continued to rock back and forth squeezing his fountain for the last pearl of his treasure.

Limp with exhaustion and humiliation Zu collapsed beside the maid, wrapping her in his arms, pulling her chest close to his so their beating hearts could drum together in a soft tattoo of pleasure.

The maid was, however, not ready to let her victim off quite so easily. Her right hand stroked Zu's chest, circling his nipples, and tracing the deeply carved channel down his midriff up to his beautiful face. Her fingers stroked his brow, curled around the turn of his nostril as it breathed, flared and relaxed. They toyed with his reddened lips until she kissed him gently, gratefully, her tongue searching for his.

Freed from such duty, her hand caressed his belly edging downward, slowly, and tremulously. Curling his short hair around her fingers, she tenderly caressed the limp body of her defeated enemy, stroking it, rolling it about in her palm, until it began to arch once more. She released it and watched it, as it rolled on his thigh, mounting slowly into its brave form, renewing its armor and flaring its helmet for a second attack. She kissed his breast, coiling her tongue around his nipples, biting them gently as her long hair covered his face luxuriantly. He breathed in the smell of her, awakening once more to her battle cry. Her tongue probed his belly button, and followed the trail of hair down where the tower of his manhood stood quivering and pulsing. Delicately she tasted him, rolling her tongue around the cleft of his ruby shield, tracing with her teeth the outlines of his armor until her tongue found the vent and began to rummage it greedily, as if more treasure might fly forth if she found the right maneuver. Suddenly, she took the entire shaft in her mouth, plunging down upon him, until her nose was buried in the fragrant thatch of his hips. His musty odors, mingled with her own, were powerful inducements to her, and her nose wrinkled with delight.

She began to rise up and down with her head so that the back of her throat battered his soldier deliciously. Her tongue wrapped around this sensual cap, seeking with every effort to increase its supple stiffness. With equal suddenness she released his warrior from this sweet embrace, and took his heavy bag of tricks in her mouth sucking in the rounded eggs it contained and massaging them with her tongue. Zu could hardly contain himself, so overcome was he with pleasure. These were not allowed in the combats. For a woman to subject a man's warrior to her teeth was deep humiliation for the consequences could be unimaginable. He sat up and took her in his arms, until she straddled his chest. Pushing her backward, his urgent need for combat was thrust upon the maid. Quickly she lifted herself on his hips and gripped his brave man with both hands. Lowering herself upon him, she slid around him slowly until she had captured the full length of him within her. She placed her hands on his shoulders and began to rise up and down—slowly at first, pausing at the rise of her hips to grip his ruby helmet with the muscles of her jade well. Then down she descended and began to ride him, as if he were a magnificent war horse with a very special saddle.

Zu relaxed his hips and his belly and let her work her wonders upon him. He closed his eyes and let all his sensations drain from his extremities, concentrating on every pore, every hair follicle where her captive met his opponent. He felt the slickness of her prison, the firmness of her door as she slammed against him repeatedly. He felt her hair meld with his; her fingers bracing upon his muscled hips; his bag grew small and tight. He felt his man's eggs roll with pleasure within it, responding to her embrace of his paralyzed warrior. He felt the warmth of her buttocks as they buffeted his thighs. He saw her arch her back, how her small breasts would quake when she descended upon him. He saw the wild look of ecstasy she wore beneath the veil of long hair, as she rose over him.

Suddenly, she stopped. Zu's breath was driven out of him by the quickness with which she turned over him. Now she had her back to him, both hands took him prisoner as his warrior arched toward her belly like a spring-loaded, heavy door knocker. She lowered herself upon him again driving this battered soldier into her woman's walls. Zu had never in his life known this could happen, never known the pressure he could thus endure on his brave champion. She shoved him into her, until, as he could see in the dim moonlight, she was impaled completely.

He saw himself reappear as she rose on her hips, and the pleasure he experienced as his helmeted fighter jammed his head against the entirety of her long burrow was overwhelming. He gripped her hips with his hands, and slowed her descent and her ascent, wanting to savor each stroke, each thrust wanting to delay the loss. She began to shorten the strokes until she seemed to bob upon him. Suddenly, she began to spend and weep with pleasure, a cascade of radiance washed over Zu while at the same time Zu's dam burst a second time. She quickened her pace now, feeling her victory as his warm fountain drenched her temple precincts. Zu nearly fainted as she pumped up and down on his too knowing dancer.

She rose off him, looked at him, his arms flung out, his legs apart. His throbbing warrior lay on his belly like the head and neck of a great turtle which has been turned on its back, its arch seeking solid ground to right itself. So too Zu's warrior turned and moved as it pulled itself back into its shell, his chest was still heaving from his exertions. The maid cradled his head in her wet lap momentarily, washing his face with her hair.

She thought he might revive, but he was out, out like a lantern extinguished in a storm. She felt his face with her fingers, exploring the muscles and bone which projected his divine features. She wondered how it was possible for the face of Bright Isis, goddess of spring and new life herself masked upon this form. She was sure this face did not belong to an ordinary enemy, and yet she sensed that this brave form with whose champion she had so recently battled, was not a friend.

What he was, she did not know. She only knew she had defeated him and that he was now hers to kill if she wished. She hesitated thinking about this heaving form before her. Should she strangle him now or wait. She knew this was the time to strike but smell of him was too near and too fresh. She wrinkled her nose pulling him in and knew she could not kill him. Set's asps hovered at her hip watching intently ready to strike should the god detect lethal intent.

Later, she thought. *Later, after I have safely delivered his child. Then there will be time to finish the work.* She rose from her embrace, tossed a robe over him, slipped back in her shift and was gone. A happy smile flooded her face. Inwardly, she knew she would conceive this night a hero, more god than man surely.

Zu himself did not feel her parting caress, he felt nothing except a deep and satiated sleep. When she left, Set's asp emerged from the bedclothes and coiled itself on Zu's belly, its split tongue tasting the air, feeling the heat of her who was gone and not gone.

A kind of steam rose from its length as it melted again into Zu's chest and arm. The second asp slithered down the valley of Zu's spine and found its old channel and the new radiance it now contained, even if it was not as much as there should have been. Cain would also have detected the heavy odor of Set, had he been there to smell as well as see.

A Test of Arms

Zu slept as the dead sleep until the discomfort of his bladder awakened him. His warrior stood vigil fully armored as if his defeat of the evening before had meant nothing. It was a vigil Zu took pleasure in ending as he filled the bowl beneath the bed with the water of his life. His morning ablutions were minor compared to what he might have had at the temple, but he'd had enough of the temple for a while.

He'd been very glad this particular opponent had not found her way into the combats, she might have humiliated many before she'd been conquered. Zu wondered if she could be taken. How he'd like to have a second attempt at those particular gates! But he put the thought of her away and put on fresh linen for the day's trials. As he moved down the hallway and out into the stair he thought for a moment he could smell her perfume yet lingering where she must have brushed the wall with her shoulder or perhaps her hair. He shook off the notion and made his way out into the street.

The day before he'd noticed a tavern in an alley near the wharf and it was to that tavern he turned his feet. The smell of the ocean hung heavy over the cobblestone pavement, the screeching of Gulls who fought for scraps around the fishing boats echoed against the buildings. The good people of Cassoria went about their various businesses with a purpose and energy that pleased and amazed Zu all at the same time. These were a people gifted in commerce and commerce was their gift. Zu stopped at a cloth merchant's stall to admire the finely woven linen and ask the price of a particular scarf he admired. But it was more to blend in to the crowd that he did so, he wanted neither commodity and they seemed overpriced to him anyway.

When he turned the corner he saw a man who looked familiar. He puzzled over this for a while, thinking it must be someone from the Temple, until he saw his profile as he turned into the tavern. It was the man in the dream who had killed the two assassins of Isis. The very man. Older perhaps, and somewhat worn about the edges, but it was the same man. Now he was puzzled. Cautiously Zu stepped into the tavern and paused. In the deep gloom, his eyes quickly adjusted to the tavern's hazy interior.

It was crowded for so early in the morning, and the loud talk which seemed to swell and collapse at intervals seemed to portend something more than ordinary. This hardly seemed like a crowd taking the noon time meal or preparing to. Zu eased his way through the thickening crows before he found a table at one corner of the room, sat back. He wanted something to break his fast, a local beer and some bread perhaps. The serving girl came to him and inquired of his needs. Though he had many, Zu told her only of the need for bread and beer. He decided to let Set worry about recognitions. As he had made his way through the crowd he'd noticed a table at which sat a likely looking foursome. He continued scanning these particular candidates as he sat waiting for his beer and bread.

One was the man he'd recognized, or thought he'd recognized. When he turned to survey the crowd in Zu's direction he observed the man wore a strange crest on his cloak, a poppy in the center of which was a skull. Beneath this a legend in Syrian, which he thought translated into something like "Sleep No More." Mumbling again, his lips made the words, "I wish I had studied languages more carefully. Maybe one of these will know the group I am searching for."

The crested man was not as big as most fighters he had seen, but he still looked formidable, decked out as he was in a heavy leather chest piece, arm, thigh and shin wards of Syrian make, heavily scarred and scratched. It was armor such as charioteers wore, but it had seen better days. He was a handsome man, but his sandy brown hair was swept back and kept short revealed a face older than he had expected.

The woman next to him was a wonder. She was tall, heavily tattooed if her arms and neck were any indication and into her braided hair were knit a string of gilded camels. She was obviously not from Cassoria, Zu thought. Unbidden he wondered what kind of combatant she'd make, and whether his tattoos would like her tattoos. Smiling he continued to scan the table. Seated next her was a second man in a charioteers mail, but this was highly oiled almost ceremonial in its tawny hue. It was hardly the attire one might wear if he wished anonymity. His cloak also bore a crest, the device of Ra. This warrior was not young, his stark white hair was just beginning to recede. Clearly, he was a Sythian, but his build was slightly larger than his friend with the poppy crest. Next to him sat another Sythian who also wore the charioteer's armor and had two swords at his side one long, one short. This Sythian had blond hair, as was common to his race, and by his features and build could be a younger brother, or at least from the same tribe, Zu thought.

As he sat in the chair the woman turned and looked at him, Zu did not indicate he'd seen her, though he certainly had. He continued to stare so that the man in the scarred leather armor eyed him and gestured gruffly, as if to say

"Have you lost something in our midst?" As he rose up from his own table, moved through the throng and sat down at Zu's the odor of Set came to Zu. It was a strong sending, and for a moment he feared others might have caught it, but if so none reacted. Zu smiled as the man from his dream settled down in the chair opposite him.

"Do I know you?" the charioteer asked in growing heat. "You've been staring at us as if we were to be your noon day repast."

"It is possible?" Zu said under his breath watching to see what effect his next communication might have. "I saw you murder two of the Hag's assassins in the forest as you rescued a young woman with the most amazing blond hair." The warrior blanched and his hand moved quickly to his sword his sword arm muscles bunching up under his tunic.

"Relax, I am not your enemy. What I saw was in a dream Set sent me to guide me to you. I seek the shadow company, and Set seems to think you might know of them."

"I might. But if I did, why would I tell a stranger who won't show his face?" Came the menacing reply.

Zu had donned his traveling clothes with its face scarf as he usually did when traveling beyond the temple. He studied the apparition before him for a moment, estimating the likelihood of an attack, or at least how much might be gained in a physical encounter. He seemed too confidant of his ability, however, so Zu answered him calmly.

"I have journeyed far from the bright desert to join a certain company of lunatics which expects to seek out the dark lady." Although the forbidden name was absent and although he was speaking casually and in normal voice, his statement brought the babbling room to an abrupt silence.

The man who wore the holy symbol of Ra blazed briefly as he raised his hand and offered Zu a seat at their table, "Why don't you two join us here so we don't have to ease drop with the whole room." When Rau and his new companion returned to the first table Ra's initiate asked "Why would you think that men might gather here to seek such a formidable foe?"

Zu gathered himself into the seat offered and said in a more quiet voice "Well for openers the I have been led here by the god. I know you from his dream and as you approached me Set let me know you were one I needed to know," he replied.

"But why would you think such a group would tell a stranger their whereabouts, especially when everyone in Cassaria knows the one you mentioned has agents everywhere?" replied the man in the leather armor somewhat taken aback by the naivete of the response. Sensing an mistake Zu removed the glove on his tattooed hand and held the glove tightly. The sign of Set visibly changed the atmosphere at the table and sensing that change he preceded.

"Of course, caution is always in order. Perhaps, I have made a mistake. But that I am sent here by those greater than myself should be obvious. While this city is handsome, it is no more so than my own and I had far rather be there breeding wenches, than here seeking companions for a death march."

The man in unkempt armor thought about this proposition for a moment and then said, "What you say has some truth in it concealed one. I speak for no one but myself. Should my friends here think they should share with you their names, that is up to them stranger. My family calls me Tristen, Knight of Sorrows. It's a bad pun as my mother died birthing me. I wear the crest of Cassoria as I on occasion serve the king with my rusty armor."

The rest of the table sat quietly trying to keep from laughing. But they settled in to a glare aimed at both the new comer and Tristen. Finally, the Sythian wearing the highly polished armor spoke up.

"I think this lad has mistaken us for fools. We know of no such men and of no such ambitions. So my friend you may continue your search elsewhere. May I suggest the island of the Damned? Mad men sometimes seek their allies there."

Zu made no ruckus. He merely rose and left.

As he left them, he heard one say, "That mask is familiar, where have I seen its kind before?"

"Maybe he's hideously scarred and is afraid to show us his face…" said another.

"Maybe he's famous and doesn't want to be recognized," he heard the woman reply before the noise of the tavern rushed in on him and hid their conversation in the clatter.

Once outside he retreated back along the cobblestone alley and out into the broad avenue of merchants. He stopped to examine cedar wood lumber from far off Lebanon and the resin of the tamarisk tree from which the best incense came. He was startled when the woman he'd seen in the tavern was at his side. "Come with me if you are what you say you are." Together they walked down the broad avenue and out towards the city gates where five horses awaited them. Join us for a little expedition into the country side, it is so beautiful just now, it is a shame to stay cramped up behind these crenelated walls.

"Gladly, I will join you. An expedition is just what I've been wanting." Zu agreed.

"So you said in the tavern" she averred.

They made a mad dash out of the city gates and into the countryside, vying with each other to see who would take the lead. It was a noisy affair, not what Zu would have preferred but it had the look of companions out for a lark in the countryside. Few would have known that a company of assassins was gathering. They stopped in a secluded glade not far from the city, and dismounted. Slowly the four faced Zu ominously, with steely determination and stealth.

"I am here to answer a challenge, if that is what you intend this encounter to be."

"Indeed it is," said the younger Sythian. "We do not ride with any who cannot kill us, or with any we can kill easily."

The young Sythian broke ranks and walked toward Zu. "I am Dormor, Knight of the shadow company and I will kill you if I can," he said.

"I am Zu, brother of Set's Chosen, I will not die easily, but I did not come here to reduce your numbers. But if you insist, you will die on the edge of my sword."

"I insist," said Dormor. Both drew their swords, Zu's two swords were at least three hands shorter than Dormor's, and he gave Dormor an impressive display of Set's sword kaat. When Dormor moved towards Zu to engage him, the double swords put Dormor at a distinct disadvantage. So Dormor tried to rush Zu, but Zu met him with such a flurry of steel he could not progress. Dormor drew out his own second sword and began again. This time the double sword attack left Zu on the retreat. Until, Zu called out, "I think we are evenly matched, do not make me kill or wound you, Dormor. What say you?"

"Nonsense, I do not feel threatened," Dormor boasted. At which point Zu relieved him of one sword and pressed him into the brush until he stumbled and Zu was on top of him ready for the kill.

"Enough" cried, Tristen. "You have proven yourself with a sword, how are you with a knife?"

"Thrown or fought hand-to-hand?" asked Zu.

"Either," Said Tristen.

"Come and die on my dagger then. My name is Zu, brother of Set's Chosen and I will not die easily."

The two met in the middle of the road and Zu stood stock still while Tristen approached him. Several close feints did not get Zu to bring up his guard. When Tristen attacked for real, Zu stepped into him, blocked his knife thrust, turned his knife hilt first, and delivered what surely would have been a death blow.

Tristen was stunned. He stood as if turned to marble.

"How did you do that," he made out after he regained his composure from the shock of the attack.

"Just a little trick assassins know," said Zu.

"A trained assassin," said Dormor. "I might have known."

"Yes and a member of the thief's guild as well. Though it is women's virtue I prefer to steal, I am a master thief."

"Catch," said the woman as she threw a bag of coins in the air to Zu. "I Quinn am, last of the Telshandra, and thief you are not I say."

Zu recognized the challenge immediately and neatly caught the bag and had it whistling back at her in the flick of a wrist, a second bag joined this one, which he returned with equal finesse. She added a knife to the bags, and returned them to Zu who completed the circuit again, before the challenge was met, Quinn had loaded the circuit between them with two bags of coins, a knife, a sword, an ax, a boot and a heavy silver bracelet. Catching them all in her turn, she saluted Zu as master thief. "By your hands, you I know, guild brother," she said with the formula of greeting.

"I thank you for the challenge, guild master," he returned.

The members of the shadow company had never seen such a challenge before and were quietly amazed. But Levit, the white haired Sythian, was not convinced yet.

"I ride with no man who conceals his face. Until I behold what secret is there, you will not have my back to guard, he strode up to Zu and tried to rip the mask off his face. Zu however met his movement with another, and quickly had Levit on his knees in a painful wrist lock none had ever seen before.

"Shall I break your sword arm, my Sythian friend? I am Zu, brother of Set's chosen, and I will show you what you ask if courtesy is restored."

"I am Levit, Priest of Ra, I yield to you brother of Set's chosen. Show us your visage, that we may know Set's warrior."

Zu let Levit have his arm back unbroken, though very bruised, and stepped back untying his mask as he did so.

"I am perfectly happy expose my face among friends. But I should warn you that it will complicate our lives to ask that I go mask-less in your company," Zu said in a tone, dripping with mock seriousness. Slowly he pulled off the mask so they could see his face.

A sudden hush came over the company assembled there as the dappled forest light struck his face.

"Gods you tell." Quinn said passionately. Zu just raised his eyebrow at the tattooed woman who only stood and gaped at the young champion in front of her. His beauty was astonishing. He seemed more god than man. His smooth skin radiated health, his eyes were large like those of a startled stag. His hair was thick and radiantly curled, a lustrous mink color. The cupid's bow mouth held the most perfect teeth of gleaming ivory white. Centering them was a Homeric nose, heroic without being arrogant, strong without being over bold. Bracing all this perfection was a cleft chin and wide jaw bones that were both strong and manly, yet at the same time suggested both strong passion and the energy to fulfill enormous desire.

"I see what you mean. Every woman who saw him would want him. Some men would not want to fight him, lest they mar so great a wonder. Others would challenge him only to ugly him up some. I can see, Levit, how our life would be complicated if we asked him to go mask-less" said Tristen.

"So do I, but I still cannot ride with a masked companion. Perhaps a cloak and hood would give equal protection. Is your mask guild associated?" asked Levit.

"It is sacred to Set, but I will acquiesce to your demands, if only to join your company of warriors," offered Zu.

"That may be good enough for you, but not for me, came a voice from nowhere.

"Ah, Boone, I wondered when you would announce yourself." Said the Knight of Sorrows.

A blur emerged from the forest, like the vibrating air which comes off a very hot fire, and rippled onto the road until it stood in front of Zu.

"I am Boone, Priest of Anubis, and Knight of the Shadow company. I will not ride with any who wear a tattoo I have not seen entirely. There may be more to you than your wrist shows. Show us your ritual blaze."

"And if I refuse, O tear in my eye? Said Zu to the quivering air.

"Then you die, before your next breath." Said Boone.

"Be warned O shivering mask of air, that the secret of such cloaks is not unknown to me, and any man who touches me uninvited will find the light of tomorrow's sun a distant dream."

Stunned by the cult words associated with the secret of his cloak of invisibility, Boone stood back and said, "I hear my friend, and I ask my friend to show us his talisman of blaze."

Silently, Zu shucked his shirt and stood naked from the waist up, on his muscular torso the serpents of Set were clearly shown, except for what was concealed beneath his waist. Two sand and rose colored serpents rose across his body. One in the front arced up his midline undulating around a point three fingers below his navel, and around a point exactly over his heart before it shot out over his right shoulder and down his arm to end in a magnificent head on the back of his hand. The second matched this ascent except it traced the valley of his spine and undulated in the opposite rhythm and exiting down the left arm and hand.

"Magnificent tattoos," said Quinn.

"These are not tattoos, Quinn; these are something far more potent than tattoos. They are actual serpents are they not Zu?" Asked Boone.

"I do not ask such questions nor have answers you might understand. These are ritual marks of Set's favor. I have had them since birth I am told, and I am forbidden to tell you about either their nature or their purpose," said Zu.

"But they do demonstrate not only an assassin's guild, but also a healer's," am I right," said Boone?

"I have some skill as a healer, but I would never advertise my skill because to do so would violate basic agreements between the gods," said Zu.

What are these four marks on your breasts?" Tristen asked, "they do not look like tattoos, more like scarification."

"I know the tooth of Anubis, and I bow before its bearer. The claw of Horus I also know, but this can only be the flail of Min and the dagger of Amun? What are you to wear such talisman of multiple possession?" Boone said with obvious awe in his voice.

I am twin of Set's Chosen, born when the Ka of the great teacher Schilo fecundated himself in our mother's womb. I do not know how I came to wear any of these marks. They have come unbidden and unsought. I know I am warded, however, and that the gods use me as a vessel as it suits them. More than this I cannot tell you."

Boone took off his cloak of invisibility and stood before Zu. "I accept your explanation and your purpose. I welcome you to our company."

"Enough of such shows of courtesy. We have completed our test and have increased our numbers. Now we have more pressing business. Will you join us Zu?" asked Tristen.

So this is the Shadow Company, thought Zu. *I hope they are better connected with their Gods than they seem. I felt nothing from the other side as I endured their tests. I wonder if they could pass mine?*

Again came the question. "Well how about it?" Tristen repeated, "Will you ride with us against Her?"

"Willingly, but I have a task to complete when we return. I must secure the mace of Ra before we attempt the most holy precincts of the Temple. I am instructed that this implement cannot be left unprotected once we penetrate the temple precincts." Said Zu.

"Now you are treading on my toes," said Levit. "As a knight of Ra, I am of Ra's order and honor his relics. Who dares give such instructions to violate the sacred precincts of Ra?"

Zu paused for a moment, looking at Levit and the talisman of Ra emblazoned on his shield. "All I know, Levit, is that these are Set's instructions. I must carry this mace into battle, or our cause is lost. I would not defile your god's precincts, nor cast you as my enemy. If I fail in this, I am assured we go to our deaths, if we challenge the Hag."

"We do not even know exactly where it is in the temple," Levit said thoughtfully. "I was told it was buried with one of the High Priests. But as that was before my time in his service, I cannot speak from personal knowledge."

"I bear knowledge which indicates to me its location. I can find it. I believe I can secure it. But I need your permission to make the attack." Said Zu.

"Attack? said Tristen incredulously. "You would lead an attack on the kingdom's most holy shrine."

"I am informed that not merely stealth will secure the mace, but that its guardians must be overcome, if we are to secure it."

"I wonder if we merely asked permission to borrow it?" mused Dormor.

"I don't think the priests would give that permission without sharing in our quest. Moreover, Set is of the opinion that the cult of Ra in these environs has been compromised by the Hag, perhaps in the same way the Temple of Set was before I liberated it. Zu proceeded to tell them of the maze and the battle on the rooftop. The nobility of this particular temple is not what it used to be. Include them and the Hag will know we are here and what our plans are," said Zu.

"But you already seem to be on the Hag's short list of enemies. You said yourself she knows you plan to come against her," said Tristen.

"I am not in charge of this expedition. I am here only because the gods command it. I will leave my fate in their hands and in the hands of Set's Chosen," Zu said quietly.

There was a long pause of stunned silence at this admission.

"How many knights will you need on this attack?" said Levit finally. "One only can succeed. I must go alone. But I will need a diversion. Can I rely on you to provide such a diversion?"

"Inside or outside the Temple?" asked Tristen

"Outside." said Zu.

"I think we know about diversions, don't we my friends," asked Tristen.

"Know we do," smiled Quinn, "Know we do!"

Now with all the cards on the table and a plan reached Zu felt more comfortable and allowed Tristen to lead on.

The company left not as they had come. They mounted up and one chariot left at a time, and in different directions, so they would not attract attention. They even gave Zu and Boone their own chariot as the others doubled up in the other two. As Boone wore his cloak of invisibility it seemed that Zu entered the city alone. Boone left him as he slowed to enter the city gates, and Zu continued alone.

Purge

For a while Set's Temple and armies were content with consolidating their gains. Things seemed to be going well in Volun as the people began to accept Set's rites and appreciate the amenities of the new baths. Yet flowers still appeared regularly where the shards of the old temple had been used in the new. Every now and again rumors would surface that the worship of the Hag was continuing in secret, and with some frequency the old cult was suppressed anew with impaling. Gradually Volun returned to its commerce and rebuilt its trade with other cities. But beneath the seeming prosperity a new problem emerged.

As the months progressed, however, it became clear what the Hag had meant. There were no births in Volun. Its citizens grew alarmed. A year came and went and still there were no new children. Finally, the grief grew too massive to be contained and riots broke out in Volun. Rau was forced to enter the city came to the city with the new army which he was assembling and set up camped beyond the city gates. When he entered in power riding in his great war chariot, the people did not cheer or proclaim his arrival with shouting. There was a universal silence, a silence which unnerved even Rau.

In the reception chamber of Set's new Temple in Volun, Rau received the leaders of the town. One very large and corpulent merchant came before Rau and after the appropriate gestures of obscene, spoke for his city. "My lord, your captured city of Volun is dying. We had been a seat of ancient power, we are now nothing. Our seeds do not spout in the fields, our flocks no longer bear young, and our wives no longer swell with children."

Rau was silent for a long while. A second man of obvious wealth stepped forward and spoke more aggressively.

"You have destroyed the threshold of entry. You have desecrated the goddesses' most sacred centers. She has withdrawn our fertility. Our wives are barren, our seed is as sand. Even the mighty Set cannot restore our children to us."

As he ceased his speech, he bowed before Rau, tears running down his cheeks. *Here was a man in obvious pain,* Rau thought, *I wonder what his wife would have to say.*

"Bring to me your wives and midwives, I would hear from them their plight," Rau said gently concealing his rage.

Six women were ushered into the audience hall. Two aged mothers dressed in black were identified as midwives. The other four were the newly un-bonded wives and daughters of the men who had petitioned Rau.

Rau spoke first to the midwives. "Tell me grandmothers what you know of this problem."

"Lord. You have defiled the city. You have broken the ancient pact between Isis and her women. Our wombs are empty, our arms are empty. Our men are strong, our women willing, but no seed takes root in this defiled soil," said the oldest.

The other stepped forward more boldly and challenged Rau, "Where is your power now Set's chosen. You have polluted our temple, you have shattered the doorway between the worlds, and no one knocks at the womb door anymore. The bright world is growing dark. Can a man create life by himself? Give us back our goddess you stole from us. Give us back the ring of entry. We are doomed without them."

Rau rose from his seat of power and strode forward. He grabbed the mer-chant by his hair and slapped him soundly. He knocked down the younger man, and ordered the guards to seize the women. "Strip the midwives. I think we will discover something very interesting if we do."

The other four women began to shriek and defend the old ones. But after a fierce struggle they were all six restrained and the old ones stripped sky clad. Tezable gasped, "They are poetesses of the Hag, look at the ritual tattoos on their hips and breasts."

"Take them out and impale them immediately" Rau ordered.

"Strip the others too." The two wives also bore the marks of the temple and these too Rau ordered impaled. The daughters were unmarked, so that Rau ordered them imprisoned for interrogation later.

He turned to the men, "Whom do you think you address here, an ignorant farmer? Do you not think I am familiar with the Hag's strength and her cult? It is she who teaches the women how to kill their children; it is she who knows how to make the seeds turn to mush in the soil. I will fix this problem for you, and it will not take long to do it either, but first I will see you as well."

The two men were stripped. The obese merchant was pitiful, his body a hideous ruin of excess and gluttony. "Lock this one away, bring him back when he is reduced to a more ordinary size." He kicked the merchant out of his way and strode up to the younger man, who was now cowering before Rau.

"Stand up man, show yourself to us, we are men here, we are not afraid of other men."

The man unfolded himself slowly to his full height. His thighs bore the marks of Amun, his warrior was inflamed. But he was strong, his chest well muscled, his belly flat. His hips clean and his thighs powerful. "I think," said

Rau "you are not beyond us. Tell me about the combat which your warrior has endured."

"Combat?" The man asked.

"Your ivory stalk is red with wrestling the guardian of the well." Rau said. The man flinched as if he had been struck.

"My wife and I want children. We have tried everything. Recently we joined a group who claimed to know the cure for the barrenness, but nothing works. I am sore with trying, that's all." Rau waved Tezable to him, "Take this one into the baths, and teach him. I will solve his problem for him.

Rau strode into the courtyard in front of the presentation chamber. Quickly he gave the orders. At first his soldiers could not believe he was serious, but his fury soon convinced them he was. All women older than twenty-five were to be impaled along the road into Volun. Those over fifteen were to be sold into slavery. He would break the Hag's power forever: it would be a brutal victory but it would be final.

The bloody business took three weeks. Eight hundred and seventy women were impaled, 382 were sold into slavery. The men of the city were shattered as they wept and fought the troops who were executing Rau's orders. Nearly 400 men were killed in these skirmishes. In the process Rau's troops found three secret chapels dedicated to the Hag, chapels they demolished and obliterated all traces of. The flowers stopped arriving at the ruins of the great Temple where the new baths were rising. The all male survivors of the city saw Volun nearly depopulated and they were pressed into Set's Temple training. Those who objected were slain on the spot, so that soon the survivors were becoming adept at the battle for the wellhead.

Furthermore as Rau's armies conquered other towns and smaller villages, the young women and children he captured were sent to replenish the Volun's population. The men who endured this devastation soon found younger arms to comfort them and within two years the city was teeming with children. Rau set up his presentation chamber in the new temple of Set in Volun and asked the fathers to bring their new children for presentation. When each father with new children came forward, Rau required an oath of allegiance to the god. Those who acquiesced were given a small image of Set for a home altar and some commercial privilege of their asking. Those who knew nothing about commerce were given small parcels of land. Those who refused, and there were some unlucky enough to have tried it, were trussed up and hung by the feet, head first into the middens with their shoulders touching the surface of the offal which held their beloved Hag. Only by considerable exertion could they keep their heads above the foulness. Finally, when in their exhaustion, they relaxed and drowned in the mire, their bodies hauled out and burned. When he finished he ordered all the men of Volun to be initiated into the cult of Set during the next year.

All who were not initiated by the new year, would be impaled on the road. Rau realized that his treatment of Volun was the only program that would permanently seal the Hag from his people. It was harsh, but it ensured a permanently loyal population. Thereafter, the word "Volun" became a term used to describe his method of conquest. Wherever the cities of the Hag were found, they were Volun'd. All treasures of the Hag's temples were also treated similarly with the result that her images permanently vanished from sight and those who knew her mysteries and rituals were as rare as comets.Finally, an ironic thing began to happen. Even before Rau's armies would focus their attention on a new fortress of the Hag, the men of the city would begin to assert themselves and demand the rights Rau everywhere gave to other men.

On three occasions Rau found that the cult of the Hag had been brutally suppressed even before his armies appeared. The Hag's priestesses were impaled and found lining the roads to the cities as the armies approached. Huge wagons of cultic treasure, absent its gold and silver and precious stones, sat as if abandoned in front of the city gates. But for Rau the really precious things, the cultic images were intact and surrendered. Soon other people got into the act and found that raiding the Hag's Temples was both profitable and less dangerous than thumbing their collective noses at Rau's army. Tribunals were set up independently of Set's demands and women who were thought to be assisting other women in controlling their fertility were condemned and impaled. Women whose husbands accused them of murdering their children in the womb were given a quick trial and burned at the stake. It was not long before the cult of the Hag was forced underground and then had to be rooted out by zealous priests of Set.

As soon as it was known that another city had accepted his law, Rau dispatched his students to set up a new temple. Always their first task after establishing their sacred precincts and, erecting a black obelisk of the law, was to demolish absolutely the sacred precincts of the Hag, and if possible to appropriate the site for public baths, or for a training center for Set's initiates. Birth rates were watched carefully and women who were infertile were sold into slavery. Women who were charged with murdering their unborn children were publicly burned, and older women who seemed especially knowledgeable of the Hag's lore were impaled. Set's priests were especially feared by women and with good reason.

The Challenge of Anarantha

Every now and again a city would oppose Rau and it would become Rau's special challenge to Volun it. One such city was Anarantha near the sea. It had been an ancient cultic center of the Hag, and was now an important military center with a huge navy and fine ports. Many who had fled other cities which had been Voluned, chose Anarantha to make their stand against Rau and its laws. One morning a traveler came to Rau's Temple bearing gifts. Seven stone urns he carried in his cart, and in each one the head of a priest of Set. It was a hideous sight, as from each mouth clenched in rictus protruded a severed warrior, like a round black tongue. Rau welcomed the traveler into the gate.

"Where did you find these urns, Stranger?" Rau asked.

"The Hag's chosen in Anarantha gave them to me after she kidnapped my children and my wife. When I refused to deliver them to you, she slaughtered my youngest child before my very eyes, stripped the skin from his body, and…" said the stranger.

"And made a drum, with which she terrorized you," ventured Rau.

"Wh…Why yes, how d….did you know?" the stranger wept uncontrollably. He was my precious son, only four years old. He knew nothing about you or the goddess. Nothing at all."

"I have fought the Hag for years, I should know her tactics well enough." Rau answered the weeping man, as Tezable swept him into his arms comforting him as we wept.

"She said she'd do the same to each of my children in monthly intervals until I returned with your answer."

"What kind of answer do you think she expects?" Rau asked.

"I think she expects you to descend on her city of Anarantus with your army, where she hopes you will be utterly destroyed. She has a huge army prepared, a fleet of heavily armed ships, and an impregnable fortress. And the Hag openly walks among the citizens of the city."

"What did you say?" Rau asked.

"That the Hag walks openly among the citizens?" the man asked through his tears.

"That's it. Describe this apparition."

"It is hard to describe, but often out of the corner of your eye you will think you see her, when you wheel around to confront her, she's not there. The citizens have learned to look away from her but watch her out of the side of their vision. I myself saw her this way: A great black form, with multiple arms. Her hands brandish terrible weapons, and one even carries the severed head of a man. The last time I saw here I was so over come with sexual excitement, I wanted to lie down and let her dance me into pulp."

"This is something new, said Rau. "Something I shall have to see for myself. Take this man and send him on his way, give him a shard from the red threshold stone. Tell him to tell the Hag, that I will shatter her as I have shattered others."

Rau left secretly in the company two other chosen, Dalinar and Tezable. They were dressed as travelers, though under their garments they were well armed. It took them thirty days of hard travel on horseback to arrive and the Hag's city. As they neared they sought the highest vantage point overlooking the city. It was set on a plain near the sea, but it was ringed by mountains, one of which was smoking. A huge port with deep harbor facilities occupied one whole side. But it was clear that this was a holy city, laid out and regulated by geomancy.

The pressures of the port and commerce might have overwhelmed a lesser city and caused it to spill out along the beach turning it into a ribbon of occupancy. But not this city. It was a perfect square. From the center rose a huge beast shaped mound, the most enormous Rau had ever seen. Radiating from this were four avenues which led to four great circular squares which cut the city into quarters which were composed of different colored buildings. To the Northwest was blue, to the Southwest was gold, to the Southeast was red, and to the Northeast was green. It was a huge city surrounded by high walls heavily fortified and well soldiered. Around it was a deep trench filled with stakes upon which unfortunate offenders were seen here and there to be impaled, their bodies rotting in the morning sun. Occasionally, other bodies were thrown over the walls and hung there by chains. Their decomposing bodies cast shadows blasted into the stone by the heat of the sun.

But the central mount fascinated Rau. "So that's how it's done." He said to no one in particular."

"What do you mean?" asked Dalinar.

"Well," he began "You remember how the messenger said Isis walked among her people constantly?"

"Yes, So…" said Tezable.

"Well she is able to project her strength by that structure on the hill. Look at it closely, what do you see?"

"I see a series of great stones, blood red. And in the center a huge image of the Hag like the one you buried in the first middens."

"Yes, but look closely at the size of that thing."

"It must be three times life size, and it is utterly black. No refection at all escapes from it. And look at how it holds open its life gate and what is in there."

"I don't see what you are talking about." said Dalinar.

"The Hag-stone is an image of the Hag squatting down and her hands come up under her thighs gripping the sides of her vulva holding open the gate of life, and in that gate is a huge blood red crystal of some sort. I can't see it very well, but I cannot imagine such a thing existing. It certainly was not made in this world."

As they watched, a procession of black robed women climbed the steep prominence and entered the circle of stones approaching the Hag-stone. The were carrying bowls of a dark liquid which they splashed on the stone. One carried a mallet and proceeded to drive a spike into the idol.

"Look," said Rau, "It isn't made of stone. It's probably made of wood because that one is driving a spike into the image. I think there must be hundreds of spikes there, but we are too far away to see them."

"Well shall we go visit," asked Tezable.

"Most certainly," said Rau.

The three began the long trek down to the city and were aware constantly as they neared it how huge and impressive the builders had constructed it. There was a regular stream of travelers down to the city and emerging from it. There seemed to be no gate patrol stopping people as they entered or exited.

"I have only two goals for this expedition. One is to make a circuit of the prominence and the second is to wait for Set to act. Should he act, you two are to evaporate, yet stay near. Set will probably lead you as well in knowing what must be done. The serpents I wear are restless and I feel they will be sent to work here somehow." Rau whispered.

They entered the city by the gate opposite the sea and asked directions to the market place. Soon they were surrounded by people busily advertising their wares and bargaining. Rau began to make some purchases when armed guards seized him and carried him off. Tezable and Tezable followed discretely but were stopped when the guards carried him into one of the Temple complex buildings.

"What are you doing? I am a simple merchant come to trade for salt and fruit. Have I done something wrong?"

A black robed woman stepped up to him and spoke softly. "You are a spy sent by Set, and we will kill you soon. First, we must see just who you are. Strip him."

Soldiers descended on Rau and shucked him of his robes and shoes. When he stood sky clad before them, even he was surprised, his skin was smooth and unblemished, and not one tattoo or blaze marked him as anything other than ordinary. Even his foreskin was intact.

"Mistress, this is not likely to be a spy from Set. He has no marks of the cult, not even the most intimate initiation scar," one of the soldiers observed. "Is it possible we grabbed the wrong one?"

"Probably, you fool, but I am still interested in this one." She approached Rau.

"So, you would like to challenge me," She said dragging her long fingers along the length of his warrior and cupping the pendulous treasure beneath it in her hand.

"I blush, mistress, I do not know what has come over me. I would offer you no disrespect," Rau feigned.

"Ah, you think you are only honoring Isis unaware? Perhaps, but we will have to see. Bring him."

The soldiers prodded Rau to follow the black robed woman down a long hallway until they came to a garden. Beds of low growing flowers and herbs were every where. She marched Rau up to one of these and rudely pushed him backwards into it. The sharp fragrance was nearly overpowering. He only had time to look up to see her shuck her robes before the most beautiful woman descended on him. She took him again and again, but such was his control he never gave up his treasure.

"Give to me what I want, or you will die right here, Spy."

"As you wish, mistress," Rau said, and expertly turning her on her back he battled her with ferocity. He felt Set enter him as he rammed home his warrior into her jade well, and such a flood of his substance left him he felt completely drained. Had not Set been upon him he would probably have fainted. As he completed his task, he was dragged off her and she was carried off by her companions.

"Give him back his clothes and escort him to the city gates. Get him out of here as quickly as possible, said one of the guards. "I have never seen anyone best a priestess like that, it was a wonder to behold. They will want to kill this bull-man if he is not promptly removed."

Rau was quickly given his clothes and thrown out the gates into the dust of the road. Tezable and Dalinar were upon him as soon as the guards were gone.

"What happened?" They asked.

"Set has begun. They are in his hands, entirely. Let us put as much distance between us as possible."

The three mounted and were off just as Rau's departure was discovered by the Hag's priestesses. They were furious and brutally slaughtered the soldiers who had permitted the escape. In fact, fresh bodies began to appear on the shafts almost immediately.

That night the dying began. The first to die was the priestess who had attacked Rau. Her belly burst from within as if she were filled with worms. Then the eyes of those who attended her became blood shot, they began to sweat from high fever. In five days their flesh turned to mush and they began to bleed from every pore. All who touched those infected also were infected. By the time Rau returned to his temple, the city lay desolate, funeral fires burning in all the rampart ditches. The priesthood of the Hag was dying everywhere, the soldiers were fleeing and the population that was uninfected was abandoning the city to its fate.

Rau moved to project his forces to the city quickly, and by the time he was back at the city gates, some three months later, it was a city of death. The streets were empty, the gates wide open. Houses vacant. The port abandoned.

"Touch nothing, Rau said. If you see a dead body, do not touch it. We won't be here long."

He took a squadron of his troops to the prominence and marched to the top. He was confronted at one point by a sick priestess, but he merely knocked her down and proceeded. At the summit, he confronted the hideous spike infested Hag. She was enormous but fascinating. In her gate were teeth, and the teeth gripped the most enormous red gem.

"Be quick, he said, as his men began to pour oil on the image. Dig a trench around her to catch the oil. And take care not to touch her."

The fire they set could be seen for miles, the entire city was left in flames, but the image of the Hag burned long after the rest of the city had fallen to ash. Rau enforced his old plague regulations so that any soldier with lesions had either to commit suicide or be executed immediately. He lost some three dozen, but he felt that was a fair price to pay. When they returned to the temple and the fourteen bathed Rau in the ritual of purgation and restoration, they were amazed again. The marks on his flesh where changed, where they had been colorful richly hued tattoos, they were now silver. Where before the snakes seemed to writhe in the light, now they seemed poised to strike through a veil of invisibility, the stone of reckoning was now golden, as was the tooth of Anubis. Rau's talismans of power were changed, and what change in his powers that portended none knew. They washed him the water of their lives again and again; they fed him and filled him with their substance until he could take no more treasure. Three weeks later the tattoos began to take their old color, but there was now a new talisman a fourth snake had begun to appear on the flesh of his skull, its tail as always sought the dark mouth of his hidden body, coiling down his spine as it went, but its flared head shaped itself on his fore-head. Its mouth open, its forked tongue extended.

The Mace of Ra

As he was riding back into city, Zu stopped at a trader's establishment he had noticed on the way out to meet the Shadow Company. Two men, one who was very tall and the other who was just a little shorter than Zu, stood inside talking. One was far too athletic to be merely a trader, and the other shorter and heavier with a distinctly yellow hue to his skin was clearly used to power.

This second man was elegantly dressed, his hands looked as if they had never done honest work, and his fingernails were as polished as a woman's. *This oily one is trouble, the second is trouble's fist,* thought Zu. Walking into the wooden building through its massive double doors, Zu still without his mask, bowed low to them and bid them good day.

"Greetings, friends. I wonder if the merchandise you have here is for sale." Zu asked looking about as if searching for his sought after goods.

"Is there something in particular you were seeking, stranger?" the stubby oily man asked.

He looked too longingly at Zu. *I must watch my step with this one.*

"Yes, I am looking for a replica of the famous mace of Ra, and a votive ear. I was just in the temple of Ra, and when I saw the mace, my hearing was restored to me. I wish to make an offering to Ra in gratitude," Zu lied.

"Well, I don't know about the mace, but the votive emblems of course we have. Do you want wax, wood or silver?" Without waiting for an answer, the oily one continued, "We have a large business serving the pilgrims to the shrine and many come to give thanks for Miracles. Now about the mace. What do you think," he asked his companion, "Wasn't there a special procession last year that required several of the maces? Where did I put the extra ones?…Oh yes, I think they are up there," he said pointing to a parcel high on a shelf in the corner of the warehouse he had wandered to as he talked to himself.

"Where are you from pilgrim?" asked the tall man.

"I have come from the bright desert to seek the cure of Ra. Even there stories of his Miraculous cures have been heard. I went deaf in my left ear after a fight with my brother last year and thought this was as good a time to make the pilgrimage as any other," Zu lied again.

"I see." The tall one replied.

The oily one swarmed up to Zu in such a way that his skin crawled with revulsion. "Here is the mace. See what care the carvers took to match the original. Unless you had the heft of it, you would not know it was not the real one."

Zu took the offered mace and marveled at the workmanship, it was a very good copy and should do nicely for his task, he thought.

"Well then what do I owe you for such things?" asked Zu.

"Oh my boy, I would rather not take your money. You are so beautiful to look at. Perhaps you could have dinner with us, maybe even spend the night? No? I thought not, that would be too much to ask. To be both beautiful and poor, or at least beautiful and willing. Ten Vulnas should do it," said the oily one.

Zu's expression had told them all they needed to know about their first price, the second Zu paid willingly and left. Had Zu thought to look over his shoulders he would have noticed that the two men were standing on the threshold of the storehouse watching him with great interest. He might have heard what Cain heard when the oily one said as he rubbed his hands lustily, "I must know more about that one, I want him in my power. don't let him out of your sight. He must have some weakness, some vice we can take advantage of. Go now and be guarded by the mother."

Had Zu known, he might have been more cautious. As it was, he was relieved to be away from that unspeakable one. Anyhow, he felt distinctly uneasy as the night seemed to have more eyes than is normally good in a new city.

He rode on to the temple following the instructions he had been given by Rau. It was a beautiful white limestone structure cunningly built of enormous stones taken from the temple of the Hag which had been overthrown by Schilo when he originally took the city, it was said. On the exterior were many paintings and a large ornate stone wall around the front more for decoration than for protection, Zu thought. Light from huge braziers illuminated the paintings showing Zu that they illustrated the Victories of Ra. They showed Ra at play spearing hippo, Ra the Sun-Priest, Ra the warrior god who banished night, Ra who sailed into the maw of night. Even the godhead Ra, giver of life and immortality.

Zu drew his chariot up to the temple precincts and handed the reins to the guardian who tethered his horses to the shaft outside of the wall. The iron gate was opened for him and he entered an area which seemed to be more royal garden than temple. It was open to the sun, and in the center was a giant obelisk on the top of which sat a sacred sun stone.

Almost as soon as he entered the garden, a great fat priest richly dressed and nervously fingering an ornate pectoral sub, opened the temple doors and stood on the steps, his hands on his hips, as he watched Zu approach. Zu paused for a moment at the bottom of the steps before he proceeded to stroll to the top of the stairs where the priest now stood.

"Stop there my son, and make an offering," the Priest demanded imperiously.

Bowing low, Zu stepped into the light where the priest could see him and placed a sack of coins on his outstretched chubby hands. The priest was overwhelmed and stepped back to allow the handsome youth enter the sacred precincts. Inside was an empty hall with a huge carved screen dividing it roughly in half. Zu knelt before the screen and admired the ornate wood carving which again had scenes from the gods myth in exaggerated display of the wood carver's art.

"Was there something you wanted pilgrim?" asked a voice.

"Zu rose prayerfully and turned to look at the speaker. It was a tall and thin priest who was fingering a tiny image of the god as he spoke.

Zu touched his ear and said, "I am deaf in one ear and I have come to ask the god to heal me. If I could only touch his sacred image and the tombs of his high priests and pray before his votive memorial in the inner sanctuary I am sure I would be healed," Zu lied convincingly.

"It is quite impossible to have access to the inner sanctum," said the fat priest who stood just behind the thin one.

When Zu took off a large ruby ring and fingered it in the light, the thin priest said hurriedly, "My associate is far too hasty to judge the quality of pilgrims, I am sure something could be arranged. Won't you follow me," he said as he took the ring from Zu's proffering hand.

The three entered the sanctuary and the thin Priest led Zu to the sacred image.

"These are such marvels of art, you won't mind if I admire them before I seek the help of Ra, I hope," said Zu. He walked up to the huge statue of the god and studied the mace there, Set told him nothing. He walked to the alcove where Ra's armor was housed in loving display. The mace there too was fake. He walked to the tombs of the high priests and knelt at each in prayer. As he pretended to pray he noticed a bas relief of Ra cut into the far wall. It showed Ra using the mace against the hag. The odor of Set grew strong as he gazed at the life sized portrait and he knew that the mace was hidden in the panel. Luckily the bas-relief was polychrome so his reproduction would be an easy swap.

Zu stood up suddenly as if in a swoon, and when the two priests moved to catch him, as they touched him he positioned his hands at their throat and the asps of Set came alive sank their fangs to the priestly jugglers. In the lore of the bright desert it is known that Set's Asps are three heart beat snakes. That is if one is bitten by them their heart only beats three times before death takes them. The priests died quietly and instantly, almost happily. Zu paused only to remove the bag of money from the fat priest and the ruby ring from the thin.

Then moving like the desert wind to the sculptural panel, he fingered the real mace. Power surged from it as if it were alive. The brother of Set's Chosen found its securing mechanism and released it from its place. With equal speed he slipped the fake mace he carried under his cloak into the mechanism which held the original. It was a good fit.

In an instant Zu moved through the shadows across the stone floor and was outside. He thanked the guardian and threw the silver ear into the sacred pool and took the reins of his chariot and was off. The chariot is not as quiet a ride as he might have wished, but it was fast so horse and charioteer moved down the road toward the tavern, quickly as a cloud crossing the moon. He rode in a most un-assassin like and fast back to the Inn where he made a small celebrating his miraculous cure.

He made sure the landlord remembered his requirements were those of a gentleman, a man of high character and good breeding. He wanted the landlord to know he would not tolerate neglect of his needs. Although, his room had only bed and a small chest in which he could place his clothes, they were of exceptional quality as befitted a gentleman. It was clean and the woodwork had been recently oiled, and more to the point had a large casement window looking to the west and the setting sun. After he had unpacked his things for the night, he sat on the bed and examined the mace.

It was heavy, obviously powerful as a weapon, but of incalculable worth to the right priest, or thought Zu to the right god. Away from the fourteen, to be possessed as a god used this Mace through him surely meant death. Zu also knew that such implements of power left their signatures, and so he quickly drew out a special bag which Rau had included in his tick. It was a bag which dampened objects of power, so that only the bag's owner could feel its presence. At least that is what Rau told him. He further concealed the bag by placing in up the chimney hanging it from a pin which must have served another purpose in an earlier time.

Convinced that he had done the best he could to conceal his prize, Zu rose surveyed his room again trying to imagine himself a burglar. Would his prize be found? He decided that any who came after the mace would not anticipate Set's dampening bag. They'd be feeling for its power and finding none look elsewhere. He decided, however to take a final precaution since his life and the others depended upon this artifact. As if in response to his decision the odor of Set was strong again so he made three swift gestures and the asp which had been secured on his back slithered free of it mooring. With another set of ritual gestures he secured it in the bag along with the mace.

Finally, he thought. Comfortable with his arrangements at last, he stretched languidly and decided to seek the company of his new companions. He desperately needed to relax and food would be most welcome, the knot in his stomach told him. Slowly he took off his garments. His remaining ally the asp was part of him, took nourishment from him, but could not be startled. He wondered what Boon would have said if he could have seen the rest of the blaze he thought as he traced the tail of the asp into his groin with his forefinger.

He loved to stroke the long bodies of the asps and though he could remove them as he always did when he stole intimacies from young maidens, he felt exceptionally naked without them. From his tick, Zu changed into long skirts made of crisp linen, an elegant shift a beaded gorget and heavy silver bracers. He threw over this a traveler's cloak with an over large hood which he had sought from the temple. *If Levit wants me unmasked, then he will see the trouble it causes tonight,* thought Zu. Zu took a deep breath, looked around one final time, exited his room and walked down the stairs to the tavern where he found Tristen and his companions seated around a large table at the back of the great room. He seated himself next to Tristen feeling almost comfortable in his presence.

Dormor was the first to speak to him, "Why don't you take off that silly hood, so we can see what you really are."

"I would be perfectly happy to my friend," said Zu in mock replay of the afternoon's discussion. "But I should warn you that it will complicate our evening to do so," Zu said in a tone, dripping with mock seriousness. Slowly he pulled back the hood so they could see his face.

A sudden hush came over the table, as the dim light struck his face. "By the gods." Tristen said passionately, "I think I'm in Love." The table exploded in laughter and the tension of the room immediately dissipated. Zu just raised his eyebrow at the young barmaid who was moving across the room to see what his needs might be for food or drink.

The maid had now come up to the table where she only stood and gaped at the young man in front of her. His beauty was astonishing and she recognized it immediately. He knew her as well, but neither wanted to acknowledge the tryst of the previous night. She still marveled at how this face came to be exposed in this place. She did not know whether to bow as to a god or beg him to sleep with her again.

Feigning that her shock was merely the ordinary effect his beauty had on maidens, Zu took great pleasure on making a show for his new friends at the table. He stood up took the young statue in his arms and gave the trembling young woman a hearty hug, a quick kiss on the cheek, a pat on her rump and said.

"I don't mean to embarrass you, but would you be so kind as to get me an ale and some of that grouse I saw on the spit as I came in?"

Leaping from her paralysis, like a struck dove, she cooed, "It would be my pleasure, gentle sir." And she quickly turned to do his biding though she lingered at the edge of the room trying to understand what she had seen he looked so changed from the previous night.

When he returned to his seat he said, "You see how it is with me. These looks have always caused me trouble, Sometimes it is trouble I love. Sometimes it is trouble I loathe. So I keep my hood up or my mask on for a purpose. From almost before I had the equipment to go camping with women, women have fawned over me so much that I have grown jaded by their demands, but somehow I have never grown jaded by their embrace." He said all this in such a matter of fact tone that his mirth was apparent.

His robe slid off his shoulders when he unlaced the tie at his neck and came to rest over the back of his chair, revealing as it did so the change in his garb since this afternoon. The sheen of his milk white linen shift was in stark to the inky color of the onyx and ivory beads which gripped the broad shoulders of his pectoral and gorget. The whole portrait was designed for effect. Clearly Zu knew what impact his looks had on people and knew how to amplify the effect with his attire and his grace. While he was about average in height and weight, he was broad shouldered and lithe in his manhood. He was powerful without being bulky, handsome without a hint of the feminine about him.

The other men at the table were all much larger than he, but their gazes were riveted on him, nonetheless, as if they suspected his beauty was a glamour which might fade under hard scrutiny. It was just the thing for this moment, thought Zu.

The waitress returned shortly and gave Zu his ale. As she set it on the table she blurted out uncomfortably, "Courtesy of the tavern holder." As she smiled and walked away Zu found a note under his ale mug. Scribbled in half legible script were the words, "The moon is full, the wind from the south. I will come to you again at midnight." An enigmatic way he thought to set up an assignation. He smiled and tucked it away quickly in his boot.

When Zu looked up again, he noticed an elegant but powerful man had entered the room. He was finely dressed in crisp white linen, over which was draped a pectoral of high honor given him by the Pharaoh himself perhaps. He wore an elegant wig and carried a whip shoved into a knotted belt which accented his form making him look bigger than he probably was. A bright silver dagger and sheath hung at his waist. He was followed by another man who looked as big as his companion but was armed with a strangely glowing longsword which he was just slipping back into its sheath. He was dressed in the same kind of mail Levit wore, and in the polished leather images of the tavern roiled, reflected in the dim light.

"Who are those two?" Zu asked uneasily, not liking the sudden appearance of so strong a champion in so clearly a flamboyant dress. This was not merely an accidental appearance, Zu felt.

"That is Bern and his companion is Rouphas. It is they who have assembled this company. Levit quickly replied.

"That's odd, I was told the temples would be gathering this force."

"I can't help what you were told, Zu, this company you have joined is under an obligation to them, not to the temples," Levit returned.

"They are powerful allies and would be formidable enemies. Treat them with respect or leave us," Tristen said suddenly sober.

"You said they have bound you to fight the Hag. How so?" Zu asked, suddenly alert to a new dimension to his companions' quest. Something here did not sound right.

"Well, it's a long story my young friend. But this is as good a time to tell it." Levit and Quinn both nodded their consent "You'll have to know someday anyway. It all began shortly after Quinn and I hand made the acquaintance of our Sythian friends here. We were going to make a reconnaissance of an ancient temple ruin near here thinking as many do that there was a lot of new activity going on in those ruins and that there may be new treasure for the taking. We had not even encountered the first earthworks when we encountered a group of Knorigh. Knorigh are fierce ancient people. They were pretty much wiped out we thought during the conquest of this temple back in Schilo's day, so we were surprised to discover so large a band of heavily armed Knorigh. I tried to avoid battle by the usual offers of truce and friendship, but the Knorigh were obviously spoiling for a fight. We were considerably out numbered, probably three to one. The Knorigh leader was particularly offensive to Quinn here, so I took his head and the battle was on."

"One thing you must know about me, Brother of Set's Chosen, is that I always fight beyond my abilities by the use of special potions. So I drained one, called the Cup of Fire, and waded into the Knorigh. I was quickly surrounded by a circle of dead, which I jumped only to find a second circle bleeding at my feet, then a third. Finally, I confronted the true Knorigh terror, their priestess. She was a huge woman, dressed in rags and fur scraps, she looked more like laundry than a warrior. She started to weave a spell just as I removed both her hands from her arms. A hideous scream, caught in her throat as her head tumbled from her shoulders. I was like a man possessed, Quinn tells me. My companions were left merely with clean up, dispatching a few Knorigh who had avoided my berserking rage and delivering the final blows to the dying. Just as we thought we had things under control, a second band attacked us and all of us were battling for our lives. But this time there was neither leader nor priestess so we eventually got the better of this lot too.

It was on the way to make camp after this battle when we passed through a small farming village that straddled the road. It was a poor lot, flat roofs, mud brick affairs, you know the type. Well, as we were leaving it in our dust, a group of children came out of one of the out buildings near the fields and began to throw stones at us. Taunting us as murderers, butchers, rouge knights. They were just kids on a lark, I suppose, but I was still in the grip of the fire cup. They tell me it was like a bear among sheep. I slaughtered all those children and several adults who came to protect them as well.

It was only when Quinn reached me that my frenzy was broken, and I knew what I had done. Her cool hand on my arm brought me to my sanity and I was horrified at what I had done. I had killed nearly all the children of the village, and two of the older women who had been left behind while the men worked the fields. In all twelve bodies lay behind me in a path of carnage I still cringe to remember. An alarm gong was ringing the men back from the field as I came to and I realized I would quickly be surrounded by angry farmers who probably would be added to the mound of bodies for the night's bonfire. Quinn helped me to my chariot and we rode hastily down the road towards our camp. In the night as the funeral fires raged on the hilltop on the distant horizon, into our camp these two knights rode. With them came a Priest of Ra who had come to investigate the slaughter.

In the moonless light of our camp, the old priest spoke to the armed men he saw who stood before his chariots and their steaming horses. He called out "Who camps on the heath before the ruins of Temple of the Hag? Speak to the god Ra or die where you stand."

My friend here, Levit, strode out of the darkness bearing his shield marked with the sign Ra to stand before the three chariots and bowing spoke to them humbly. Speak my teacher, one of your own stands here, in reverence to god is my life devoted." I can tell you, that priest was astounded to find a Knight of Ra in what he had believed to be a band of murdering Bedouin.

"What is your name? The light is dim and I cannot tell if we are known to each other? this priest said.

Levit here bowing in that peculiar gesture of Ra's order said, "I am Levit. I have served the god for twenty years."

"Though I do not know you, I have heard of a Levit. We have come to investigate your campfire. There was a terrible murder in the farming community behind us. You can see the mourning fires that take the victims to the underworld. Do you know what happened there?"

"Aye, sadly we do. One of us is a warrior of the Cup of Fire. We were set upon by Knorigh before we entered the village, our champion of the Cup was forced to enter the Fire to save us. He was still ablaze with the Cup when we passed through the village. The children came at us with rocks and taunts and he slew them all, and the old women who came to their aid, he slew them as well. It was a terrible mistake, but a Knight of the Fire Cup is a berserker and who can tell what a berserker does or will do when he is in the fire."

Hearing Levit's explanation the priest began a loud lamentation intoning prayers of savage forgiveness. You should have seen it Zu, it was quite something. I don't think I've ever seen its like. He drew himself up to his tallest apogee and gave us his best senatorian voice: "Bring me this Knight of the Fire Cup I would question him," the fellow bellowed to the darkness. When I emerged from the shadows I was well into the grief madness which follows the cup. I was sky clad, my hair was matted with blood and dirt. Quinn here kept picking up the blanket she draped over my shoulders as it fell off. Otherwise I would have presented a truly bizarre aspect.

"It was bizarre enough as it was," offered Levit.

Only the tear streams down my face which exposed the true color of my skin, told our visitors I was not a creature mud, a creature of the world beneath the earth.

"What is your name?" the priest asked me.

I was unable to speak. After I take the Fire Cup the road back is not marked with a fluid tongue.

"Tristen called he is," offered Quinn. "When emerges he does from the fire unable is he to speak days several. See you can unable to respond to you he is, but knows what he has done he does. The fire cup steals not your memory, but catch up it has to with voice his."

The priest began to mutter arcane words that could only mean that he was casting a spell of some sort. He asked me directly this time, "Do you know what you have done?"

"Quinn tells me I fell to the ground and began to dig in the dirt pouring it over my head and shoulders in the universal sign of despair," Tristen continued. The Priest apparently convinced he was being told the truth by Levit and this tattooed princess here began to wail.

"Ah, what a tragedy is here" said the Priest. I can see this was not an intentional act of slaughter, I will come again in the morning to see what I can do for you. I the meantime I will set a guard on your camp. Do not try to leave."

"My friend Levit was stern with his rebuke. 'Brother, do you forget, a Knight Ra shares this company's honor and its shame? I too grieve that I could not stop Tristen, but it was done before I knew it was happening. The Cup is sometimes like that. We will not leave camp until you return. This I pledge on my sacred oath to the god."

"These two chaps, Bern and Rouphas, stayed the night as our guards, though that function was hardly what they had expected when they started out. They told us there would be a trial in the morning and that the priest would probably defend me from the wrath of the village. But that there would be a cost, nonetheless.

"In the morning the priest returned with a huge crowd of angry villagers. I was still in the agony of the Cup, and they saw with their own eyes what they had only heard about. As I learned that day, the Cup of Fire was invented by the Hag. It belongs to her rituals. Schilo fought whole legions of Cup Knights in the conquest of the Hag's Temple whose ruins we were near. They were the most feared of her troops and always led the attack. They were defeated only because the Ra-Prime knew how to trigger this grief response which disables them for battle. So the story was well known to the farmers. How these legions were slaughtered in their grief, as they sat naked on the ground pouring the bloody soil over their heads is the stuff of local legend. So when they saw me, they knew themselves what had happened.

"The priest told them I had been possessed by the hated Hag herself and that she was to blame for the terrible slaughter. Even so, the villagers demanded a punishment. That was when Bern strode before the villagers and announced "I say we bind him and his party to scouring the temple anew. We know that the Hag is loose among us again and we can never be free from her power until her priestesses are dead. Should they kill him in the process, so what. He deserves to die."

"The villagers thought this a sensible project and hoped us a speedy death. The Priest called Levit to him and bound him and through him, us, to carry out this task. So we are bound, because of my slaughter of the innocents. But at the same time, we would never have survived the attack of the Knorigh. So who is to say who bound us to what? Anyway that is the story."

Zu sat back in his chair, and gazed at the direction of the two men, who were now seated several tables away. They were staring at him. Zu nodded at them and turned back to his companions.

The Temple

Inside the Temple of Ra there was an unnatural silence as all ceremony and all who might witness ceremony were either gone or in their rooms asleep. Terjon, the priest who had stopped Zu from entering the temple, lay beneath the toppled form of his superior Didnor. Their bodies seemed locked in a fraternal embrace as if sleep had over taken them as they held vigil before the tombs of the High Priests.

Deep in the darkness of the night a tall man had witnessed Zu's entrance to the temple and his departure. Wrapped in silence, he lay where for a few minutes longer to insure he would not be seen then stole across the pavements and into the temple. With as little noise as possible he slid into the temple and looked around to see what might have happened. The outer precincts were empty, and probing further into the temple he noticed the light in the inner sanctum. The bodies of the two priests he saw but did not examine as he heard noises he suspected were officials of the temple. He did not want to be found in the sanctuary of the enemy, so as silently as he came, he fled. Confident of his anonymity, he crawled back into the darkness toward the trading post.

"Ari, you should have seen those priests, they were either dead or unconscious." the tall one said to his fat friend.

"Thank you, Gremeg. I believe we may have found the very angle we need to take this one," he purred thoughtfully. The tall man languidly stroked his chin, the muscles of his neck rippling dangerously as he considered what his friend had in mind. He knew Ari's lusts and his scheming mind. He did not approve always of what Ari had in mind, but he knew there were few better at what he did for the goddess. As he watched Ari's dark eyes sparkling unnaturally in the dim light of the lantern hanging in the store room, Gremeg knew he was in for trouble.

"I'm thinking," Ari mewed, "we should pay the young scamp a visit this very evening."

"Yes, I believe that would be a good idea," said Gremeg who knew the only correct response was affirmation. With that Gremeg changed into clothing more appropriate to merchants than thieves, and they left sure that their prey would go to cover of a public place as soon as possible. When the arrived they quickly spotted their objective, but were taken aback to see who he was keeping company with.

"By his throat, this one is deeper than I suspected, "growled Ari. "What else is afoot that we may profit from, let us watch." The two crypto merchants settled into a table near the fire, watching their prey through the great arch that connected the public area to the tables for feasting.

The two watched as Zu and his new companions were quickly surrounded by a throng of women, women who laughed and giggled at each and every little pearl that dropped from Zu's cleft chin. There were young women, older women and even a few matrons who hungered for just the slightest touch of this young demigod, though truth to tell they should have known they were well past their prime. Finally, even the most masculine among the company had their fill of the attentions and pandering of voracious women, who became insincere and over witty in the extreme as the night wore on. To Cain, it seemed harpies had come to pick the flesh off Zu's bones, rather than women who all had homes and hearths and men-folk to tend them.

Clearly, this was a dangerous scene, and the companions recognized a compromising scene when they saw one. One by one, they finished off their drinks and left for other lodgings. Soon, Zu was left alone with a few women who were obviously compromised by drink and with whom Zu did not care to be further compromised by. Making a few lame excuses about a long day, and a longer day forthcoming, Zu extricated himself from their company and began to finish his last mug of beer.

Unexpectedly, an oily voice cut through Zu's meditations. "Young man may we be seated at your table?" Gremeg stood at Zu's side, hands on the back of a chair, gesturing at the empty seat.

Zu paused for a moment recognizing the two of them as the traders who had equipped his evening's adventure. "It would honor me to have you two sit at my table. Be seated and drink with me." Zu lied as he waved a bright arm to the chairs in front of him.

Zu thought, I wonder what has brought these two to my table. Perhaps word out about the dead priests. But it only happened an hour ago. Something I do not like is afoot he worried.

Ari and Gremeg seated themselves directly in front of the languid young man. They were amazed anew at his beauty and could not take their eyes from his face, as he sat relaxed across his chair, his legs cocked in the chair next to them. Ari was the first to speak. "Forgive us for being so forward, but we are business men and have a nose for opportunity," the smaller man said laying his finger to the side of his rather large snout. Wrenching his eyes off this handsome young man, Ari began again:

"Obviously, a man such as yourself is here on business. You are a man of means and of breeding. Men of your kind do not come here aimlessly, we venture. So we would like to know who you are and what your purpose here in Cassoria is. Perhaps, we can be of assistance. We have many resources to offer you. We are sure your venture will be more successful, if we are part of it."

Offended by the unctuous self-ingratiating speech, but loath to say so, Zu dismissed their inquiry with an feigned innocence: "I'm only here to find wealth and power, the same as any other adventurer." The hair on the back of his neck began to stand up, and Zu knew instantly that answering incorrectly might cost him his life. More to the point he feared he had begun badly. These two were not what they seemed to be.

"Do not be flippant with us youngster. We are offering you a business deal which might be more valuable to you than any brash adventure your other companions might offer," Ari got out between his gritted teeth, as he had reached out and laid a hand on Zu's arm, half caressing and half griping it.

"What would you say if we wished to employ a resourceful young man?"

"I would ask why and how much?" Zu parried softly "And I would say there are some things that cannot be bought." he shook off Ari's hand.

A silence descended on the table and Ari hissed, "Do not get too cocky my young friend, ours is not idle talk, and we are not men to be toyed with, as you have been toying with these tarts tonight. Further, I am of the opinion that anything is for sale if the right price is offered. You, for example."

Zu understood that he had almost over-stepped himself. Consequently, he spread his wiry hands out on the table, and hunched his neck down between his ample shoulders in a gesture of willingness, if not outright submission. Still his silence left him enough room to save face.

"We are not fools. We have both eyes and ears, and the feet to move both about without being seen. And we believe you are just the man we need. You see, we wish to hire you, young thief." Zu sat there stunned. "Yes, we saw you pick people's pockets this night. You were lucky that you were not caught for this is not a city which tolerates thieves. Punishment is always swift and severe. If Bern would have caught you, you would surely be dead. And as for the Temple….while that was a lovely piece of work, it would surely be fatal if certain people knew what we saw." Again Zu was stunned into utter silence.

"Gremeg followed you this evening…saw you enter the temple, saw the unconscious priests." Zu was reeling, but at the word "unconscious." He sat bolt upright in his chair, his mind caught in a whirl wind of possibility and implication. As the first threads of panic rose in his chest he began to think to himself, I am surely dead for these two have witnessed my every crime this day. Why do they toy with me? But they said "unconscious" not dead. Have Set's asps misfired. Impossible. So they do not know as much as they think they know, perhaps.

"What a pity it would be to have such a handsome head on the spikes of the town gate. Women would probably go mad as you were led to the scaffold. You are very lucky, young thief, that were in need of your services, my friend here would give a very high price indeed if you were more accommodating to his tastes." Gremeg spat out clearly enjoying the discomfort he was creating within Zu's breast.

Ari made his play. "I want you to return with us so I may get to know you more intimately. Knowing me would certainly be better than knowing the sharpened end of the post. For surely they would impale you for what you've done tonight. My post would make a less intrusive entrance surely. You will be my companion tonight or my entertainment tomorrow."

Zu was enraged but he concealed his anger. "As you say, I am yours to command. Shall we go now or do you wish to come to my rooms?"

"Ah." Said Ari. "You are an accomplished young man, are you not. But let us go to the trading post. I have rooms there more than adequate to our needs." Zu rose with his new companions and adjusting his robe exited with them. Ari had a litter waiting, Gremeg and Zu walked behind it as the four slaves carried the oily merchant along the cobbled avenue.

After a silent walk, the litter and its occupant arrived at the warehouse. Gremeg and Zu came up behind it, and watched as Ari stood up and opened the doors of the large building. Slaves inside scurried to provide light for their master and his friends. Ari waved them off and escorted them up some wooden stairs to his private compartments. When they were inside and after the slaves had lit the oil lamps, Ari shooed all but the two of them away.

Zu was uneasy, but confident he and his remaining asp could dispatch these two quickly. Gremeg and Ari sat down at a large round table and gestured Zu to sit next to Ari.

"Thief, we have a simple task for you. Information, is all we need you to steal, Simple as that. Not gold, or silver. Not even gems. Just information. You see, we want to know who killed a good friend of ours recently. A man by the name of Larath."

The tombstone, Zu quickly thought!

"I am new here. I know almost no one. How am I to find out this information? I don't even know who Larath is," said Zu playing for time and an opening.

"Who he was is not of any importance to you. The only thing you need worry yourself about is finding out who killed him," Gremeg continued.

"You can not expect me to just go up to murderous types and ask first this man and then that one if they killed Larath! I'll need more than that surely."

Ari sat there for a moment considering how much they should tell this enigmatic young man. It was true that they had him at their mercy, and it was true enough he seemed to have the skills required to ferret out the information they wanted. But there was much unknown about this seemingly competent young man. Why had he journeyed all the way from the bright desert to here? Was he sent here by some powerful family? It is often said that only the mighty survive the trip through the bright desert. What alliances did he have that they might be playing into? There was no small risk, thought Ari, but how he wanted this lad to be more than merely an ally or employee. Such beauty was too infrequent in Cassoria, he told himself.

Finally, Ari spoke up laying a hand this time on Zu's thigh under the table moving towards his warrior, "I have decided to trust you, my beauty, but be warned if you betray us, it is dead you will be. Very dead and slowly killed. Our colleague, Larath was a powerful mage-Priest of Isis who controlled a mote house on the outer limits of the town of Nolbe. He was a loyal servant of our masters, and when he was found slaughtered, our masters sent us to discover how he was slain, and by whom. Then we are ordered to kill those who murdered Larath, and to extract no small vengeance in the doing."

"A Priest you say? That must have taken some doing. Sounds as if he had powerful adversaries. Surely such a death should not be difficult to trace. Surely such information would be valuable. So all we have to do is to settle on the terms of my employment," Zu replied. Thinking to himself, *Or the manner of your death if you do not remove your hand.*

"Yes indeed. There is no small risk to be taken in this effort. How does fifteen gold a day sound?" Ari said.

Zu struggled to maintain his composure, but he could hardly contain his self control as he mused to himself, fifteen gold that's a lot of money. They must need this information badly. Or needing it so badly they would promise me anything with no intention of delivering. *Either way, I had better play. But I'll wager they've never met Set's Asps before.* He stroked the forearm where the remaining snake lay embedded in his flesh.

"I am ill equipped to deal with those who can murder a mage-priest of Isis in his own lair. Clearly," said Zu seeing what advantage he would wrest from Ari's lust. "I will need some new weapons. I imagine I'll need a good coat of leather mail, a set of throwing knives easily concealed, and several vials of poison. Several snares and some darts may be of use as well…Does this sound like too much to ask?" Zu added thoughtfully.

"It is more than we had anticipated," replied Ari. "But if you spend the night with me, I'm sure we can provide you with things that you need. Humor an old man with a taste of your beauty and it will all be made open to you." Zu saw that Gremeg was scowling, but Ari seemed pleased with himself.

"I can understand what you want Ari, and I am willing enough, but you should dispatch Gremeg here to assemble my price while we talk. I prefer privacy for such conversations."

Ari was astonished. "You are a willing lad, are you skilled at pleasing men?"

"Skilled enough to be legendary where I come from," Zu teased.

"Gremeg, be a good fellow and go about your business preparing for the boy's needs. He and I have some business to discuss. We'll come down after a while," Ari said wistfully.

Gremeg rose and strode out angrily and shut the great sliding doors as he left. Ari rose and walked behind Zu petting him and cooing. Zu rose and pretended to embrace Ari only long enough to let his asp sink its fangs into his neck. Ari stiffened and slipped noiselessly from Zu's arms. "One down and One to go," thought Zu. Quietly, he searched Ari's body. Astonished to discover a quantity of gold curved barbels piercing the skin of his belly in a peculiar wedge formation. His knife relieved Ari of these, as well as a great seal ring he wore on the thumb of his left hand.

Zu rose to search the room but took the precaution to move Ari's body to the bed and to disarrange his own clothing in case Gremeg returned unexpectedly. The room had many secret compartments, which Zu ferreted out as only a trained thief might. Unfortunately not many of Ari's treasures were of the sort Zu might usefully carry. He was readjusting his clothing when he heard Gremeg's heavy footsteps on the stair. Zu met him at the top of the stairs, pretending to be leaving an exhausted Ari to his rest.

"Ah Gremeg, have you gathered my tools?"

Gremeg, snorted disgustedly and turned to lead Zu to his workroom. Zu unleashed his asp a second time. Gremeg stiffened and fought the poison longer than Zu had ever seen any manage. But even so six heart beats were not enough to mount a useful brawl. So Gremeg slipped into death a grim look of surprise and defeat on his face.

Zu saw several bundles on a work table near the door, and decided these were his prizes. He upset several lamps among the wooden crates of fine linen and waited until he was sure the conflagration was fierce enough to defy rescue. He gathered up his bundles and moved into the darkness. Against the bright flames, Zu stole invisibly into the shadows. He turned to wonder at what he had done, but only for a moment and then he was gone.

The Green Man

In the days that followed the it soon became clear that the real question was how to attack that which was hidden, that which Rau knew was growing silently in the green glade, festering readying its attack on the gods. This, Rau set his mind to as he left the Temple for a meditative walk. As he walked, he purged his mind of all save the magic name of Set. He began to sing his name and the names of the other gods now allied with him as he searched. He tried to imagine them all seated in a circle around a great drum, each sacred presence, each with a stick beating the sacred drum of his heart.

Down the sacred way he walked the way now growing up with saplings and brush now that no one was there to keep them cut, and without the heavy tread of hundreds of feet. He was saddened by the transformation even though he had been its architect. The great stones were gone now underground or shattered into fragments and pressed into service as building materials. Only two were left, their shaggy sides' spoke of what had been and what would be, healing power shed from their green stone. He began to walk the circuit of the ramparts, thinking of the great orchards and their heritage of health and their final desolation. On the back side of the rampart he came across a body long dead, bones bleaching and covered with ivy, so that its skull was wreathed in leaves, only eye sockets and upper jaw were visible. It struck him that here was his answer, a cadre of green men, invisible for all practical purposes, but the hand of death itself veiled within its greenery. He smiled and continued his walk around the great enclave of millennia already planning how to set things in motion, the kind of training which would be needed.

He was very pleased with himself, he felt as if he had just accomplished something important. As he walked he was struck by the silence of the place. No birds sang, no crickets called, no flies buzzed. His movement through the knee high grasses did not even disturb insects trying to evade his footpads. Alarmed he stood still and listened. A soft keening came to him from within the sacred precincts. He was not really surprised.

Women had been coming here for months since the desolation. In twos and threes, they came. They would leave small wreaths of herbs on special stones, at special locations where once cult statues had stood, where shrines had stood before the desolation. They sometimes tried to tidy up the debris. They planted flowers, herbs, trees anything which might restore the beauty they'd lost. But this was something new. Keening, not that mourning was unexpected. But this was different, entirely. There must have been thirty voices in this sound. They were quiet, but strong and virile. There was a power here Rau had not felt for a long time. Quickly, Rau put his new plan into effect. He wove a garment of vines and supple young branches, until he was a moving bush. Quietly he climbed the rampart which now that it had been damaged was accessible. As he came to the top he moved with increased stealth so his appearance would not draw attention.

He was not really surprised by what he saw, but the cold he felt in his spine was nevertheless a worthy warning. There were women dressed in the black robes of the secret mothers, the hems of their garments were blood red, and their cowls were thrown back. The heavy gray hair grew from their heads like dense mats. Thorns pierced their ears and their nostrils in grief and mourning. Their heads rested on their dark legs as they squatted before great piles of odd looking tubers. To Rau it seemed as if they were sorting roots of some kind of winter harvest.

Then one crone held up one root as if to examine it and he saw it for what it was, saw them for what they were. These were severed warriors. The maleness of a thousand men had been harvested and was being sorted like so many tubers, like so many herbs for the goddess's tea. Rau was profoundly shocked, sickened. What had they done? Was this the repayment for his attack on the sacred precincts? Was this the revenge of Isis?

Reeling, he noticed a train of carts with three or four great bags each over which other women were working as they sang their low chant, their keening for the departed goddess.

Horrified and mesmerized, Rau lay there in the tall grass at the crest of the rampart watching the sorting. Then one of the Hags produced a handful of long pointed objects, needles he recognized, and proceeded to thread the harvested roots individually. Soon the circle of Hags was stringing the blackening warriors into long bunches like so many winter carrots for drying. Several came from the wagons and confirmed Rau's worst fears as they dumped out new bags of blackening roots into the circle where the great harvest was being preserved. Every now and again, a crone would take a root into her mouth moistening it for the thread. Others culled through the pile in front of each of them arranging with infinite care their produce so that their strings might be attractive and of a size. Rau began to grow angry as he shook off his fascination; his nostrils began to flair, his teeth to grind.

It is not certain how his attack would have begun, had it not been arrested by the sudden appearance of a great woven basket carried by three of the women in black. They set it down to one side of the circle and gave it a good kick, dumping its contents out unceremoniously. In it was a youth with flaming red hair who uncoiled as he found himself on the cold grass. He stood up as if he were in a dream, stretched like a young lion, the afternoon sun catching the red flare of his arms and thighs. He was a Miracle.

Rau had never seen such a being, such color. Taut, lean and tall, Rau estimated his age at about fifteen. The boy rubbed his hands down his thighs and across his back and belly as if to reacquaint himself with land masses long forgotten in his basketed hibernation. Several of the Hags shed their robes and began to run their hands over his ivory skin, through his red-orange hair which cascaded over his shoulders and down his back. The kissed his shoulders and the small of his back, and the backs of his thighs until his warrior was armored and dripping treasure in anticipation. Serially these abominations embraced this solar lad for wild rides of abandoned lust. He seemed insatiable as he loved them, caressing and cooing, riding and being ridden, sucking and being sucked. Three at a time worked him, covering him with kisses as he mounted them, pushing his tongue into their gushing furrows.

As one completed untangled herself from the lad's unquenchable embraces another Hag would rise up from her labors at the threading and take her place. And so it went with this voracious lad whose remarkable red crested warrior neither wilted nor showed any incapacity even when confronted by the ugliest and most horrible of the women. Indeed with these he seemed more compassionate and tender and almost more aroused than by the less objectionable of these she-beasts. Seldom was he entangled in fewer than three and sometimes as many as five as they took refreshment from him and anointed him with their vile liquids.

As the circle of women grew sated, two brought blankets and jars of ointments and set to work on the boy. Laying him down, one crawled between his legs where she stroked the still armored warrior of the purpling cap. Another cradled his head in her freshly plowed lap as she caressed his breasts and chest. It looked to Rau as if they were kneading bread as they worked the golden unguent into his flesh, turning him on the blanket and kneading him thoroughly across his strong back and hips. When they finished their chore, the righted him, caressed him lovingly, and then with quick surgical motions slew him.

As if a silent scream had howled across the clearing, the Hags converged on the trio, knives flashing. The orgy of blood and butchery stunned Rau; he was frozen in complete bewilderment and horror as he watched the bright youth being devoured. His flayed hide carefully removed and laid aside, and the lad's flesh was stripped away from bone and gut like taffy being pulled from a spoon. The meat was eaten raw, and then the organs consumed, first the young liver, large and healthy.

The still beating heart yanked from its cavity was a delicacy offered to the eldest and most horrible of the Hags, the very one the boy had lavished so much tenderness and passion on. His skull was shattered and his brain dumped into a dish. His tongue quickly severed and halved lengthwise for distribution. Eyes greedily consumed like over-ripe olives. In what seemed like long hours, though must have taken only a few minutes the bright solar boy had been reduced to reddening bones and discarded gut.

Rau slumped back out of sight on the ramparts and coughed out the contents of his stomach. He was thoroughly sickened by what he saw. Isis was indeed insane, Amun had been right. There could be no place for her in the lives of men. Gathering his strength he took one last look, only to find yet another horror forming before him. The Hags had taken the lad's flayed hide and stitched closed the openings through which they had eased out his body, and the openings the boy had used in life to take in sensation and nourishment as well as to expel the waters of his life and the earth of his garden.

And they began to inflate the body like a balloon, as children sometimes do with a pig's bladder to make a ball. They hung him by his wrists from a cross bar supported by two uprights firmly planted in the earth. His feet were bound each to an upright so that he was spread eagled in death has he had been in life beneath the Hags. The bright red mane rose again, and the sun caught once more the golden hairs of his chest and thighs and the bronze of his groin and arms. Bright in the sun he stood. And then he became a drum. From somewhere they produced the thin arm bones of the dead lad still bearing shreds of his muscle and sinew. On his hollow form with his own bones they began to beat a strange and wild rhythm as twelve danced in slow cadence in spirals around him, chanting as they stepped.

Who he had been, Rau could not guess. He had never imagined that any man could long survive in the presence of such women, and this confirmation of his suspicions that even so beautiful a lad had not been able to long endure such treatment. Rau summoned his patience and lay quietly as the remaining Hags reformed their circle and more of the grim bags were unburdened of their cargo and the strings of darkening warriors began to be draped in the afternoon sun across the remains of the orchard. Rau wondered how many battles had been waged to deliver such a harvest. It was unimaginable. The depopulation of whole cities must be represented by this harvest he calculated.

He was about to leave when another basket was produced and another lad unceremoniously dumped on the grass beside the circle. Another solar boy seemed to be in a stupor as the sat on the bloody grass in the afternoon sun. He stood unsteadily, watching the drumming and the horror of the circle of women threading one severed member after another like so many fish caught of an afternoon. He stretched and wiped his bloody hands on his hips as he tried to regain his full form. He was very like the original, though less tall, better muscled however and with hair more blond than red.

Nevertheless he shown in the afternoon sun, radiant with maleness and with fecundity. One of the Hags brought a long stick to the lad who now lazed propped up on his arms, legs wide spread, warrior armored proudly even in the midst of all this death. The boy raised his golden arms to accept the offered stick prayerfully as if it were a sacred relic. Soon from the thin belly and broad chest of this second stripling came the most amazing sound of the flute. Rau had heard of the cowherd and his flute. He had been told that in the most solemn of the Temple rites this music was possible, but he had never imagined that it would sound so, so compelling, so intoxicating. He could almost believe that this was the way things were supposed to be if he closed his eyes and disregarded the odor of decomposing flesh that as the wind shifted reminded him of the harvest he had witnessed.

"Krishna can this be?" Rau mumbled as he recoiled from his hiding place. Silently he moved down the ramparts and made haste to retrace his steps for his temple and his springs. He moved as if in dream, as if walking through honey in the afternoon light. When he found himself back at the Temple gates his own did not initially recognize him, so effective had been his green disguise. However, once it was known that he was back his fourteen came to him and began the long procedure of restoration. But they could not stop his weeping, or make sense of his inchoate muttering. They were completely mystified until when they disrobed him they found a bag containing several dozen dried warriors, neatly strung in a wreath as if ready for hanging above the shrine of Isis.

Then they knew then that he had traveled further than he seemed and were content merely to wash him in the waters of their lives and feed him as he required. Rau was in more need of their attentions that evening than he had been in many days. The warmth of their bodies, the strength of their gentle chests and strong thighs restored him as they fed him. He could not get enough of them, continually stroking their bald heads as they held him. He stayed with them longer than usual so they had to call in the second fourteen to provide him with the spiritual food he needed. Finally as they held him in the warm waters of the springs, he revived enough to tell them what he had seen, verification of the wreath's portent they all knew.

They were wise to tell him nothing about its existence until a few days later. The profound shock it produced they had expected, since it demonstrated how completely the Hags had known of his existence and how they could have slain him had that been their goal. That night and for several days thereafter there was stunned silence in the temple of Set as the enormity of what Rau had seen set in. News that dozens more carts were seen on the road heading toward the temple precincts chilled the priests, the Ackilons, the soldiers of Set, cast them into a veritable paralysis of mourning and sadness.

Rau understood what Amun and Anubis had been trying to tell him, understood how great her rage had been and how great her insanity was becoming. If ever he had doubted what had to be done, these doubts were now obliterated totally. A ferocity was rising in Rau he had never known before. Yet it was modified somewhat by the knowledge that Isis could have been drumming on his hide as easily as that boy's or so he thought. A transformation was settling in and nothing would ever be the same.

Rau's Desolation

Success after success had given Rau no ability to deal with defeat. Surrounded now by the few remaining remnants of his priesthood and haunted by the memory of his valiant followers protecting him from the murderous swords of the Hag. Never had they seen such weapons that could cut arms from shoulders, heads from necks, and legs from knees. The short javelins and the slaughter of horses utterly destroyed chariot warfare.

Never again would war be the same. Whole worlds would collapse underneath those new swords and short javelins. Nothing could keep the Hag's armies from wiping Set and his temples from her great back. Not his beloved chariot armies, not his brave infantry, not the presence of Set or the other gods. This was not magic or sorcery. This was something on a whole other order. Something had gone terribly wrong. Even now he longed for sleep, but he dared not sleep. The screams of his beautiful horses obliterated sleep. The terror in their eyes when the javelins began to fall rose before him. Huge brown eyes, wide with fear.

Nostrils flared, teeth bared, blood jetting from their brave throats where the wicked barbs tore arteries and flesh. The great herd they had nurtured, many he had seen born, watched as yearlings, trained, ridden and broken. All were carrion bloating under the October sun. Men knew that death was the consequence of battle. Horses, his horses did not know such death. Always they had been protected as war booty. The greatest treasures of the battle. Now they were reduced to meat for jackals and hyena. They had been betrayed. He had betrayed them. They had come for him and now they never left him.

Rau knew his world was larger than Thebes, Schilo and he himself had added many cities to Set's empire. But nothing they had could compete with these new weapons. Even if they managed to steal copies of these new swords, it would take months to fabricate enough to make a difference. And months they did not have. The Hag's armies would sweep across Set's empire now like fire in dry grass. Worse he did not know where they would strike next.

They had made camp near a spring they had discovered; as luck would have it they had a small tent in which they planned to continue their ritual cleansing. In this they sheltered, in this they grieved.

In the midst of his meditations on his defeat, the odor of Set came to him. He knew what came and he made himself ready. Even though the fourteen had been decimated, he would risk a possession even if it meant his life. Set took him with a force he had seldom known. It was as if he were being executed on one of he Hag's great spikes. Then the blessing of sleep without dreams took Rau. To his small band of followers it seemed as if Rau had been restored to his former status. He was robust, full of confidence issuing orders.

"How many of us have survived?" he asked.

"Chosen there are sixty-three of us here, ready for your commands. Send us to do your bidding or find our deaths."

"Three things must we do. First, we must find a strong hold where we can rebuild our strength. Second, we must warn Set's temples that the goddess is coming in force to obliterate all traces of Set's Rituals. Third we must launch a preemptive strike against Isis in her high place. She must be sealed up forever so that she cannot spread her disease among men again."

In rapid fire Rau issued orders to teams of three dispersing them across Set's kingdom to take the grim news of his defeat at Thebes and the way in which it was achieved. When he finished he had only eighteen of the faithful remaining. These saw Rau's eyes roll back in his head and his body go limp and knew they had been dealing directly with Set himself. Of the remaining eighteen Set had kept all the surviving members of the fourteen. These ten took Rau to themselves, commanded the others to prepare the stones for Vivendre and themselves for sharing. Rau was utterly depleted by Set's visitation, and although the ten worked to restore him their radiance seemed dim. One saving grace was the presence of a youth among them, a youth just recently made an Ackilon. It was this youth who restored Rau, and who became Rau's constant companion thereafter.

These mounted their six chariots and rode towards the great citadel from which Schilo had originated many of Set's greatest ritual traditions. They rode through the night and for the next three days until the old citadel came into view. Never had the old temple looked as good to Rau and his party. Even the thick temple walls they had laughed about as they campaigned against the Hag, looked fragile and delicate, though they must have been at least fourteen feet thick. The gate keeper did not recognize them at first, but once he saw more closely, the heavy cedar doors swung forward on their great stone pins admitting Rau directly into the arms of his brother and the waiting temple community.

He did not know how good familiar things were, until he suffered the loss of Thebes and returned to the home of his childhood. His brother was there still, ready to serve, and glad to step aside as the representative of the Chosen in this place. Rau could not get enough of Zu's company that afternoon and evening. They were constantly talking in private as Rau poured out his heart to Zu. When night came, Rau asked Zu to share his bed as they had as children, and though this was a startling request, Zu did has he was asked. Zu understood the need when the dreams came. By dawn the both of them were drenched in sweat as Zu struggled to keep the thrashing Chosen from doing himself an injury as he slept, if that's what it was. Zu had never seen Rau in such a state.

By the third night, Rau calmed to a point where as long as Zu was holding him, he could sleep. At the end of the second week, some normalcy had returned to Rau, and he seemed much restored. Rau found comfort in the ancient darkness of the subterranean caverns of initiation. He would go there for hours of meditation accompanied by his ritual crew.

Horse Murderer

The morning sun struck him hard. It wrapped his fair skin in a blanket of searing heat. His wrists hurt where the ropes pulled him tightly in the spread eagle between the two upright posts. Luckily, he thought, they'd left most of his weight on his feet rather than pulling him off the ground as he thought they were going to. He looked around him and saw that he was nude; his clothing lay in a torn heap at his feet. The soil at his feet was dry and there was no shade for a great distance. He seemed to be in the middle of a camp of refugees from the battle, he summarized finally by the number of wounded who were being cared for.

He remembered the fateful battle that had brought him here. How the chariots of the gods had faced the troops of the golden one with what they thought had been overwhelming force, seven hundred chariots fourteen hundred horses, thirty thousand men at arms. They made a proud show of their capability before the attack. The golden chariots and their brave archers careened just out of bow shot before the attack. What beautiful horses they were. How proud they were of them.

The ships of the golden one had unloaded he estimated about ten thousand men which met another ten thousand already on the ground at Thebes. They had no chariots at all between them and the chariot army of the gods. When the attack came the earth thundered with the hooves of so may brave animals crashing into its thirsty breast. When they died spilling their blood over the dusty soil of the battle field, no one had ever imagined there could be so much blood.

When the slaughter began there were places where it was ankle deep. Many lost their footing and were covered in the gore of dying horses before they continued their slaughter. Never had such a defeat been possible before. Such a victory, his victory! Isis had known what it would mean, and yet they had not known how terrible her victory would be.

Yet here he was captured by the gods, the liars. He shook his head to knock the sweat out of his eyes. His tender skin exposed now to the harsh sun was beginning to burn. If they left him here he'd be carrion in three days or sooner. What did they plan? They had told him nothing. The golden one's army had come ashore to certain defeat, they'd thought. The Chosen had even planned a huge celebration for after the slaughter. He remembered the use he himself had been made of the sharpened stakes they'd prepared for the captives they planned to sacrifice. And how they now adorned the very stakes they had prepared for his troops.

Isis had been clear, exterminate the liars. So he had ringed the city with impaled priests and warriors three times Thebes became a city of flies. But the ravaging of the city itself had been the greatest victory. With no walls to protect it, the city of Set had been easy prey. They had trusted too much in their heroic chariots and their beautiful horses. But never in the history of chariot warfare had horses been slaughtered. Never in their wildest nightmares had Set's Chosen dreamed Isis would slaughter such beautiful animals.

When the first horses went down Set's troops could not imagine what had happened. None could imagine what was happening in the clouds of dust kicked up by the thrashing horses. He remembered the screaming of the horses, the unexpected short javelins that took them down. How vicious his soldiers had been slaughtering them first, fast. Those wonderful short spears, only about three feet long, nearly as thick as a thumb and with their razor sharp barb and puncturing heft they were very deadly. A soldier could carry about ten of them at a time and account for both horse and archer. They penetrated leather armor as easily as horse hide. It took a little practice, but soon even the lightest foot soldier could stop a charging chariot.

He remembered how the heart had gone out of Set's infantry when they saw how quickly the horses went down. Line after line of chariots fell when the runners raced directly at them. Never had soldiers behaved this way. To race directly into the face of the horses was unnerving. But it was the best way to pierce the large arteries in the horses' necks. Most stumbled and fell when struck. The chariots often cart wheeled over the horses creating an awful jumble of wood and flesh when they crashed down with such headlong terrific charges.

When the god's infantry saw the Chosen's chariot go down, they'd panicked and ran. Without their god on the field with them, they were lost. In this panic, Zadog unleashed his warrior troops to a ferocious slaughter. The new swords that slashed as well as pierced were everywhere unexpected and deadly. Many of Set's troops were only armed with bronze rods and short swords which were no match for the new swords of the golden one. Many pitched battles were won only on the merits of the slashing swords. Everywhere the rods of the god were discarded as worse than useless in the face of such technical innovations.

In the grim dusk, when the battle Zadog watched as the black robed priestesses harvested the field of battle. How they would expose the dead and in quick movements gut the heaps of severed warriors they had mounded in front of his victory tent were horrible. Thousands upon thousands of them in eleven heaps over sixteen hands high stood in grim reminder of the price paid by the armies of the god. The palaces had given up their treasures and the streets of Set's cities ran with the blood of those who tried to defend the houses from the sackers. The heaps of gold and silver plate torn from temple walls, the mounds of golden goblets and assorted treasure seemed endless as they made their way into the holds of the ships on the backs of newly made slaves.

Zadog had collapsed in his field tent that night in exhaustion, only to awaken in the enemy's camp, a prisoner, a living sacrifice it seemed. How they had effected his kidnapping he could not imagine, not unless there had been a terrific battle which had not awakened him. But that could not be. Zadog's attention was brought out of his reverie by pain and thirst. A youth was poking him with a sharpened stick.

"So are you ready to die, murderer of horses?"

"I am at your mercy, aged one." Zadog hissed. The youth was using his stick cruelly, jabbing it at his chest and neck.

"Is this how you planned to destroy our beautiful horses? Stabbing them in the neck?" The youth struck a particularly vicious blow drawing blood from the side of Zadog's neck. "Tell me where this came from, this strategy which has destroyed Set's greatest army and his finest city?"

"The goddess delivered you into our hands. Just as she will avenge my death."

"Think so, do you?" The youth slapped Zadog brutally with the back of his hand. "You are nothing. Worth nothing. Less than nothing." By this time a group of youths had gathered around Zadog and his tormentor.

"Show him what happens to horse murderers." One of the others yelled out.

"Soon enough he will know, but for now simple humiliation is enough." They youth grabbed Zadog's hair and spit on him. The others jumped on him kicking and prodding him with sticks. Zadog's face burned with the degradation of it. He hoped it would soon be over. Then he saw a troop of soldiers approaching him.

"Get out of here, off him, you dogs. Steal our fun would you? They dashed him with cold water, and now they began to humiliate him in similar fashion. Where the lads had been playful, these men were vicious.

"It will soon be over," he thought to himself trying to keep back the agony. But then he saw them bringing the horse to him.

"Since you have slaughtered our horses, it is only right that your death will come from them."

The soldier slapped Zadog's buttocks cruelly as the soldiers untied his restraints. They led him to a flat platform and tied him spread eagled again to it. They intended to quarter him a rope on each limb and a horse at the other end. He knew he would never see the morning light. Yet the animals were not allowed to pull his limbs from his body as he had thought they only prolonged his pain until he passed out.

Sometime later, he was awakened from his blissful unconsciousness by a terrible pain, only to discover that his warrior was being hacked off by one of the youths, he was bleeding profusely weak as wet cloth. As he tried to focus on what was happening around him he realized he was about to be hoisted on a tall post. A mallet drove the post high into his belly, but the pain was now no more than expected. He was so exhausted by the ordeal; he thought even this he could endure in silence.

But when they heaved him upright and he began to slide down its great length, he screamed with all that was left in his body offering himself up to the goddess as intensely as any noble man had ever done. He realized as he died he would not have done a better job of it, if he had planned it himself. And inwardly he was pleased. As the sharp post entered his chest, he had only enough strength to see the army of the golden one descend on his tormentors before he expired.

When Zadog's troops saw what had been done to their commander, they went into a murderous frenzy and slaughtered everything and everyone they encountered. At the end of the day, Zadog's broken and torn body and been retrieved and in his place nearly a hundred new posts marked the ground of his humiliation. The bodies of young men and warriors, Zadog's tormentors, now like hideous blossoms on tall stalks bloomed in the afternoon sun. The great stallions themselves had been beheaded and that great head now decorated another post in their midst. His aides wrapped the body of Zadog in the garments of the Chosen they had found in the temple of Set. They carried him to their black ships in high honor and left the field to the vulture goddess and her carrion birds. Of Set's city only smoldering ruins remained. Of Set's army, only the great black pigs and the ravens and vultures were left to number the dead, and their rituals of praise lasted long into the night.

Again and again in the following months, the black ships of Isis attacked Set's cities. Those which had walls fared better than those who had trusted in the gods and their chariots. But even those cities protected by high battlements left mounds of their dead on the plains before them. Before they attacked each new city, they sang of the noble man, Zadog, who had given his life in intensity for Isis.

In The Beginning

Rau sat on his haunches before the fire, the heat warmed him, but the coolness from the lake hidden in the darkness behind him reminded him of the seriousness of the occasion as it blew over his back and shoulders. Between him and the fire were forty-two young men, initiates into the sacred circle. They glistened in the firelight, swept clean of all body hair and oiled in the ritual baths before being brought into the absolute darkness to this hidden recess at the shore of their underground sea. They were well prepared and as he knew from his observation of the process, this was as fine a group of warriors as they'd seen.

Behind the fire, a crowd of Minotaur and other sacred beings stood in the shadows. The ritual masks shown in the shadows, their legendary persona seeming to float above the clean shaven flesh which supported them.

This was the night of the telling. The initiates were at the end of a week of exhausting physical training. Into the subterranean caves they had been borne by the Minotaur as they slept a drugged sleep. They had awakened into the utter darkness and had bathed in the cold waters of the sacred sea. They had fasted in the oppressive lightness caverns. They had taken as much treasure as they could willingly accept.

Then came the enkindling of the sacred flame, a fire that would burn away the darkness. In a golden Porphoi, Set's wine was enfolded. It was a sacred brew of visions and dreams would burn away the interior darkness which hid the eternal from ordinary eyes, just as the fire in the huge bronze hearth on the ledge of sacrifice that would burn away the exterior darkness that hid the gods attending the ritual. On occasion some never realized that the world of the Porphoi was not the world of eternity, it was always part of the mystery unwrapped as the darkness was rolled away.

Rau had himself overseen the blending of the flesh of the gods, and the blood of the black bull, Set had given his temple. From the sacred Porphoi a radiance burst unlike the fire enkindled for the ceremony. It was a thickly sweet concoction which transformed men into time walkers and their warriors into fountains of radiance.

He remembered his own initiation, how he had trembled in the darkness. How he felt as helpless as an infant in their care. How the cold water had shrunk him and taught him. But the wine of Set had liberated him from the darkness and in the moment when the light was struck he had seen the god for the first time. And he had been chosen by Set. He remembers what he was told of the experience because he was, of course, absent from his body, walking in eternity with Set, seeing reality as it truly was for the first time.

But his teacher told him how he had suddenly stood in the middle of the rocky ledge and began to recite the sacred story even though he had never been told or heard it before. Even how he had included an ancient passage that had not been used for several generations. How suddenly at the completion of the ancient tale he collapsed in a fit of enormous love and the sacred fire burst into sapphire blue flames, as if in that moment there had been a divine consummation. And he heard how the flames greedily burst through the wood as if it were oiled.

Now from within his great earth pig headdress of Set, Rau began the intonation of the sacred story. The resonance of the mask melded with the strange echoes of the cavern producing the most amazing sound from his voice, a voice of power and remembering. Rau began in silence until all he could hear was the fire's noise a divine roaring that took him as he sang. Remembering the first time he had heard it, remembering his teachers Tezable, Polandus and Dalinar and his murdered friends Laurentilo and Polandus, those who had died in the plague and all who had nurtured him in the ways of Set, Rau began, tears welled up in his eyes as he sang in honor of the teachers whose dust now mingled with the ancestors. From deep in his belly came the sound as he began.

"In the beginning all was chaos save for Set, the single point of order in all the void. Set saw the void and fell in love with it and was aroused by it. He took it in his arms and made love to it. From the sacred pearl of his loins he created the world and all the seas and lands. He fell in love with the land, took it in his arms and impregnated it. From the sacred pearl of his loins burst all the creatures of the earth and all the plants. He fell in love with the sea, took it in his arms and impregnated it. From the sacred pearl of his loins came all the fish and creatures of the sea. He fell in love with the wind, took it in his arms and impregnated it. From the sacred pearl of his loins came all the birds of the air and all the insects. Set looked at the results of his love realized that it was good.

But there were none to worship him. A golem of mud made he and he fed it daily with his godly treasure. The golem grew in beauty and in strength. Set named this golem Mortalis and it was good. But Set saw that Mortalis was sad and asked why he was sad. Mortalis said he was lonely.

So another golem of mud made he. Set filled Mortalis with his pearly treasure day and night for twelve days and twelve nights. And so Mortalis fed the second golem with borrowed fluids. As this new golem grew in beauty and in strength, Mortalis and Set washed her with the water of their sacred lives until she was complete. Then was Mortalis happy. Mortalis named the second golem, Horea. Together they were blissful, for a while.

Gradually Mortalis began to sense that Horea was a threat. He came to Set and asked, "Father Set, Horea troubles me. She seems not to need me. She seems to be gathering her power and I am lost before her."

Set was troubled for he loved Mortalis. He examined Horea and found that indeed she was powerful, more powerful than he had hoped. To correct his creation, he began to wash Mortalis in the waters of his divine life, to feed him with the milk of immortality and fill him with generative power until Mortalis was as bright as the sun, and as strong as the river in flood. Horea saw Mortalis as a threat and released from her body a cloud of blood which blotted out the sun of Mortalis. When Set came into the blooming world to greet Mortalis, Set found him close to death. And Set knew a terrible fear and a greater anger. Death had come into the world and it was not good.

Set instructed Mortalis on how he might regain his health. Mortalis began to sing to Horea, and Horea came to Mortalis. Mortalis and Horea sang together such divine harmonies that flowers were created in their joy. Yet Mortalis denied Horea his pearls of life even as Horea let hers' loose. Again and again, Mortalis and Horea sang in their bower of bliss. Again the flowers bloomed and birds of the new Paradise were created. Again and again the golden liquids of her power flowed over Mortalis even as he withheld his own. Finally, with one last embrace as Horea exclaimed her adoration of Mortalis and poured out of her ivory gates the amber waters of her power, Mortalis strangled her. All that she was, all her powers, all her golden liquids filled Mortalis. And she was dead. Death had come truly to Set's beloved world.

Mortalis was bright again, strong again. But he was also alone. Now when he sang alone his harmonies were discordant and only fungus bloomed in the midnight sun. So in his love for Mortalis Set made him another golem, like himself. Together they washed this golem in the water of their sacred lives. Together they fed him with the treasure of their souls and filled him with generative power. Mortalis named this third Golem Alantus. Alantus and Mortalis were happy and complete. Never had two men loved each other so entirely. They were inseparable. What one lacked the other had. What one desired the other gave. Set believed that harmony had been restored to his beloved creation.

But one day as he swam in the crystal streams of the earth, Set saw in the water threads of blood. In his nostrils Set once more knew the odor of death. Then Set discovered that Horea had created herself others like her who were spreading across the earth like vermin. Such a thing had never been known or intended. Horea had been more powerful than Set had dared to dream.

Angry at this violation of his creation, Set ordered that his Temple be built, a vast fortress against the death. Set trained Mortalis and Alantus to combat this scourge and to offer these renegade creations to him in ritual sacrifice. He also trained the two men in the secrets of controlling Horea's children, and in creating more bright and strong children of Set like themselves. So it was that Set instituted his Temple and created the first Lords of Thunder, the Chosen."

When he had completed his singing, Rau let the heavy mask fall to his chest in a reverential exhaustion. Across the stone walked the majesty that was Zu in a golden Minotaur mask, he came to Rau and took his place and began again to sing the song. And so on into the night until the rocky ledge of opening was filled with the chanting of men retelling the story of the creation. As Rau left, the fire was extinguished but the chanting continued. In the darkness he shed his magnificent sacred mask and passed it to reassuring hands. Other hands took him and led him carefully into the dark recesses of the Temple where among the closely pressed bodies of Minotaur he was bathed in the waters of life and cleansed of the telling.

Subterranean Treasure

Claire walked carefully down the path behind her village to the small building where the old mother lived. It was a fabled old woman she was going to visit. Some said she had lived forever, others said they remembered when she was a young woman. No one seemed to really know how old she was, but that she served the women of her village as healer was well known. Around her small home was a rich garden of herbs and medicinal plants the old woman had nurtured for years. Claire didn't know the uses of each one but she recognized a few of them, peppermint and feverfew and psyllium, Queen Anne's lace and pomegranate. But others she simply did not know.

Claire wasn't sick, not really. She had simply missed a month of her flow, and was concerned that it might mean she was going to be sick. The winds of change were blowing through the countryside and there were rumors of all sorts of horrible things that came to her village. It was known for example that the armies of Set were extending their influences into every village and province. The precincts of Mohibhar had been reduced to rubble. Its great Temple to Isis and the mysteries of Har which were celebrated there had been utterly destroyed. It was as if a darkness had descended from the heavens and obliterated the sanctuaries of light which had brightened women's lives for centuries. Even the sacred priestesses from the most venerable to the teenaged neophytes had been left hideously impaled on trees pruned and branches sharpened. When visitors to the town found the cold ruins, the trees and their abominable fruit stood as a mute testimonial to the power of Set. No two stones of the fabled Temple remained standing on one another. And the sacred image of Isis and Har were gone entirely. Huge stains of defilement were all that remained of their sacred sanctuaries.

It had been a great loss and the women of the area grieved at the loss of their mysteries. Claire remembered her visits there. Her last visit had only been several months ago, during the great summer solstice festival. It had been a time of great comfort when she had traveled with her mother and sisters to the Temple for the ceremonies. There had been nights of singing and story telling. In the morning baths in the cold springs of the goddess were followed by fasting and ecstatic dancing. The descent into the depths beneath the Temple to the hidden garden of Isis had been astonishing and filled with marvels men never dreamed women knew about. It had given Claire a sense of purpose and community which had refreshed her secretly and continually. Now it was gone, and in its going she felt bereft and lost.

So she had decided to visit the ancient one. At least, she in her hidden garden was safe from the predations of Set, Claire thought. At least this much of the women's mysteries and wisdom remained. She found the old woman sitting in the sun on a stone bench making bundles of her herbs, tying them with string to dry.

Claire had to touch her shoulder to get her attention, so wrapped in her work was the old woman that she had not noticed Claire's arrival.

"Oh! Who's that? Is it you my dear? No? Well then, come close and sit with me so I can see who it is then. You're a healthy young one, what could you possibly want from such a worthless old crone such as me, I wonder? Come on, out with it."

Claire came to the other side of the old woman and sat beside her keeping her silence as she had been taught when asking for assistance from ancients such as this. It was a kind of game the women played among themselves. A reverential game, one achieved at great cost over centuries of practice.

"What still silent?" Came the ritual question. "Well then let me look at you. Let me see if I can guess."

The old woman's bony hand let loose her bundles of sage and rosemary, and with their strong scent of herbs still clinging to them moved to caress with the back of their bony fingers Claire's cheek, and gently stroke her ear, drawing it out tenderly from under the long dark tresses. Pleased with her inspection she began the ritual probes.

"Now, tell me about the young man. How long have you been singing with him? How long do the body songs last? Is he young, or older?

Clair was plainly taken aback. Could she read my mind? Claire thought.

"I've lived with him only for about three months. We plan to make our offerings to the goddess soon, but now that the Temple at Mohibhar is gone, we'll have to wait until we can travel up river to make proper ceremonies."

"Tell me about him, is he young or older?

"Oh yes, so young. He's about sixteen winters, but he has the most wonderful touch. He is gentle, but he has great stamina. We sing nearly all night, over and over, again and again. I have never known such harmonies. I love the way his bow caresses my instrument, the chords of my soul soar when he plays. It is how Isis described it, exactly. I have shown him the mysteries of the well of life and he draws me to him every day to drink and feed there. He is everything to me. But the flow has been broken, and I am afraid something is wrong."

The old woman looked at her with glittering eyes and a broad smile. "Are you ready to start a family?" she asked quietly, her voice full of compassion.

"This is what I fear most. No we are not ready; we are just beginning to know each other. It is too soon. And anyway with the armies of Set on the loose who knows what might happen. My singer might be called to defend the village. We do not know what stalks our lives. And he so young and filled with dreams I would not like to dash him to earth just yet. There is time, isn't there mother?

Claire paused in her narration, searching the old woman's face for some sign of recognition or denial. But there was none. Her face was a wrinkled mask of aged care. Claire feared her problem was of such little consequence that such a wise woman as this would not want to be of assistance. So she continued.

"This is no time to be with child. Besides we are not ready to set up our own household. And as I've said he is too young. Anyway he is not set in his craft as potter. He still is learning from the old clay-man. He makes wonderful things and is always bring me little jars and pots he has fired. But he could never support a family just now."

"I see how it is." The old woman sighed and settled back on her benches. She took up the herbs she was working and began again. Claire was afraid that this would be all there was.

Then the old woman asked, "How will you pay me for my help? What can you offer?" Again Claire recognized the ritual inquiry. And as she had been taught, she said. "Old mother, I will give you what you ask, but more than that I will promise to help my sisters in my turn when you are gone."

"That is enough then. There is a flowering plant with red and pink blooms by my back door. Pinch off three flowers and bring them to me."

Claire thanked the old woman and moved quickly to do as she was asked. When she returned the old woman was no longer in the garden, but working at the hearth in her house.

"Come in little one; bring your treasure to me." She had a mortar and pestle and was working some dried herbs into a fine powder. "Let me bruise the flowers on top of this lot."

Claire set the flowers gently in the mortar and pestle and watched as the old woman pressed the pestle into them turning them a dark red as she worked. Then she took a kettle off the hearth iron and poured hot water over the mixture which she had transferred to a drinking bowl. A rich and heady vapor emerged from the heated water and herbs. Drink this quickly, it may be bitter, but that is the medicine."

Claire did as she was told, and drank down the broth.

"Now go sit in the sunlight with me and help me make my packages for the fair."

Claire was enormously relieved and felt as if a great burden had been lifted from her shoulders. She began to dream again about her young lover and his tight belly and chest pressing her into his bed and his life.

The old woman amazed Claire as she bustled out of the house into her garden and seated herself again on the stone bench. It was such a beautiful and cloudless day that Clair hesitated for a moment at the door surveying the wondrous garden the old woman had established. It was a magic place filled with butterflies and blooms. The dark moist soil around the individual plants had been recently reworked with compost so that Claire could see it was alive with all sorts of helpful bugs. A huge preying mantis sat on a large daisy at the side of the bench where the old woman sat. Claire shared the bench with her in the morning sun for what seemed like several hours though it could not have been anywhere as long. Soon she felt moisture descend to her gates and she looked at the old woman.

"Has it begun?" the ancient one asked noticing Claire wince and look her way.

"Yes, I think so," said Claire.

"Good, you will find some cloths on the table beside the door, you may use them. Your flow will be heavier than usual this month as the springs of life renew your well. You may even have some cramps. If you do, take these bundles and make a tea. When you're better, bring me a fat young hen that I may serve you again. Now, until you are ready to start with the gifts of the goddess take the skin of the pomegranate and make a tea. Drink that tea every morning after a night of singing with your young musician. If you think that insufficient take these seeds of the goddesses fan here and take three pinches of them in a cup of cold water. Then bring me a fat hen that I may serve you again."

The old woman pushed toward Clair some of the small bundles she had been gathering. But just as she did almost with the same gesture, she grabbed Clair's arm and whispered.

"Sit very still, we have visitors. I can't see them yet, but I know they are here."

Claire was suddenly aware of an odd silence in the timber around the old woman's hut and it's clearing. Even the wind seemed to have died down.

Six armed men burst from around the house and confronted the two women. They were hideous to behold. They wore helmets fashioned from the skulls of huge dogs and horse hair; they had an offensive stench about them as if they had been rolling in filth.

"That's the bitch," one of them growled. "Take her. From behind the warriors came a man dressed entirely in greenery. Like a moving bush.

"It's the other one. I've cut the tree, bring her."

Three men grabbed the old crone and tore the robes and clothes from her aged back. She tried to fight back, but she was too old. Her frail old body was beautiful, Claire thought. Her skin was nearly translucent and her thinness made her look like a young bird dropped too early from its nest.

The old woman began a chant, which Claire recognized immediately as one of the songs sung at the Temple. With an aching suddenness Claire recognized it for what it was, a death chant. They disappeared behind the house for a moment, and Claire heard the chanting stop, the silence punctuated by a terrible scream.

The green man beckoned the others, "Bring her that she may see what happens to such demons."

"The remaining men dragged Claire to the rear of the hut and there she saw such an apparition as she never could have imagined. A young apple tree had been shorn of all its limbs except two bottom ones. On this central spike, the old woman had been driven right through her gates of life. Her trembling feet balanced on the lower limbs, her hands waving in the air, tearing at her hair and pushing at the sides of her hips as if that might disentangle her womb from the torment she felt from the sharpened tree. She suddenly she lost her footing in her agony and slowly slid down the length of the trunk as the length of the tree was pressed through her chest to emerge through her breast bone until it finally lodged its sharpened end in her lower jaw. Her old flesh quivered for a long while, as her blood and rich brown entail fluids soaked the trunk of the tree.

The armed men laughed at her agony. One of them said, "Let's see how she likes the embrace of this lover."

Another jibed, "Let's see her shed this inconvenience."

The green man now pointed at Clair, and barked orders.

"Hold her to the ground; I must examine this monster's friend. He quickly raised her skirts and found the blood soaked rag. What have you done here, what have you done? He asked her. Claire was so terrified the truth came to her lips unbidden.

"I was sick, my flow was blocked, and I had to restore it."

The green man struck her hard on the side of the head.

"You murdering bitch, you demon whore, you have murdered your children. You are damned beyond all reclamation. Never will you have another chance to do this kind of murder. Strip her, bind her and take her to the pits."

The armed men fell on Claire and though she fought them, she was quickly pealed like a ripe fruit and trussed up like a deer newly slaughtered. They laced her to a pole and after they set the old woman's hut on fire the formed a column of twos and set off through the woods.

Execution

Claire was senseless with terror. The worst that could happen seemed to have happened. From the midst of her safety she had been snatched and thrown into the jaws of death. Happily she fainted and did not know where she was being taken.

The men jogged at a rapid clip, not wanting to be found in the midst of their predations. As they moved they changed their garb, throwing over Claire a bloody tarp such as one might use to protect slaughtered game. Soon, they looked like any hunting party bringing meat home from a morning's hunt. Of the green man, nothing could be seen; he had remained behind to continue his reconnoitering of Claire's village. On the outskirts of the small city of Tarn where the temple of Set had from the earliest time been revered, the men found the wagon which had been waiting for them. Quickly they placed their captive on the wagon bed, and themselves around it like hunters coming in for the day.

Claire remembered nothing of this journey. She only awoke when she was laid down on the cold stone of the temple compound. She was on a short block of rose granite, her legs and arms secured to rings in its side. Her head hung back so she could not see much except that which was directly behind the stone. When they began, however, she knew there was not much left.

"Boys, boys, boys. We've got a little present for ya. You've been working too hard so it's time for a little recreation. There's a woman in the reception room needs a little loving. Do you think you could oblige? The six stable lads looked up with evil grins on their faces. They were young, and part of the outcast society consigned to handle the really foul jobs of the city. Cleaning the sewers and the stables were two of their better jobs.

"When may we have her, lords?"

"Why now, right now. Go to her, but remember you must not kill her with your love, and you must take her as usual." The six leapt to their task with joy. Stripping themselves of their rags they ran to the reception room like dogs after a kill and began to worry Claire wordlessly. One after another they used her again and again. One after another they pinched her and slapped her to keep her from fainting. It was a good show the hunters thought. It's what the bitch deserved. "Fill her up the shouted. Stab her with your spikes." When one of the outcasts preformed with exceptional vigor, the hunters applauded and threw him coins. When they began to tire. One of the hunters called out, "Bring out the oil she needs a little lubrication." A fine oil was poured over her sacred mound and breasts, and then over the outcasts as well. Quickly they were on her again, aroused as if they had never known her.

When they dragged Claire off the stone, she was completely exhausted, and utterly ruined. She was sore and bruised in places she had never even known could be bruised. Her life was over, she knew. They meant to kill her; she could only hope that it would come quickly. She lay there in her cell on the straw for what seemed like hours, the dust and bits of yellow stem clung to her oiled flesh. A noise in the corridor awakened her.

"Where is the Bitch?" Claire heard some one say.

"She's in cell four."

"Is she fit?"

"Fit enough."

"Give her to the lads again this morning and we'll take her this afternoon. That is if they don't kill her first."

"Whatever you say, though she can hardly walk."

"Walking isn't what I had in mind for her, or the lads either, for that matter. Claire turned her head to the wall. The tears would not come. There weren't any left.

Rau walked out of the stone building where prisoners awaited their execution and into the sunlight. A commotion at the temple gates caught his attention drawing him towards the noise.

"What's going on, Dalinar?" Rau asked.

"The young woman we seized yesterday had a man who claims her as his own, and demands to be heard," Dalinar said.

"Well I don't just see anybody. Is there anything interesting about this one?"

"He's very young, he seems strong enough and there is something about the way he holds himself."

"Investigate, will you, Dalinar? If you think I should see him, prepare him to see me in the usual way and let me know what you find."

"Yes, Set's own. It will be done."

"And do be more careful with the interrogation, we don't want a repeat of the last debacle."

"I will see to it myself, you may be sure."

"I will be, Dalinar, I will be."

Rau strode off towards the Temple into the dark recesses of Set's holy place thinking about other matters. Dalinar, on the other hand strode magisterially to the precinct gates. The scene he was presented with was not unexpected. A handsome young man was being restrained by three of the initiated as he demanded to see a priest. He was in a rage and nearly incoherent, but it was clear he had done some damage. Several of the initiated were showing signs of considerable wear and tear.

Dalinar looked the boy over. He could not be more than sixteen or seventeen. He was strongly built, tall for his age, just a stripling really. He still had a lot of muscle to add to his frame, but by the looks of things he was in command of a considerable bulk as it was. Dalinar stepped forward, and instantly the initiated ceased their struggles and let the boy drop. The sudden silence which descended on the plaza before the temple was salutary as even the enraged boy fell silent as well.

"They tell me you asked to see a priest," Dalinar asked in quiet tones of command.

The boy launched himself at Dalinar thinking to take him hostage or some such, but Dalinar knocked him senseless on the stone stairs. And he waited. The boy roused himself and made a second effort and again Dalinar sent him reeling.

"You've taken my Claire, and I mean to have her back, you bastards. What have you done with her?" The boy stood there shaking his clenched fists.

"Do you mean the young woman we seized at the midwife's this morning trying to murder her unborn child?"

"Wha…She was trying to do what?"

"She had asked for herbs known by the midwife to empty the sacred cup again to its monthly cycle of filling and draining. The foul Hag had given her the drought already, and the young woman had already begun to bleed. If she is your mate, she has murdered your child. This is a criminal offense for which she is being punished. The Midwife was impaled outside her hut; we rammed a post through her gates and stood her upright. It did not take long for her to see the errors of her ways. Now what is it you wanted from us?"

"I don't believe you, let me see Claire. What have you done with her?"

"She is a murderer and a demon. She does not deserve your concern. But if you wish I will let you see Set's Chosen. He is the only one who can give you what you want."

"Yes, take me to Set's chosen, who ever he is. I must see Claire; I know she did not do this thing."

"You understand that Set's Chosen is a holy being who does not see the unprepared, are you willing to submit to preparation."

"Whatever it takes, just get me to Clair."

"If you will follow the initiated, they will prepare you."

The young man was led off into the buildings surrounding the Temple. He was stripped and bathed first in hot water, then in icy cold. Sacred unguents were applied to his skin to rid it of blame, and then he was led to the knife. Here he nearly changed his mind, but he finally submitted as they shaved him of all body hair. He balked when they came to shave his warrior, but with the encouragement of five stout priests he was shorn. Since he was young, there was not a lot of body hair, but he regretted losing the hair on his head. Again he was bathed in hot water and then cold, wrapped in heavy blankets and placed in a special room in which a roaring fire was prepared. When water was poured on the hearth billowing steam engulfed the lad and his guides. In this steam they sat for what seemed several hours.

He was taken out of the purging room and wrapped in fresh and dry blankets and laid on a slab of wood, slightly inclined, to continue his purification. As expected, Set took him for the first time.

It was if the boy's ka left his body and looking around saw a strange earth pig headed being staring at him. The Earth pig beckoned, the ka hesitated and then fled to the Earth pig and lay prostrate before him overwhelmed by the field of force bathing him. The Earth pig raised him up, sniffed him rubbing his muzzle over the ka inspecting him, tasting him. Satisfied, Set released the ka which fled again to the heavily wrapped lad.

When the guides saw the lad's ka had returned, he was liberated from his blankets and led sky clad to the sand where he was rubbed down vigorously and then rinsed in cold water. The nearly exhausted youngster was brought sky clad before Dalinar in the temple. His skin shown brightly as he walked across the stone floor. He was dazed and his eyes glistened, his walk was somewhat unsteady.

"This is a fit youngster, Dalinar thought, as he admired the young man. He has a fine head and strong chin. Dalinar wondered if he could be turned.

"One final preparation you must endure, Set's chosen does not see the uncircumcised. You are uncut. Do you wish to continue the preparation?"

"What do you mean, un-circumcised?" The boy asked.

"Our laws require that all men who enter the sacred precincts have sacrificed their foreskins to Set. It is the sign of obedience Set requires. None who are uncut may enter. Set's chosen resides in the sacred precincts. Do you wish to continue?"

"Let me get this right, you intend to cut the cap from my warrior?"

"Exactly." Dalinar replied. "Is she worth that?"

"She's worth that and more, but won't that hurt?"

"There is a special salve we can use which chases away the pain, but it will not bring you any honor to face the knife without pain."

"I wondered why your initiated as you call them were so odd looking. It seems unnatural for a warrior to go sky clad into battle."

"What is your answer?"

"You say she was with child and emptied it into the path?"

"She did indeed, and she will be exquisitely punished for it."

"Is there no other way to see this Set's chosen?"

"Yes there is another way, but I'm not sure you'd prefer it."

"What is it?"

"You can become an Ackilon. But I do not think that process will get you in to see Set's Chosen before we execute the woman."

"And an Ackilon is…."

"Every year a number of uninitiated young men are permitted to enter training to become warriors of Set. The training is hard, but there are benefits such as you cannot imagine. The title we give these young men is Ackilon. There is a training session going on just now if you would like to watch, and perhaps to join them for the session."

"Sure why not," said the youth.

They led the sky clad youth from the room and out into the corridor where voices of many people could be heard. When they turned the corner, the young man could not believe his eyes. There were twenty or so young men such as he who were being bathed by about fifty women. He turned and smiled at his attendant, and said.

"Don't you think I'm clean enough? But I do think I would like to share this training."

His guide stepped forward and made a gesture. Several young women came running, their breasts bouncing on their chests as they came.

"Yes my lord, how may we serve?"

"I have a young guest, who wishes to train with you. He has already been prepared, so move him directly to battle."

"As you wish," said the tallest of the pair.

"A word before you go. The object of these battles is to keep your treasure. To give up your man's milk is to be humiliated. Your object is to make her give up her treasure and to allow your warrior to drink deeply in the jade spring. But then you seem to be a practiced lad, you should easily defeat your opponent. We probably have nothing to teach you," his guide said mockingly. His sarcasm was however lost on the dazed youth.

The women each took one arm and led their captive away. Aladre, for that was the youth's given name, followed gladly, and his warrior began to take on his armor for battle. By the time they reached the far end of the room, his warrior was saluting at a sharp angle, his treasure stored close up.

A beautiful woman, probably the most beautiful woman Aladre had ever seen, came to him, ran her hand over Aladre's shoulder, down across his chest and belly until it cradled his warrior.

"And so you have come to challenge me, have you? I will have your treasure from you before you take the third breath."

Aladre smiled at the thought, as he smiled at the coming battle. She stood close to him; the silken robe she wore grazed his nipples. Aladre stood as a man polaxed. Never had he felt such magic. Her nails gently raced down his back, as her assistants removed her robe. The slithering of the cloth from between their close nearly touching bodies set Aladre on fire. The odor of her was like a hand at his throat. When she ran her tongue down his neck until she found his nipple, he could stand it no longer and gave up his treasure in a powerful jet, followed by two smaller bursts. She clapped her hands and instantly two of the initiated were upon them, a silver cup and a curved blade caught the man's milk as it curled across her breast and belly. Aladre was blushing, embarrassed.

"So little man, you could not even wait to knock on the garden door? Perhaps you need training." She smiled and turned on her heel. Aladre watched the ample hips move away, a feeling of great need sweeping over him. His guide touched him on the shoulder, Aladre nearly jumped at the coldness of the touch. "Well what do you think; do you want to become an Ackilon?"

"What else is there to it?"

"Much much more, but that is hidden from you now. All I can tell you is that this is one kind of training the temple of Set takes very seriously. But we train you in the mysteries of Set, and you will ultimately become one of the guardians of his ways. It is a life of great honor and dedication. You will have many women; you will sire many children, as many as Set asks of you."

One of the initiated who had taken Aladre's milk into the silver cup came running back, and whispered something to his guide.

"Well, it seems that you have an exceptional quality of mans milk, Set's chosen will be pleased to add you to his Ackilons, I think. What say you lad?"

Aladre's eyes were big as he gazed across the room where many young men were engaged in battle. I had no idea this was possible. Yes, I think I would like to take this training."

"What about the young woman who murdered your child?"

"Let her burn," Aladre said softly. "Let the bitch burn." The odor of the older woman still filled his nose.

"Then I think we must see Dalinar immediately," said his guide.

The guide led Aladre out across the room and into the corridor back into the temple where they found Dalinar.

"My lord, this one wishes to take the training, and he withdraws his demand to save the demon bitch who murdered his child."

"Excellent, that's excellent. But you must understand that this training is hard and difficult. There are some things you may not like, but this is a path of honor and power. Any path to honor and glory has hardship. We are about to execute the demon, perhaps you would like to watch?"

Aladre's eyes grew big, "Yes, I want to watch."

"Actually you have no choice, bind him," Dalinar said, "and take him to the execution."

Aladre's feet and arms were bound, and he was carried on a liter to the execution grounds. They raised Aladre's litter so he could stand and watch. There in the center of the arena a young woman was being ravaged by a group of young men. A bellowing came from the earth and a monster, half man, half bull rushed upon the crowd around Claire. He was a huge man, and he wore an enormous belt to which was strapped a massive leather ram, jagged metal razored down its head. The group gave way before the Minotaur. Two of the young men jerked Claire to her feet, whereupon the Minotaur embraced her, his ram penetrating her gates and ripping into her belly. He threw her down on the earth and reduced her to shreds within seconds. Her screams of agony were enough to rend Aladre's heart, but he could do nothing as he watched. The Minotaur turned his head to where Aladre stood tears streaming down cheeks only recently shaved of his boy's beard.

With her gore dripping from his leather ram, the Minotaur disengaged himself from the corpse and half scrambled half ran to the trembling Aladre.

"So, you liar, you want to take the training and yet you weep for this demon bitch who murdered your children? How many times had she done this? Do you know? Do you care? No more horrible crime exists than to murder a man's children. And you weep?"

The Minotaur cuffed Aladre with the back of his gloved hand knocking him down. The Minotaur hovered over Aladre, the blood dripping from his leather ram on Aladre's chest. The great stench of his breath was overpowering. His gloved hand pawed the lad.

"Perhaps you'd like to join her; perhaps you'd like me to love you too."

Aladre was suddenly wide awake to the possibilities as the Minotaur grabbed his feet and shoved them up until his ankles touched his ears. He felt the hot soil of the leather ram dripping on the back of his thigh.

"No." He screamed in terror.

"Never. She deserved to die." He said hardly believing the words might come out of his mouth.

"Such women are monsters," said the Minotaur, "all women are our enemies, and you must understand that. No man can ever trust a woman, never. They will deceive you, betray you, they will murder your children, and they may even murder you with diseases or with knives. The initiated are the only ones you can ever trust. We know who our enemies are, and we will defeat them. And you will help us, won't you."

"Yes, yes, I hate women. I hate this one who murdered my children. They are our enemies," the boy screamed trying to make himself heard as his knees were roughly pressed into his chest.

Dalinar rushed out just at that moment, "Be gone Astrel, you have fed enough tonight, you do not need to feed on the flesh of this boy. Be gone, Set's Chosen banishes you to the underworld, never touch an Ackilon again."

Aladre was shocked to see the Minotaur quail at the sight of Dalinar's staff and shocked to see him actually slink off into the abyss out of which he had emerged. Dalinar took a knife and cut Aladre's bonds. Helped him to his feet and back to the litter. Aladre collapsed upon it and was borne swiftly out of the arena and back to the baths where he collapsed into the gentle hands of the priests. Between the heavy steam and the gentle caresses of sand heavy hands, his body was cleansed of the execution and of his innocence.

Initiation

When he awoke, he was in totally dark room on a palate. He had a blanket over him, but he was aware he had been bathed again as a new scent rose from his forearm and hand as he swept his hand over his bare head. He sat up trying to think about what had happened to him. He looked around trying to see the light, but there was none. He was in total darkness. It was darkness unlike any he had ever known. As he sat there he realized he heard nothing except his own breathing and the sound he made as he moved on the pad and blanket, the beating of his heart.

He spoke out; thinking someone else might be in the room.

"Is anyone there?"

Nothing.

"Hello! Can anyone hear me?"

Aladre stood up and stepped off his pad onto the cold stone floor. Hands out in front of him, he took several steps, then several more, feeling each time with his foot the floor in front of him before he took a step.

Aladre heard a sound. He froze and dropped into a crouch listening. It sounded like something big was being dragged across the stones. Then he heard an enormous hissing noise and Aladre realized he was in the room with an enormous serpent. Its musty odor hit him like a wall. And not knowing what he did, he ran, and then he fell for what seemed like forever until he hit cold water and sank like a stone.

The shock of the water and force of the blow nearly knocked him senseless, but as his lungs were nearly bursting, he struck bottom with his feet and pushed off mightily. When he burst out of the water, moments later, he inhaled deeply and righted himself. Out of the darkness, a light erupted across the water at a distance, showing him the enormity of the cavern in which he found himself. He began to paddle towards the light and had just reached a shelf of rock and had just begun to scramble out of the water when the Minotaur appeared again with a three pronged spear and stopped him dripping wet at the edge of the water.

"That's far enough. Why have you come to my lair?"

Aladre froze and didn't know what to answer? He looked carefully at the Minotaur and noticed he was missing the leather belt and its man ripper, though his own warrior looked enormous enough.

"I was trying to escape a python, and fell into this lake. I don't know how I got here, honestly."

"Well step out of the water and come to my fire. As I said you look like you need feeding."

"I am hungry," Aladre said. He crouched by the fire as the Minotaur receded into the darkness. When he returned he had a troupe of monsters with him. Aladre moved back towards the water, not knowing what to think. But from the water a huge head reared and glared at him evilly.

"Well," said the Minotaur, "It seems you have a choice. The Python or us. At least we're partially human."

"Aladre, moved back towards the fire until he was surrounded by these hideous men. Aladre noticed that their bodies were beautiful but their heads were monstrous. Two of them came close and took his arms; two more came and stood before him and two behind him.

You are going to be initiated in to the mystery of life, Ackilon. The truth is that only men create life. Women would have you believe that they create life, but it is not true. Man's milk is the sacred breath of life itself. It is powerful medicine, and it heals the spiritual ache contact with a woman creates. Women drain us of life milk, and into their bellies we pour ourselves. We give them the flesh of the new life, and they add to it only the blood.

Set has taught us the mystery of life; he has set us on this path of liberation and power. Since you have chosen to join us, Ackilon we will feed you. Do you accept our lives willingly? Will you give us your life?"

There was a long silence as Aladre stared at the men surrounding him. He knew there was only one answer which let him live.

"Yes," he said, "I accept your lives and give you mine willingly."

"Do you swear on pain of gruesome death never to share our secrets with others? Never to speak of our rituals or our faith except as required by your duty to Set?"

"Yes," Aulander said, "I swear."

One of the men in front of him set his hands on Aladre's head and said, "I offer you my treasure." He felt a surge of power rush through his body like a lighting bolt charging through the sky.

From behind him a deep voice said, "I offer you all that I am, always will I be ready to sustain your life." Hands spread across his back. Suddenly with a little pop, Aulander felt himself filled with pain, as a power surged through him. Darkness descended onto the stone shelf as water was thrown on the fire.

Aulander was not left alone however; he was carried by many hands, carefully, quietly. How far he could not say since it was pitch black again. But before long he found himself on a padded surface again. Finally, he was completely exhausted and sated and he fell into a deep sleep.

When he woke, he was dressed and laying on a bed of straw outside the Temple compound. Every bone his body ached, it seemed, but he felt wonderful, and oddly at peace with himself.

He tried to remember what had happened. When he ran his hand over his bare head it all came flashing back to him again. He was an Ackilon. What was he doing outside the temple? He got up and ran to the temple gates. One of the initiated stopped him.

"We have nothing for you here outsider."

Aulander, stopped, quite amazed.

"I am an Ackilon and I wish to continue my training."

A big smile spread across the initiate's face who led him into the temple precinct. He strode up to Dalinar and said softly.

"Tell Set's chosen that his newest Ackilon is here to continue his training."

"Excellent," Dalinar smiled. "I will take the Ackilon to his quarters. Thank you my brother."

"Will you come with me Ackilon; there is much to do this day." Aulander walked with the initiated across the courtyard into a new life.

Contagion

Summer gave way to harvest, harvest to the barrens, the barrens gave way to spring and so on it went for many years. Rau's stewardship of his lands brought prosperity to his temple and the surrounding villages. Soon a walk of one hundred days could not discover a village where Set's laws were not supreme. Riders from the North came in the spring of the seventh year after the destruction of the Hag's Temple. They brought startling news. The riders were escorted into the main gates where Rau's public throne was set. He met them courteously.

"What brings strangers to my land in such speed and alarm?"

"Chosen, we are all that remain of great temple of Set at Laruinth. We were attacked in the night by the legions of the Hag. Great corroding fires spilled over our walls, huge stones smashed our gates. All who could not fight fled, all who fought died. Our teacher, Melindar who studied with you, set me on urgent dispatch to warn you. We left his side with reluctance, but he commanded us to give you warning. I fear that all at Laruinth are slaughtered, so great was the Hag's host."

"I have heard," Rau replied evenly, "that the Hag's legions were on the march, restoring her sacred precincts where Set's Chosen had destroyed them. I am even told that hideous tortures are reserved for Set's holy ones. I have been preparing now for months, but I had not known they were at the borders of my lands. Set thanks you for your message. You will want to retire to the baths, I'm sure. When you have purified yourself, meet me in the great chamber of Set. We'll continue there."

The travelers were led away and Rau licked his lips and smiled. There was a strangeness about these priests of Set. He would know more about them before he spoke further. Rau left his seat and stole into the inner chambers of the Temple. From there he entered the narrow passageways behind the baths and tiring rooms. He always placed watchers here to observe blemishes on the skins of his temple community. At the first sign of lesions, the offending man would be isolated. If he could be healed he was, but very often he was sacrificed out of fear of contagion.

This day it was Rau who watched as the newcomers were ushered into the baths, stripped and oiled and shaved. It was the tattoos that struck Rau first. They wore the rams' horns of Amun on their thighs and on their shins the delta of the Hag. Moreover, they were too dark, their warriors nearly black, although their belly and backs were tan.

Stepping out into the chamber he clapped his hands and warriors came running.

"Seize these men. Take them to the chamber of knowledge."

"My lord what have we done, but serve you? What have we done, but bring you valuable news?" The leader asked.

The long flail of authority came to Rau's hand and with it he traced the cultic tattoos and raised the black warrior for viewing.

"I would question your bodies for their mind's secrets. If you are Set's, no harm will come to you, if you are not hideous pain will be your lot."

"So Set permits, so Set allows." The lead visitor replied smiling broadly.

The strangers walked proudly out of the bath down a long hallway into the chamber of knowledge. The three were placed in a cell, while the leader was directed to lay on the central stone of inquiry. Fourteen of Set's inner circle surrounded the stone. First they bathed the stranger in the water of their lives. As they did so, the deltas on the man's shins began to glow and he began to cry out. The Ram Horns of Amun began to seethe on his flesh. Ropes were attached to his legs and arms and he was elevated and turned over so that his blackened warrior hung over the stone of inquiry, even as his back bowed powerfully. Rau approached and with a double handed grip yanked mightily on the black warrior until it came free exposing the mound of a woman.

"Who are you that you should think yourselves secure from Set's detection?" Screamed Rau. The fourteen fell back securing the ropes to rings embedded in walls.

The disfigurement of the leader who now hung above the stone of inquiry was terrible to behold. His chest produced pendulous dugs, his face grew old, wrinkled, and his chest and thighs grew thin and covered with folds of flesh. The glamour of the Hag had been rolled away, and she was exposed, a warrior priestess. She began to scream obscenities; blood began to pour from her mound. Lesions grew across her body like cracks in dried mud.

Rau began to issue commands, and the fourteen scattered. Quickly a metal cage was produced and clasped around her. Her hands and feet still bound by the ropes were extended beyond the cage where Rau amputated them with swords heated to white incandescence. With a second blade equally heated but differently shaped, Rau penetrated her bloody maw. The ceiling of the chamber opened and the cage was drawn out into the hot sun where it was positioned between the twin obelisks at the fount of the Temple. A great fire was built beneath her and she was incinerated.

Rau did not enjoy this procedure, but he knew the contagion she carried and it was all that stanched it. When he returned to the cell where the remaining three visitors were held. Rau was shocked to discover three of his students who had been sent to the East to found a new temple. They were covered with lesions and as the glamour of the Hag slipped away, their agony was revealed.

"Don't come near us, beloved teacher. We are the contagion, the Hag hoped to destroy you with. The best way we found to handle executions of the Hag's contagion bearers is to wrap them in rugs and crush them beneath a cairn. We were successful in defeating the Hag's messengers until she sent us diseased children. They were so piteous we could not refuse them. Our temple was utterly obliterated save for us in whom the Hag suspended the course of the infection."

"So Set permits, so Set allows," Rau intoned bitterly, echoing the fraud now screaming in the fires of purgation.

"Lay out the rugs, do as they request. Bury them in the Hag's ramparts. None of us go there, so we will not risk infecting our own. But if the Hag's own investigate they will be brought low by her own disease." All was done as Rau ordered. And great fires were built in the chamber of inquiry to purge the infection.

Rau sat in his inner chambers thinking about this attack. The form was insidious. It was devastatingly thorough. It was unnerving to confront the Hag's potential. She was the great death maw, and who better to destroy adversaries than she who feeds on our bodies at the end. His precautions had held him safe, this time. But he would have to be made of sterner stuff if his students who were even then being entombed in the Hag's ramparts were right. Rau called his inner circle together and said,

"We are going to the stone of sacrifice to see if Set will give us a presentment. Prepare yourselves as if for initiation." As always his students obeyed him completely and soon joined him in the utter darkness of the caverns. There they bathed in the cold waters of the lake and drank Set's wine before settling down and to listen. After what seemed like hours as the cold chilled them sufficiently and the Amanita laced wine had its effects Rau saw the pinpoint of light in the distance. As it began to grow larger, he said to his ritual crew, "stand ready, it comes." A lens opened on the burning city of Laruinth, the dark horsemen were slaughtering women and little children, all who were not already dead of the infection. A veil was drawn over the presentment and another city lay in rubble, its fires quenched by recent rains. Rau recognized Pladio, home of his student Davendarus. Another and another presented itself to the watchers, until the iris blinked out and was gone. The darkness covered them again, leaving only the sounds of weeping.

"Silence," Rau thundered. "Who dares to weep for valiant brothers of Set? Life is always challenged and challenging. Sometimes we survive; sometimes we dwell in the underworld. But always we live, we love and we die. That is the Hag's way. We dared to hope for something new and she would return us to her maw. Well she has forgotten or never knew that I possess the Stone of Reckoning which told me one of these strangers was not of Set's family. I will seek her out with its powers and there will be a reckoning. On that you may depend."

The fourteen and Rau lit the fire of celebration and danced themselves into exhaustion, burning away the toxins of Set's wine. When they felt cleansed they would one by one exit into the darkness, until only Rau was left. Out of the inky waters stepped Amun, ram headed god of the sun. Set possessed Rau instantly, so quickly that he hardly had time to assume the ritual posture. The two gods faced each other as equals.

"I am come as a warning, Set," Amun said. "The Hag has gone mad with grief, she has become insane. She sweeps all life before her. Even my Temples are not immune. The ancient maw of life is closed to us, only the grinding of bones is heard across the land. I have come to join you in your effort to birth the new order."

Then out of the darkness came a second figure, Anubis, jackal headed guardian of the dead rose out of the black coruscating light, his movements sounded like dry bones grating against stone. Slowly he turned to face the two gods. When he spoke it was the sound of granite sarcophagus lids rasping closing sealing for eternity the beloved of Amun.

"The Hag is demented. She is crowding the world of the dead with multitudes dead before their time. She is the she bear defending a dead cub. If we do not stop her, the doors between the worlds will be sealed forever. We will be locked away in eternity without purpose, without nurture, without joy. I too will join you Set, that we may put an end to such torrents of the dead. I bring you a talisman which will revoke her contagion's power. Wear this over your heart and your champion will walk uncontaminated, uncorrupted into her worst defilements. There is, however, a price you must pay. Never again will your champion sire sons. His fountains of futurity will be as dust. So be sure when you confront her that his enkindling days are over." From the god's hand fell a stone out of eternity, out of fable into time and space, into history? Such things had seldom happened in the fore time. As it fell it shimmered and grew, as if it were processing toward Rau-Set from a great distance. Rau had thought to hold it in his hands, but he stepped back and in the place he had been standing a huge megalith stood, a giant stone of the purest white shot through with fissures. Rau-Set approached it and thought to caress its warm sides. As his hand approached a small piece detached itself and fell into his cupped fingers. It was shaped like a great tooth. Set-Rau held the tooth before him and bowed low.

"Oh great god of the hidden way, the world of the living is sustained today. We will send our champion against the Hag's kind and rekindle the world in loveliness. The doors between the worlds will remain open so long as Set rules." The megalith shimmered again and began to regress as Anubis reclaimed his gemstone and was gone.

From his place on the shelf Amun stepped forward out of the darkness and touched the tooth Anubis had given Set-Rau. In a rich tenor voice like a praise singer's, Anubis intoned a sacred blessing, "What the lord of death has given you, the lord of life seals forever in the material world. Only Rau-Set can give this stone to another willingly. He who steals it or tries to take it by force will themselves be stricken with the dread defilement for which it is an antidote."

Rau-Set felt a great weight move through him, as if his limbs had swollen to lead briefly. Then Amun was gone, his going made a sucking breeze stirred the chilled waters of the subterranean lake. Rau raised his hand in salutation and then collapsed as Set left him. The fourteen caught him before he struck the stone; they carried him to the fire and warmed him. When he did not revive easily, they carried him to the stone of sacrifice and once more washed him in the waters of their lives. They fed him with their substance what he would take. When they lay him gently in the warm waters of the volcanic spring he opened his eyes with difficulty, even though the light was dim.

"What did you see?" Rau asked.

The youngest of the fourteen spoke, his beardless face still quivering from the cold so that his teeth would sometimes chatter. As he spoke he ran his hand up his belly in a gesture of nervousness and wonder.

"We saw only a strange light moving on the waters. We could not understand what you were saying or to whom you spoke. It was a language we had never heard. But we have seen the new marking on your chest. What does it mean?"

"It means that Amun and Anubis are with us, and that the Hag is so insane she is frightening the immortals themselves. It means we have much to do. It means that this battle is about the doors between the worlds: It means that the Hag is trying to close us off forever from the gods so that she alone will rule as she had done forever until she herself opened the doors. It means that we have powerful allies but it also means that we have a terrifying adversary against whom we must be utterly cruel and ruthless. We will have to steel our hearts from her, if we are to prevail. It means that we must prepare for death and welcome it if the cause demands it. It means that we must preserve our sacred songs and histories so that our defeat will not plunge our wisdom into everlasting silence. We have much to do, but first I am still too weak. Feed me with your youth; repair my soul with your flood."

The God-King's Laws

With the destruction of the old order, the Hag's desolation and the weakness of the other temples, Set's Chosen took preeminence among the Council of High Priests. The first order of business was to confine the plague and the Hag and, at the same time, to rebuild the other temples of the gods. Even though the plague had soon exhausted itself after the Temple of the Hag had been desolated, Rau knew there had to be greater action in order to confine the Hag, herself.

He approached the problem at first by seeking advice and counsel from the other High Priests, but they seemed genuinely at a loss for a concerted program of action, besides obliterating the Hag's temples wherever they stood. Rau consulted his elders. Dalinar had some particular thoughts about military expeditions. Tezable was oddly unhelpful. The guardians of his youth were growing old, it seemed. The god no longer walked with them. But old Bendilho was particularly useful suggesting some mechanism to change the way women were regarded.

As he wrestled with the problem, the gods seemed to have deserted him. Though he had made all the usual preparations and summoning, there was no response, as he might have expected. Rau began to think there was something terribly wrong. He began to go days without real sleep or food. Finally in frustration, he decided to leave the security of the temple complex and go for a long walk in the night.

Most of the temple guardians were unsuspecting, so it was not difficult for Rau to exit through the secret passages only he and a few knew about. The late September winds were cool and he remembered that it had been the night birds which had called him from a fitful waking sleep. He walked out onto the pavement outside his temple apartment. The temple was dark, heavy clouds covered a full moon into a moonless night. Silver light and silence seemed to fill up every emptiness.

A wayward breeze crossed the ground beneath the temple walls and played across Rau's brow and caressed his back bringing with it odors of the grasses and savannah. He undid the string of his long skirts and the black cotton fell to his feet exposing warm skin to the cool air. As he stepped into the night air, onto the wet grass, his feet arched at its near cold touch.

Boldly Rau strode out wanting to make the tall grass of the fields beyond the temple wall before the clouds broke. The leaves of low hanging trees at the edge of the grasses brushed his thigh as he passed and sent shivers of pleasure through his belly. He stopped as if he heard a sound. Standing stock still, motionless he suddenly crouched as if he felt the thousand eyes of the night press in on him. Finally, wanting to be invisible as possible he allowed himself to lie flat on the grass at the edge of the field, his back wet and crisped by the cold.

When the clouds obliged with heavy cover once more, Rau stood up and moved through the high grass. He grabbed a thick thatch of them and mashed them into himself feeling the coarse seed prickle and anoint his chest with their fragrant greenness. A little further out the grass grew chest high, and without much difficulty he could imagine himself hidden completely from view. He was luxuriating in the movement of the long grass against his body when he heard a cough.

He dropped to his haunches as if he had been struck. Who was there? He wondered. There it was again. Just ahead of him. With the grace of a cat in inky night, Rau moved forward nimbly. Every sense straining for news of his visitor. A clearing in the grass opened up where it had been trampled, on the crushed grasses a green blanket had been thrown and there someone lay apparently asleep. It was too dark and Rau could not make out who it was. Rau edged more closely, as quietly as any hunter after prey. Until he was beside the sleeping form.

It was Polandus! Polandus, asleep under the moon clouded sky, in this hidden bower of grass and cloth. Polandus whom the Hag had murdered, in whose ashes he had bathed. The delight in his lost Polandus' form taught Rau that his vision might be real, in some unexplained way. Perhaps it was a gift from the gods. Perhaps it was a vision of great portent. Rau eased himself down on the blanket as near as he could without awakening him. The remembered fragrance of his friend came to him powerfully as Polandus' moved his arms over his shoulders to cup his head. Rau took a heavily bearded stem from the matted grass and feather stroked his friend's belly imitating a fly. A hand moved forward unconsciously and rubbed the place Rau had stroked before returning to its resting place beneath his head. Rau waited awhile. No response.

"Polandus," Rau whispered his voice nearly breaking. "Polandus come run with me." Nothing. Quietly, Rau moved back into the tall grass crouched down so he was quite hidden but not far from Polandus' head.

A little louder. "Polandus." Motion this time, a hand tousled his hair. "Polandus, come run with me." He was now awake. He reached for the blanket and drew it around him.

"Polandus" more softly this time.

"Who's there?" Polandus said quietly.

"Who would you like to be here?" Rau answered.

"Who is Polandus?"

This quite unexpected response caught Rau off guard. He fell silent. After along while Rau stood up slowly emerging into view like smoke. "Who are you, if you are not Polandus?" Rau said quietly as stepped forward into the full moon light. Rau seated himself ritually on one end of the blanket opposite the truant and asked again. "You are clearly an Ackilon from Set's temple. I am Set's Chosen. I have a right to expect an answer."

"Who would you want me to be? Won't Polandus do?" He said.

The answer so struck Rau that he knew instantly he was in trouble. This was no ordinary being, no Ackilon, no friend of his youth, no sending from Set or any of the other gods Rau knew. The boy's shape began to slowly shift through all the forms of physical perfection, male and female.

"I was made for you. But you have denied me."

"What did you expect me to do? Force myself on you?" Rau asked clearly astonished.

"Isn't that what you are best at, murder, rape, slaughter? You have destroyed my temple. You have murdered my priestesses. You have stolen my talisman and profaned the most holy places. Why should I not take your flesh from your bones?"

"Because I have offered you only my love and sorrow, Polandus." He now spoke with more than Rau's voice for Anubis had entered him unbidden. The shape shifting form returned to the noble Polandus' elegant body. Tears came to Rau's eyes, to have Polandus so near and yet to be unable to embrace him. But he knew he could not embrace him. To do so would be immediate death. "I honored you. We could have lived in peace. Why have you attacked us?" Rau asked.

"I was not made for negotiations. I was made for death's touch." The body of Polandus rose as if to strike Rau, but the Stone of Reckoning prevented it, that and Anubis' knowledge of its lore. The apparition evaporated like a fog. Rau-Anubis rose and walked through the high grass for hours it seemed, his arms leaden his feet felt like bricks.

Rau's breathing was labored; his heart was like ice in his chest. He walked as if in a dream, until he heard another sound, close by but different this time. He stood stock still. A clawing at earth, a sniffing and rooting sound. His momentary paralysis in the tall grass was replaced by a familiar odor. Set. Rau knew instantly what he heard, earth pig.

Stepping into the moonlit clearing, a large silvered earth pig was tearing at a huge termite mound. Its tongue slithered in and out, devouring the tiny white termite soldiers who fought it to protect their high walled citadel. Fascinated, Rau felt Set enter him, and together they entered into the earth-pig, tearing, digging, scratching the earth away from the secret chambers. Snorting, tongue slithering in and out with its sticky surface emptying small reservoirs of eggs and larva with its precocious tongue. Bursts of honeyed sweetness inside soft shells. Odors. Rau was astonished by the fantastic sharpness of scent the earth pig was capable of detecting. The sturdy mound seemed suddenly so fragile, made of layers of crusts each with their own scent. He smelled the markings of many animals. The different sorts of soils, some new some old, some from deep in the earth. He felt the air rising from deep in the ground. There were many strange odors, hardly recognizable to his human experience, but Rau knew they meant pleasure indescribable.

Finally, with a massive sweep of his clawed forehand Rau-Anubis-Set-earth pig opened a deep corridor and was confronted by the most amazing perfume. It was intoxicating, compelling, some how addicting. The earth-pig went frantic digging faster and with lunging claws succeeded in opening up a subterranean chamber about the size of a large melon. For a brief moment the earth pig confronted the Termite queen. Large and swollen it was covered by a heavy layer of her children who waved their antenna and mandibles trying to protect their queen. Rau-Anubis-Set-Earth-pig swept them away with one lick of the long silk-sticky tongue. The great termite raised her ivory head in the moment before her death and looked at Rau-Anubis-Set-Earth-pig through those huge segmented eyes and in that look lay everything Rau had sought. He knew!

The honeyed juice of her entrails were like creamy ecstacy to the earth-pig as he darted his tongue repeatedly into his prey. Rau-Anubis-Set withdrew, and through the tall grass Rau began to run. On his back he wore wild knowledge, burning truth, piercing recognition. The grasses tore at him wildly as if trying to slow him down. He ran heedlessly through brambles and scythe grasses which razored him bloody, but still he ran.

When he broke into view, the temple guardians could not believe their eyes. Set's Chosen, outside the temple walls! He was bloody, running. Alarms sounded. The great door of the temple swung open only enough to permit a few guardians to meet Rau. When he reached them, he collapsed. He was carried to the Stone of surrender, where the fourteen were hastily gathered. They bathed him in the waters of their lives and would have fed him, but he waved them aside and demanded wax and a stylus. Quickly he wrote what Set-Anubis had taught him. When he finished he yielded to the fourteen and he slept as one of the dead for three days.

When he finally awoke and broke bread and beer with Zu he narrated such a tale that Zu could only shake his head in disbelief. That morning Set's chosen ordered a great black granite obelisk to be erected before the Temple of Set on which was to be inscribed the narrative of his becoming the Earth-pig and how the laws of Anubis-Set were discovered. It became legend among the chosen, this revelation. The laws, when they were announced to the Counsel of High Priests were immediately recognized as inspired and cauterizing of the ancient wound.

And these are the laws of Anubis-Set:
Of Young Men:
Let your sons after eight winters enter the Temple of Set that they may be approved of the gods.

Of Women
Let any woman who knows the Temple lore of the goddess be stoned.
Let any woman who worships with the goddess be stoned.
Let any who protect the priestesses of the Hag be impaled.
Let no man be bonded to any woman.
Let any man own as many women as he can afford.
Let families sell their female children to men at puberty.
Let Women bear children as soon as menses begin.
Let Women who displease their men be cast out by three public declarations.
Let no woman be taught the skills of the scribes.
Let no woman be allowed to own property.
Let no woman conduct business.
Let no woman move outside uncovered.
Let women who make public display of their charms be considered runaway slaves.
Let any single woman unaccompanied by a man be designated a runaway slave.
Let any runaway slave be considered a whore.
Let any midwife who performs abortions be impaled.
Let any woman who murders her children born or unborn be impaled.
Let any woman who takes a lover unapproved by her owner be stoned.
Let barren women be cast off that they may serve Set.

In each city which Rau conquered a similar black obelisk was erected. Such was the effectiveness of the laws promoted by Set's Chosen that in one generation men never again knew the oppression by women, and families flourished. Women children were highly valued. Men never sought pleasure outside the family, and many children were born. Although there was some opposition to these laws, they were enforced ruthlessly and soon the Hag's dominion was broken wherever these laws were upheld.

Visitor

By the time he returned to his rooms in the inn, the sky was ablaze with the fires. Zu looked out the windows of his apartment watching the night sky light up in the conflagration. Soon he was aware that his fire was spreading to other buildings on the wharfs. He had ignited a general catastrophe for the port city. Fascinated as he was, however, he soon became aware of something else. He was not alone.

A fragrance lit the room. He searched his mind for its like, and found none in memory. It was sweet but it also smelled of decaying flesh and spices. He turned to examine the room which lay mostly in shadow as his fascination with the fires outside had not given him time to light his own lamp. Then he felt his asp begin to move, the hair on the back of his neck stand up. He leapt on the great chest beneath which he had positioned the Mace of Ra. "The Mace of Ra" his mind screamed as he recognized what was coming. A huge form hurled itself at him, only to grasp empty air as the nimble footed Zu found it expedient to be elsewhere just then.

Turning, Zu saw who confronted him. "I have come for the goddess's gold you stole tonight, villain. You have no idea who it was you murdered, or what it was you consigned to the flames. I have you to thank for my liberty at least. Ari had imprisoned me below his warehouse for months. Now I am free and I will have his gold."

"I am willing to part with it. Indeed it is yours for the asking," Zu said relieved enormously. "But there is no reason we cannot conclude our business in the light." He moved to ignite a lamp when the voice from the shadows said quietly.

"If you don't mind, the darkness is better for our business."

"Fine, darkness it is," Zu returned laying aside the flint and reaching inside his pouch for the barbels. "Are these what you are after?" Zu said laying them on the table in the center of the room where he stood.

"Yes. They are very important."

"Would you mind telling me who Ari was and how it was he came to imprison you in his warehouse?"

"Ari was a thief, he was a wizard of a kind. He specialized in stealing the lives of young men, sucking their energy from their bodies and leaving dry husks behind. Had you not moved when you did, I suspect you would have been yet another of his victims. How did you kill him? I have tried many times and never succeeded."

"Well," said Zu, "that's a trade secret."

"Ahhh," came the sibilant voice, "Ari chose an assassin as his victim. How is it that one so young as you is so powerful? No mere assassin could have killed the Wizard. It would have taken a mighty poison." Zu held his hand up in the light of the fire raging outside, the asp's head briefly writhed when exposed to his visitor. "Ah, Set's asp. No wonder Ari fell so quickly. Not only was it a physical poison but it was also a magic one as well. Nothing less could have taken him. I assume his assistant fell beneath the same blow?"

"Gremeg, you mean? Yes, it was the same. He fought harder than I have seen, however."

"Yes he would have, he was also a Wizard of a different order, but just as foul. The two of them joined their forces to betray me into my prison. I owe you my liberty it seems, Set's assassin. Tell me why did you give up the barbels so easily? They are powerful talisman. Many would have fought ruthlessly to keep them from me. I am surprised you gave them up so easily, even more surprised you took them from Ari in the first place."

"Well, you know, easy come easy go. I really didn't think they were that valuable. What do I know, anyway?" Zu lied.

"I thank you. I was prepared to take your life, and I see it would have been no easy thing. Let me be of service to you in your journey."

"How do you know of my journey, dark one?"

"I know you are angry with yourself for causing such a general catastrophe when you only meant to destroy the ware house. But then you did not know what it contained, and could not have known how it would spread. I know that you are not going to be able to find the ship you wanted, and will have to travel overland to the next port."

"What are you that you can read my mind," Zu said alarmed.

"I am a Fore-Crone," she said as she lit the lamp with a look.

Zu stared at her. She was an ancient woman, huge, nearly seven feet tall, entirely hidden in a great black robe, her hair wild and matted covered her nearly to her waist. Her hands which she held in front of her bearing the gold, Zu had given her, were huge, long curving fingernails descended from knobby powerful fingers. She was weaving the gold barbels into a circlet, Zu could see the mystery of it, and how they fit precisely together.

"Now I would ask of you the same question. Show me who you are," she said.

"I am Zu," he began but was cut off in mid breath with a wave of her hand.

"No, I said show me!" Slowly Zu understood she wanted to see his body.

"And if I oblige you, how do I know you won't attack me once I am sky clad?"

"O I very well may, I very well may, Set's assassin, but it will not be the kind of attack you will resist," she said quietly.

Zu understood suddenly she was talking about combat. So he obliged her, doffing his pants, and his shirt until he was quite exposed. The huge Fore-Crone came to him and ran her fingers over his ritual blazes. She caressed his face with the back of her hand and let her long nails trace his midline down to his navel and below. Zu's warrior arched fiercely, painfully in response to her. She avoided his warrior and let her nails move down his flank and caress his hips.

Zu did not understand what was happening to him. He felt himself opening to her as he had never opened to a woman before, yet she must be incredibly old, beyond the need of combats.

"Where is your other asp? she asked suddenly as she felt the empty channel running down the valley of his spine..." there was an intake of air as she expressed surprise at what she felt in his mind. "You have the Hag-stone?..." another gasp as she read his history in his mind. "You are the bearer? Yet you don't know? Ah...Yes. Show it to me. I will not challenge your right to bear it. I merely want to see what was lost so long ago."

Compelled beyond his ability to understand, he moved forward to retrieve the bag, as he bent over to lift the chest, she caressed his hips sending chills of enormous pleasure through his chest. When he stood up, holding the bag with the Mace of Ra she smiled broadly. Carefully, he eased the second serpent out of the bag and she watched appreciatively as it took its place on his body. When he eased out the Mace, she began to glow with excitement and the stone itself responded to her.

"Zu do you know what this is?"

"I only know that I am to wield it against the Hag."

"Wield it against...Ha Haw, that is really special. Now I have told you I know this stone, What would it be worth to you young assassin with the curving warrior? Would you try me in the combats?" She placed the circlet on her head and before him stood the most beautiful woman he had ever seen. She was exquisite and powerful and huge. Hair enveloped her and she moved toward him. He held the mace between them. She reached for it and the stone came loose from its handle falling into her hand.

"This is Quell-me-not. Stone of dominion. I was present when Isis gave it to Mira on Gallendra. It is power beyond power." She held it to her chest as one might a beautiful flower, then she brought it down to Zu's warrior and let the stone caress the underside of his manhood. Zu felt himself splitting in half as she lifted him to her with one great hand, lifted him as if he were a child. She plunged him into her and held him there as wild energies flowed through the

Hag stone into the joined couple. Zu woke. Finding himself on the bed, sky clad, his warrior fully armored, his muscles tight as if he had been laboring in the fields all day. He remembered with a start the Fore-Crone and raised himself on his elbows to see her standing at the foot of the bed, Ancient, black shadow clad. "What have you done to me?" Zu asked quietly.

"Nothing, nothing at all," she smiled.

"Where is the Mace of Ra?"

"You bear it as you bear other talisman of power. Did you think it would be carried like a weapon and not be taken from you?

Zu searched himself and found it where it should not be. He grasped his treasure sac and realized what she had done to him. "What does this mean?"

"It means that I am going to accompany you bearer of the stone. It means that you are going to need me and the others. It means that I am yours to command. "At which point she transformed again into an enormous winged serpent, glittering green golden.

"This is what Ari thought I was, and this is what he captured. I never showed him my others as I have shown you, but then you are the bearer and from you I will keep nothing." With that she curled her great tail around herself and vanished utterly.

Zu was nonplused. What did this mean? He felt himself again and confirmed that the Hag stone was lodged beneath his warrior, which now was priapic and un willing to lay still. A great crash outside brought his attention to the window again, and he noticed that the fire was encroaching on the Inn where he stood. Quickly, he dressed and gathered his few belongings and made for the stairs. Once outside he found himself in the street filled with fleeing people.

"The city is burning, the fire has spread from the port."

"Tear down the houses in its path, that's the only way to stop it." Frantically teams of men with huge sledge hammers were dismantling buildings. Homeowners were trying to salvage what they could. It was chaos Zu had let loose, and he was caught in it. Carefully, he made his way towards Set's temple, only to discover it was being besieged by hundreds of people seeking shelter within the stone ramparts. When the priests saw him, they waded into the crowd and snatched him to themselves.

"Let in only those who are circumcised or who bear the mark of Set," Zu said. "The night is full of evil and this is no time to contaminate what we have cleansed. I am going to the baths, send me three Ackilons and the fourteen to attend me."

"Yes Lord," the representative of the Chosen responded. In the baths Zu shed his clothing and let himself settle into one of the pools of heated water.

The three Ackilons let themselves into the water as well and waited for him to command them.

Bring the Ackilons, let them take my radiance as well. Before the night was over all had been filled with Zu's radiance. Old men who had white hair for years now had lustrous black hair, as they had when they were young. Men who had lost their hair were now maned again. Men who were sick, were healed. Young Ackilons who had never known combat glowed with such radiance as had never been seen. The god walked in all of them as never before. And still he was untouched by them.

"Bring me the women of the combats, and pregnant women as well." Zu fought combat after combat and it was as if he had no control at all. He gave the women radiance over and over again, until they were hardly able to crawl away from him. Pregnant women were filled to bursting with his vitality and still he had no comfort.

"Give him to me, I will bring him comfort," rang out the voice as the Fore-Crone strode into the combat hall veiled in her radiant golden otherness. Set's priests stepped aside as the huge woman took Zu to herself and watched him collapse in her arms as the radiance enveloped them both. When he awoke, she was by his side caressing his flank and stroking his breasts.

"Is there no rest from the Hag-stone? Is that what I have to go through daily to find rest?" Zu complained.

"Not as long as I am here. I will give you rest. I will serve the bearer as long as he carries Quell-me-not" the Fore-Crone said.

But you must understand here after that this is not something to be avoided, but it is something that comes from ancient times to be borne again. And you are its bearer."

Zu did not understand entirely, but he was willing now to accept the peace she brought to his aching warrior.

When he woke refreshed the next morning, the Fore-Crone helped him bathe and dress, as if she had been doing this all his life. When he entered the temple proper, all who saw him bowed before him as if he were Set himself. He went to the parapet to look out over the city. It was nearly razed, blackened, burned and smoldering ruins confronted him on all sides.

He saw the Shadow company at the gates of the temple demanding entrance and quickly ordered one of the Ackilons who followed him everywhere he went now, to admit them immediately. When he found them in the fore court, they were astonished at the transformation they saw in him.

"What has happened to you?" Tristen asked.

"More than I can tell, apparently by the look of your gaze. Have you had anything to eat? Perhaps we could have something to break our fast so we can plan our journey."

"Yes, that would be good," Boone offered.

Zu looked them over and realized they had not slept or bathed since the fire took the city.

"Perhaps food should await bathing and clean clothes. You will feel better and have a better appetite." Zu gave orders that his friends might be satisfied, and he watched as they were led away. The Fore-Crone who was at his side asked, "Ah, the Shadow Company? Yes, I see these are the champions who would storm the island with you."

Zu looked uncomfortable and said. "You know this is not right. You know too much. Is there anyway you can be less conspicuous?"

She looked at him, radiant in her health and beauty. "I had hoped you would welcome me as a companion to your company. I am a great fighter. None can best me when I am aroused. I am wise. As a counselor I know where you are going and why. I could save you many missteps. And then there is your discomfort."

"Look," Zu said, "for all I know you are the enemy here. I do not feel myself at all and do not trust myself when you are near me. How can I explain you to them?"

"I tell you what, I will serve you only as you ask. You have only to ask and I will appear. But, I will not let you fail. So I reserve the right to rescue you if I think you are in serious trouble. But do not take foolish risks. Even with me watching, you are not immortal. You can die hideously. Otherwise I am the unseen companion of your pilgrimage to the holy mountain." With that she metamorphed into the Ancient Crone and then into the Dragon and was gone.

"Ah, that's much better." He arranged his shirt and marched to find his companions. He did not have to look far, for they were enveloped with steam soaking in the warmth of the baths. Zu doffed his clothing and joined them.

"Well you seem to be better, now that you are in Set's embrace," Zu laughed. The five gathered around Zu and looked at him carefully. They had never seen him entirely sky clad before, and they were amazed at his body.

"Say, haven't you grown since we last saw you?" Tristen laughed. "You are beginning to look like a teapot," he laughed as he pointed to his priapic warrior

"Yes" said Levit, "but you look bigger somehow. It's as if you have grown another layer of muscles or something."

Quinn said through the steam, "Not it, it's not at all. His hair, it is. Golden now where brown it was and thicker it is."

Zu had never seen Quinn sky clad before, and came closer to her. "Quinn, your blazes are wonders, what do they mean?"

"History, they are. People mine, emblazoned Quinn with tribe's story. Live they would, dying they were. But mine are like yours not at all," she said as she traced with her finger Zu's blaze up his chest and down his arm.

"That painful looks," Quinn said pointing to his warrior.

"Now look here," Tristen said, "We did not come here for rape and I won't stand by while it happens."

Zu looked astonished at Tristen. "Rape? What's the matter with you Cup warrior, have you taken leave of your senses? It was not me who began with the sexual observations. I am changed yes. I bear the mace of Ra within my body. Don't ask me how, I don't know how. It wasn't supposed to be that way. But it is a stone of awe, more powerful than anything I have ever encountered. And my brother bears the Stone of Reckoning, so I know something about these things.

This is the result of bearing the stone. Yes it is painful, but it is also a great treasure of radiance. What you notice about me is that radiance, my radiant body is filled to bursting and there is nothing about rape in that."

"All I know is that you're the only one here ready for sex. The rest of us are politely limp and to see you like that is embarrassing. Tristen said.

Dormor had been very quiet, but he said quietly. "I think we are in the presence of greater mysteries then we know, and of that which we cannot speak we should be silent, Tristen." He put this hand on Zu's chest and bowed to him before rising up and exiting the steam.

"If you think I'm going to bow to you, Set's boy, you are very much mistaken, that I will never do." Tristen and Quinn quickly rose and left following Dormor. Levit and Boone remained behind.

"I too bow to you Levit said. I have heard of the stone you bear but I have never seen it. May I touch it?" Thinking it was in his head or chest Levit moved to touch Zu. Zu grabbed his wrist and moved it down until his hand cupped his sac. Levit jumped as a man nearly burned.

"Forgive me Zu, I did not know. I would not have asked if I had." Boone smiled and took the old man by the shoulders and led his aging bones from the steam leaving Zu alone in the enveloping clouds. He also rose but did not exit as they had, he turned rather to the room of cold pools, and sought relief in their icy waters. They helped immeasurably and soon he was restored. Dressed and already attacking the food laid out for them, Zu's five companions acted as if nothing had happened.

"When you are finished, come into the council chambers and we will plan our attack." Zu offered.

The Journey

Another day had passed as Sobec told his story and it was here that he took a long pause and took a deep breath as he looked up into the black sky littered with little diamonds that glowed with an unusual intensity tonight. The moon was full and bright it shown down on them with such a bright light he could easily see the rocky landscape around them. He took another deep breath trough his nose and he could smell the cool desert and the coming change of weather. He knew that fall would soon be upon them. When he had started this story on the new moon this young lad had just come out here to find himself little did he know that Sobec had followed him out here and it was he who had set up this 'chance' meeting.

The boys prone form had grown lean in the last several days from the lack of food not that it was not offered. His warrior was armored more often than not. This was curious but it was of little concern. He knew that he had to complete the story.

"Ancient one. Are you ok??"

"Yes it is just that we are nearing the end of my story and the beginning of yours. It is a sad time I am about to tell you and this is the most complex."

"Well now I will be the judge of that why don't you continue and we will deal with it together." Jesuwa said gently.

With no more coaxing needed he began to sing and what came next was the journey that would change everything... Secure in his possession of the Mace of Ra, Zu was anxious to redirect his colleagues to the real target of their quest: The island home of the Hag. Crete. He assembled the shadow company in the temple of Set's great council chamber where he drew down Set's great maps of the region showing the temples of Set and the Hag's great kingdom as it had been found in the secret chambers of Volun.

"Well," began Zu, "What we know of the Hag's empire is very old. Much has changed in the intervening years. It has gotten bigger in places and smaller in others. We can see by the great map discovered in Volun that the ancient central temple was on an island called Gallendra. But I am happy to report to you that it was mysteriously destroyed several years ago. What great hero was responsible for this catastrophe we do not know, but he surely was one of Set's greatest sons. According to the Volun map the second great temple was on the nearby island, Crete which was much damaged in the explosion that destroyed Gallendra. Many of its warships were sunk, and most of its great trading fleet was crushed against the rocks of the harbor. Thousands are supposed to have died. But it is here that the power of the Hag was transferred, and it is here that we must reconnoiter. My brother will land his fleet here," Zu pointed to the destroyed harbor, "and we will sack the city and destroy the island sanctuary. But he has to know where the power sits, and that is what we must determine."

"But," said Dormor, "How are we to get there? Shipping has been completely destroyed here because of the great fire. If I could find the fool who started that fire, I would strangle him."

"Strangle away, Dormor, I started the fire when I slew two wizards who hid themselves beneath the calm exterior of tradesmen in the great warehouse at the end of the wharf."

"You!" Dormor looked at Zu with shock and disgust.

"Two wizards you say? How do you know they were wizards?"

"Well I apparently liberated a great daemon when I assassinated those two, who came to thank me. I am reliably informed of their character by her testimony," Zu said as nonchalantly as possible.

"Demons have sex? How do you know it was a female daemon, "Tristen began, "Did you, I mean with your ever ready stiletto there, did you…well, you know?" He stammered hoping for a good story.

"Well yes, I think there was an encounter and I have never been the same since. She did this to me," Zu said quietly.

Great guffaws of laughter rocked the room, as Boone and Tristen thought about the joke the demoness had played on Zu.

"Come back for more, will she?" Tristen asked hardly able to keep a straight face.

"Probably," said Zu calmly. "She's here now somewhere lurking about after my scent, I suppose. She just couldn't get enough of me." Gales of laughter left the company on their backs until Levit wiping tears away from his face, said.

"What a good joke. I haven't laughed that much in months."

"Oh I assure it is no joke," said Zu rubbing the aching bulge in his robe. Which comment put the five on the floor again rolling in laughter.

"When you can calm yourselves, we have much to talk about," Zu said stonily.

"Alright my beauty, alright. We are all ears. Tell us how were going to get to this place of power," Tristen said still laughing.

"I propose that we travel along the coast East until we come to a large port where Set will arrange for us transport. Then a sea voyage on a trusty ship, disguise as merchants in search of fine Cretian wine. We will take up residence in the city and discover what we need to know. Then when Rau arrives we will have reliable information to direct his attack."

"How are we to travel?" Boone asked?

"It's clear that chariots will not be reliable so far from the city, so we'll have to take pack animals. Dormor, don't the Sythians have a way they can ride horseback and maintain there seat over long distances?" Zu asked.

"Indeed, yes, we have a large strap which encircles the belly of the horse in which we strap our legs. It's not perfect, but it is far better than riding bareback."

"Then it's settled, we'll ride horseback and take some pack animals with us to carry provisions. I would like to recommend that we leave at dusk tonight, so we will not call attention to our leave taking. With the crowds of refugees exiting the city we should blend in, I suspect. I suggest that everyone use the hospitality of the temple to rest up, go to the armory and select what ever you think you need, together with your own equipment, of course, and we will leave at night fall."

"I have a question," Tristen said."

"Anything," Zu said.

"Who put you in charge of this expedition?"

"Set did, that and the Hag-stone I bear, Quell-me-not. But I will defer to you Tristen, if you have other ideas about how we should organize our travels."

"I certainly do my beauty. First, Levit and Boone here and I have much more experience on the road than you. Dormor is no slouch either and well Quinn is a tracker without peer. So far as I can see you are mostly a priest and a temple trained assassin.

Significant qualities I'm sure, but if you continue to make decisions like the one you made to burn the port down, we'll be dead before dawn. And I do not intend to die anytime soon. "Tristen sat down in his chair quite agitated, and Levit rose to back him.

"I agree, Zu, you are too young to lead this party. Advise us, guide us, but the decisions about when and how we do battle or set up camp and such should be left to your elders."

Dormor, Boone and even Quinn chimed in their agreement. Zu quickly saw he was being demoted and gave no dissent.

"I surrender to my elders. However, if Set commands, we must listen."

"If your daemon lover appears, can we watch?" laughed Tristen.

"If you dare, you may do whatever you please, Tristen," Zu said having just about enough of Tristen's teasing.

"Maybe she'll come to be for solace when she discovers you are not up to her needs. Just send her over laddie, I'll show her how a man treats a woman, daemon or not."

"You may get your chance, Tristen, You may get your chance," Zu said only half in jest.

As the Shadow party broke up their meeting and exited, Zu gave directions to the temple guardian that their needs should be met as if they were his own. When they had gone with their appointed guides, Zu took the guardian aside and spoke softly to him.

"Honored guardian, we will be leaving at dusk and that I do not know if ever I will return. I go into certain danger, a great battle looms as you know. Indeed the Blood Mothers may find you before we staunch them at their source. I would know if there is any service I may do which would repay you for your service to us."

"Lord, the Miracle of last night still reverberates through us. There are many who were not here because they were fighting the fires. They are wounded and weak, the fourteen have treated as many as they are able to but are quite depleted. Could your supply the fourteen with radiance and heal those who have not had your radiant touch?" the temple guardian asked, his head bowed.

"Lead me to them, I would do you this last service," Zu said quietly setting his hand on the older man's shoulder. The temple guardian led Zu to the stone of surrender, and there found a room full of expectant people, waiting for his touch. When he appeared to the sky clad, they were astonished at the vibrance of his radiant body. Zu filled all who asked, fed all who came, and anointed with his shining substance the burned and wounded. Many just touched his body in worshipful respect and asked for nothing. When at last the fourteen came to him, he saw that a second fourteen had been assembled. Even so all who asked were saited. The brilliance of his body never faded and indeed seemed to flare brighter than when he started. When he had completed his tasks, he donned his robes and descended to the baths. The rooms were crowded with Set's Ackilons and Priests who vied to serve him. They could not get enough of combing his hair and oiling his body. Finally, he asked to be left alone in the warm pool, and the room emptied noiselessly. As he lay in the warm waters, he felt a touch on his forearm which he recognized instantly, the Fore-Crone. When he looked up he was pleased he had taken her golden appearance as she joined him in the water.

"I did not know your status, assassin. Here you are more god than man. Has it always been thus?" she asked.

"No, ancient one, it has not. It has only been since you embedded Quell-me-not in my body, that its radiance has blazed through me. I am quite changed as a result. And I can now do things I could not before. I am grateful to you, and at the same time very angry. You tricked me, and I will never be the same," Zu said quietly his voice tinged with awe and irritation.

"That is right, but I have only made you what you were destined to be. But enough of this, I have come to ease your pain." Slowly the Fore-Crone took Zu into her, opening to him in ways he had never known possible, and triggering in him a cascade of sensations he had not known were possible. Exhausted Zu fell into unconsciousness as the Fore-Crone left him, Shadow clad. And it was none too soon as Tristen burst into his heated room just as she vanished.

"Alright, where is she? The Priests told me a woman was in here with you. They could hear her voice, but not understand what she was saying. Is it the daemon who has claimed you?" Tristen saw that Zu was quite asleep, and that his priapism was broken entirely.

"Curses on you, Zu, you said I could watch. You should have called for me. She'd never have left had she known I was nearby." Tristen swaggered about for a while until he summoned the Priests and demanded they dress Zu and make him ready for travel. While they seemed to acquiesce to his commands, they respected Zu enough to let him sleep after Tristen had departed grumbling and stammering.

When he awoke, Zu felt oddly refreshed. He was himself again. Quickly he checked to see if Quell-me-not was still in place, and was at once relieved and irritated to discover it was still very much accounted for. But his warrior was quiescent, and for this he thanked Set. And quickly the Fore-crone as well. When he stepped out of the pool he was instantly surrounded by priests and Ackilons who dried him and helped him dress. As he was leaving the baths, the Temple guardian stepped forward and offered Zu a sword.

"Lord we have little to offer one such as you, but this sword has come to us from the battle at Thebes. It is new in design. We would have you take it, that it might guard your life as you have guarded ours."

Humbled by the gesture, Zu accepted the gift and Gave them Set's blessing.

The company of six exited the temple grounds and entered the flow of refugees who were leaving the burned and still burning city. They had purposely dressed as refugees themselves, wearing cloaks which were soot stained and burned here and there. But their horses were not those of poor men, and many gave way before them. When they had traveled only a few hours they discovered themselves quite alone on the road as most had camped for the night outside the city. Boone led the party with his mage light and they continued on into the night. The moon lit the road brightly where it was not blocked by the occasional tree. But at about two o'clock, as Zu later reckoned it, the first attack came at them. It began as a rain of stones, and then became larger rocks. As they were quite exposed the six dismounted and Tristen called out to their attackers.

"Show yourselves cowards that we may gut you like fish. It's the work of women and children to throw stones. Step into the light."

And so they did. A huge woman stepped into the road as the stones stopped falling. She was surrounded by dozens of little children each with knives clutched in both hands.

"Who travels at night with the Hag-stone without paying proper courtesy to the Crones of the night. Set her loose your devils." The giantess pointed at Quinn as if she thought she must be the bearer of the sacred talisman.

As Quinn did not move, and as none of the men made to secure her. The woman was puzzled.

"Why do you not run to us sister? We will protect you from these insane men. Get away from them so we can kill them without hurting you."

Quinn took her time and walked toward the dark giant. "Enemy am I to you, hag bitch. People mine destroyed you did. Breasts from you will adorn my horse before we leave this place."

Shocked at this betrayal by woman kind, the great crone boomed her challenge. "Then you all will die, and we will take the Hag-stone from you."

"Wait, Wait." Tristen shouted. "I cannot kill little children, not again. Send them away, let us fight with warriors."

"You will see who is the warrior and who is the child, after tonight, murdered of children and women. I know who you are knight of the Cup, and you will I kill first."

Zu stepped into the light, and raised his hand. "Since its I who bear the Hag-stone, Shouldn't you discover who you fight before you begin a battle you cannot win." The Crone stepped closer to see who it was who spoke. A shadow passed between them and the Crone ceased her advance.

"Ah! Stone bearer, I did not know it was you. Your passing has been foretold. You are powerfully warded, even Nemesis will not block your way. But these others, they should die. You should let me kill them for you. Then you could travel in my protection."

"Nemesis. You are Nemesis? Even I have heard of her," Tristen said, "but I always thought you were something out of grandmothers stories."

"You are right, child butcher, Grandmothers know many things. You soil the night air with your noise, bring me this stone bearer that I may know him better," Nemesis said with a bellow that filled the valley they were traveling through.

"I am here Crone, may we have safe passage if I do as you ask?" Zu answered.

"Yes, Stone bearer, come to me and your company may travel safely."

Zu walked toward her and the little children surrounded him menacingly until a shadow passed over them and they broke and fled. "Show me Quell-me-not, stone bearer, I would hold it in my hands. It has been lost for so long I no longer know what it looks like."

"You will forgive me Nemesis. I bear the stone in my body where it was placed by the great Fore-Crone herself. It is not possible for me to draw it out like a false tooth," Zu said as politely as it was possible to speak in such intimidating company.

Nemesis looked at Zu and said, "then show me your body stone bearer." Quickly, Zu shed his traveling robes and stood moonlight clad before her, his warrior arching up in crimson defiance.

"I see how it is. But tell me what of these other things.

Of what do they portend?" Nemesis asked of his ritual blazes. "Nemesis is wise enough to know the meaning of such marks," Zu replied, I would not tell you that which you already know well enough.

"You are right Set's Chosen, I know you. Were you not warded by she who is far greater than I, you would be broken at my feet for daring to disgrace Quell-me-not with that god be sotted body. And I would be greater than I should be. Go now and be damned for I know you and your fate."

Zu donned his traveling clothes again and asked. "Why did you call me Set's Chosen."

"Did not Set himself chose you for this journey, did not he separate you from that precious murdering brother of yours, did he not humiliate you over and over? You are just as surely Set's Chosen as that dark brother twin. You alone refuse to admit what is clearly written in your flesh." Nemesis rose up to her full height in the bright moonlight and let them look on her. Terror moved through the shadow company shaking each of the hero's to the very marrow of their bones. Zu alone did not quell before her.

"No I should have known that you alone would stare me down, with Quell-me-not between your legs, you could withstand flood, fire, pestilence and bloody death itself. Be gone Zu and never pass this way again without your ward for on that day my teeth will be in your bowels grinding you into dust," Nemesis howled as she abandoned the field with her army of children.

"Ra, help us," Levit said as he rose up from the road where he had fallen in abject terror. Dormor wept openly as he regained his composure. Boone was nowhere to be seen until Zu saw the rippling light a little off the road. Tristen and Quinn held each other as the fright left them.

"I think we should travel out of this valley and make camp. I would not have that hag watching over us during the night, safe passage or no," Dormor offered.

"Agreed," said Boone who materialized as he removed his cloak. "We need to be out of here that is certain." The party remounted and made haste to put as much ground behind them as possible. When they were quite distant they found a glade where they dismounted and set up a hasty bivouac. Their horses relieved of their blankets drank deeply from the pool nearby and were tied to stakes on long tethers so they could graze. The shadow company spoke little until they saw Zu was not among them.

"Where's Zu?" Tristen asked quietly of Quinn.

"Zu here was now just," she replied in her heavily inflected tongue.

"Zu?" Tristen called.

"I'm here, over here by the spring," Zu answered.

They followed his voice to the side of the pool where a gushing spring had made a depression filled with clear water just deep enough for bathing.

"I'll be damned, how did you now this was here?" Tristen asked.

"Nemesis told me," Zu said quietly as he stood clad only in the moonlight hip deep in the icy water of the spring. "Join me if you like, Tristen."

"I've bathed enough this year, I think. You come along when you're dry and get some sleep; Dawn is not long in coming. "Tristen said quietly watching Zu's beautiful body in the blue white light of the moon." Damn me, but you'd make an astonishing woman, Zu. If that sword between your legs were not there I'd rape you myself."

"You certainly, have an odd way with women, Tristen. It is too bad you never encountered Set's rituals as a youth. You would have made a fine Ackilon."

"It is too late for me, and it may well be too late for us all if you can't find some way of making the presence of that stone more difficult to detect," Tristen added.

"I may have an answer to that," said Zu thoughtfully as he immersed himself under water. When he rose into the moonlight, the Fore-Crone was with him in the pool. Wordlessly they embraced and the water was filled with radiance.

Zu slept like the dead until Dormor aroused him. He was laying sky clad on his blanket in the morning sun.

"Cover yourself man, do you not think we have enough trouble without you exposing yourself like this?" Dormor said as he knelt by his side.

Zu roused himself, surprised to be found laid out like a goose for the spit. Quickly he checked himself and was pleased to find himself intact, still stone laden. Dormor watched all this in amazement as Zu quickly dressed.

"Either you are insane or there is more power in you than any of us dared hope," Dormor said helping Zu gather up his bedding.

"Well let us hope, gentle Dormor, that it is the latter and not the former," said Zu as he plaited his long hair into a traveling knot.

Battle

As Zu mounted and fell in the troop the six made, he noticed they had prepared themselves out for battle, rather than travel. This seemed most peculiar,
since they had not discussed a coming encounter with the enemy but perhaps
they knew something about the terrain ahead of them that he didn't. When Zu
drew his horse up alongside Tristen's he asked, "What is this Tristen. Everyone
here but me seems to expect trouble."

"Well you still can talk, amazing. I had assumed the demon women we have
met recently had drained you of all your sweet senses. After last night, I'm surprised there is any stiffness left in you at all, my slack jawed friend. Some of us
are able to read the signs and we are beginning to enter territory marked out by
the Knorigh. So we are expecting trouble. If I were you I'd get my sword where
it can be easily reached," Tristen offered.

Zu became apprehensive, and drew his cloak more closely over his face. He
sat silently on his horse, letting the morning sun warm him as he followed his
companions into the countryside. By mid afternoon the trail they followed
moved into a small but thriving forest. It was a peculiar forest, Zu thought.
Peasants had swept the forest floor clean of fallen branches and limbs in their
quest for firewood. No undergrowth of any kind crowded the tall oaks and
heavy maples. They all stood like sentinels watching over an ankle deep blanket
of golden leaf mold. Here and there a heavy root coiled out of the mold like
some large viper wrinkling its long length just under the surface of leaves and
soil. The companions grew quiet, watchful. A ring of stones could be seen
though the trees; stones hoary with lichens and moss, they claimed the only
clearing within the darkening canopy of over arching limbs.

Zu felt the hair on the back of his neck stand straight up; he reached for his
sword and felt his horse bunch his shoulder muscles as if about to spring. Zu
could just see the broad backs of Levit and Dormor who made up the van-
guard of their troop. Tristen, Boone, and Quinn rode in a small clump just in
front of Zu.

Without warning Zu noticed everyone reining in their mounts, and he could
barely bring his up before he noticed that there were twenty massive creatures, the
like of which he had never seen before, standing in the road before them. They all

wore simple gray cloaks and they reminded Zu of something akin to the Knorigh, yet something more. Eyttie, Zu suddenly remembered, Eyttie from the stony circles. He remembered his brother telling him of the giants who lived in the north and made their dwellings in burrows under huge circles of monstrous rocks. The rituals they performed on massive stone altars within these primitive circles were unspeakable and void of humane content. They we revile and hated creatures capable of incredible feats in battle.

Zu noticed that in this forested tracery their skin shown a sickly yellow which with the unkempt brown fur would have made them appear to be unhealthy creatures had not sheer size indicated powerful frames and formidable intentions. Clearly, these were not beings to treat lightly. They looked dangerous and seemed willing to give ample demonstration of their willingness to offer combat. Zu instantly turned around to find a way to escape his odd predicament, but there too he found five more of these strange creatures, to his right two more strolled out of the surrounding forested area. To their left two others ambled out of the underbrush. To Zu's surprise, he noticed that even though these creatures looked clumsy with their meandering gait they moved with surprising agility and stealthiness.

The most massive of these ugly creatures opened his toothy yap and managed a hawking imitation of Common speech, "You Give thirty gold all us, maybe you leave holy ground undead."

He hefted a huge double headed ax and made meaningful arcs with it around his hideous form. It did not take very much imagination to understand that he meant to separate the companion's heads from their bodies, if they did not cooperate.

Hesitation was not something that the companions believed in, Zu noticed abruptly. Tristen threw the empty vial of the firecup to the ground, leapt off his horse and drew his long sword in a seamless gesture before he ever hit the ground. As he charged the grim speaker, he yelled, "To the nine hells with you and all of you walking dung heaps."

Before the huge leader could anticipate his charge Tristen had planted his sword under the meaty chin of his adversary and with a savage thrust sent the blade clean through his skull. The Eyttie slumped like an ox pole axed, his heavy body reduced to so much wolf meat. As his companions charged into the battle, Zu drew out his long sword and dagger as he slid off his horse, mumbling to himself, but perhaps to his guardians as well, "Well let's see what Zu, Set's vessel can do on his own.

Tristen slew a second adversary almost instantly when he lopped off his head with one mighty sweep of his sword.

Dormor drove his sword deep into chest of the huge female Eyttie who opposed him, piercing one milk dug before it cleaved her heart in two.

"That's one little monster who will have to eat solid food sooner than he might wish." Zu heard Dormor shout triumphantly as he yanked the sword from her bleeding form. One of the female's fellows, perhaps her mate, it was hard to know, tried to cut him down, honking as he did:

"You stinking filth, my blade hungers at rotting heart beating in soul box! Come to me, you die horrible."

Dormor had to move quickly to evade the fury of this charge, but evade he did, catching his foe behind the knee, and sending him screaming to the ground with a stump spurting blood. Whirling around, Dormor swept the Eytties head from his shoulders, as easily as he might split a pumpkin. The lifeless body fell across the female's corpse in a terrible embrace of fists clenching and toes jerking.

Each member of the small group now confronted at least four adversaries each. Not to be outdone by the heroics of Dormor, Levit raised his mace and brought it down mightily on the skull of an approaching assailant, caving that haired orb in so neatly his eyes looked out at the world from the vicinity of his tongue. Such a mighty blow gave his other three opponents pause to think about hazards they had not expected in this fray.

Zu, himself, was in deep trouble. Four Eytties had him surrounded just out of sword length, and took turns swinging at him. He had dropped his cloak to free his sword arm, and heard the Eytties growl that they faced a particularly ugly woman. They seemed to be teasing him with their plans for him if they caught him alive.

Zu's temper flared and when he feinted at one, the whirled mightily with his sword and cut deeply into the belly of another leaving his entrails cascading across his knees. As the other three gawked at the pitiful scene of their companion vainly trying to put his intestines back in his belly, Zu whirled again and slashed the throat of another, leaving twin fountains of blood jetting heavenward. This second victim's eyes bulged out with surprise as he fell quite dead to the ground. Mustering all his energy he turned to confront the remaining two screaming:

"I am Set's Chosen and I will not die easily. My sword longs to drink your blood." These two did not know whether to attack this black robed demon or to flee. Their hesitation was their undoing, as Zu relieved one of his left arm with a mighty swing of his sharp sword, and plunged his dagger deep into the side of the other.

Meanwhile, two hefty Eytties opposed Tristen with surprising coordination. They both swung at him at once, and while Tristen succeeded in blocking one attack, while the other succeeded in hitting him. The Eytties wicked blade cut deeply into Tristen's side, creating a flow of crimson which stained his breeches and began to fill his boots with blood. Tristen seemed to shrug off the wound and answered the blow by splitting one of his tormenters nearly in two with a mighty swing. The gore from this corpse was more than Tristen could stand and as he stepped back to avoid the stench, his companion tried to strike but missed miserably. Tristen took two powerful swings but as his strength was filling his boots, he was only able to connect lightly with both.

The fight ended as it began when Dormor stood flanked by two Eytties. He swung at the huge Eyttie on his left who was wielding a massive club, and missed miserably on his first swing. However, with the other swing, he cut a long gash down the center of the second Eytties chest dropping the beast to the ground, his heart's blood soaking the ground at Domor's feet.

The fight gone out of them, the surviving Eytties retreated into the forest sensing that to stay would only bring about their collective demise. In the stillness of the forest, the companions stood stock still, as if worried that this might be some kind of ruse. When Tristen exclaimed after the retreating Eytties, "What's the matter, 30 gold not enough for a good fight? Holy Ground not worth protecting?" A howl of rage echoed from the forest in response.

"That's enough," counseled Zu, "they have gone and we are yet alive. Do not taunt them into a second attack.

Tristen scowled at Zu, but was too drained by the battle to continue his attack. He sniggered at Zu, "Well at least you might do us the favor of raping the bitch we slew. She at least won't offer you much resistance. Tie a sword across your narrow ass so you don't fall in.

When they grew more collected, the companions found they had only suffered minor damage, and that the Eyttie had left behind considerable booty consisting mainly of body armor their huge weapons. On the corpse of the female, Levit found an ancient golden medallion engraved within a circle of pigs what appeared to be a great fat Eyttie female suckling two infants, one on each dug.

Levit retired to his horse, retrieved his medicines and began to bind up their wounds, focusing most on Tristen's side wound. It would not do for them to look as if they had been in a battle if they encountered another adversary. Already dark shapes were to be seen slinking between the trees, and overhead through the dense canopy, Tristen said he could see vultures gathering. The companions made haste to remount and move out, leaving the trail littered with the bodies of the slain, and the soil enriched with the blood of their foes. Even though they had just been though a rough battle, Zu noticed that he had never seen the one they called Boone remove his cloak even for the briefest of a moment. The potency of the cloak was apparent since he left a trail of surprised corpses as he waded though their attackers.

"Now that is a cloak I must own one day," Zu thought greedily. "How impressive I would look in it," he imagined.

As Zu regained his saddle, he drew himself up nearly standing so he could see the trail behind and pondered this incident. He remembered Tristen's high valor in the fight and his continued taunts. Was this an enemy? He thought about the Eytties and their losses so near their holy shrine. Perhaps he should have let the Eytties know he was the stone bearer. But since he had wrapped himself with the special cloth which dampened the Signature of the Hag-stone none had recognized it. Zu began to wonder if that were an especially good thing. Perhaps the Eyttie would have let them pass unmolested if they had known they confronted the stone bearer. Questions like this tormented Zu as he rode in tired silence trying to map out the relationships between the companions, and how he might manipulate them for the success of his mission.

A New Adversary

The Shadow Company rode along the sea coast for five days in a relatively uneventful journey. It was an idyllic time. The azure sea. The breakers along the coast. The salt sea canopy of odor that enveloped them with the fragrance of Isis constantly.

The gulls and small strand birds which flew in great clouds over the beaches and shoals. The nights when the six camped by the sea gave them sleep unencumbered by their journey or the great Hag who waited for them at journey's end. Unbeknownst to Zu, he was being watched over by Oceaniads who detected the passage of the Hag-stone now that Zu had unwrapped the dampening cloth from his body where it hung. They came in the night and made the flowers bloom around his head, drove away the black flies that would disturb his sleep, brought sea winds to freshen his dreams, and left sea shell offerings to the Hag-stone. Zu always woke refreshed on these nights, and Quinn never ceased to wonder at the profusion of flowers that bloomed where he slept.

The worst that could be said of this period of time was that the rivalry between Tristen and Zu increased into what almost might be said to be hostility. What had begun as good natured sniping turned into something quite different after the attack of the Eyttie. Tristen was no longer sure that Zu was really on their side. Perhaps he sensed the presence of the water folk.

Perhaps he sensed the presence of the Fore-Crone. Perhaps he was angry that the Mace of Ra was beyond his ability to see or to test its heft, or to wield in battle. Perhaps he loved Zu and it made him so uncomfortable he had to act as if hatred and loathing were his true response to Zu. For whatever reason, Tristen began to have doubts about Zu's real mission. For all Zu's protestations, Tristen began to develop the most uncomfortable suspicion that Zu was really working for the goddess against the gods. At every opportunity Tristen tested his suspicions until the others began to have their fill of them.

For his part Zu's defense of his integrity quickly subsided into silence, when it became clear that nothing except action would clarify his position. Zu hoped that Set would provide such action before long. But Set seemed unwilling to cooperate and the adventure seemed destined to descend into an ordeal of patience. That is until they heard the pipes.

"Hold," Dormor commanded to the party when he heard the noise. "Listen." The six strained their ears to catch the sound but all they heard were the ordinary noises of the seaside road curling through the hills and beaches of the shoreline. Then it came more clearly, the skirling of pipes, the sound of marching. Some kind of procession came their way, and the six decided it was better to avoid it than confront it. Hastily, they detoured into the hills to conceal themselves and watch what passed. Their wisdom was not long in being repaid as a large column of the Hag's army came into view, some eight hundred fully battle armored warriors marching under the banner of a golden sow. They were a marvelously diverse group. Ranks of archers followed ranks of javelin runners, followed ranks of skirmishers followed by wagons of supplies and provisions and not a few wounded. There was an odd humming welling up from them as the piper passed. It was not a sound such as men make, but more like the contented noise a mother makes as she nursed her child. It was a very odd sound to emanate from a well disciplined armed force. They watched the lengthy procession marching with sure procession, as a quick time as if the were hastening to battle. This was not an army of defeated warriors; they were proud, well provisioned and well generaled. Tristen had expected to see a ragtag lot, but these were a formidable force.

"Bless me, I'm impressed. That's as fine a troop of warriors as I've seen anywhere," Levit observed quietly to Quinn and Boone.

"I'd not like to confront that lot without overwhelming force, I can tell you," said Dormor.

"What about you Zu, perhaps they have come to protect you from us or other adversaries who might be searching you out.

More of your backup plans?" Tristen taunted.

"That's enough, Tristen," Boone urged. "It's quite unwarranted, this attack of yours. What do you want? Zu to charge down there and defeat the whole lot of them single handedly? Would that convince you, perhaps?"

"No, but will I tell you what I do want to know. What is that army doing following our trail, not an hour behind us? Very convenient wouldn't you say," Tristen hissed.

"More like a colossal failure of communication, I'd say," Boone added. "If they're following us and tracking us why didn't they see that our horses left the road? They seem to be possessed of no particular hurry, and quite capable of discovering our where abouts if they were after us. No, I think something else is afoot. I fact, I'd guess we were riding into a battle of some sort, between the Hag and I don't know who."

"No, do you think it is possible? Might they be on their way to attack Set's forces? What is up ahead that might draw them?" Zu said concerned now for Set's probable army's plight.

"Quinn says look we should ahead. Army of friend's trouble may have, sooner than later," she advised.

"Good idea lets mount and get ahead of them. That shouldn't be hard," Tristen agreed. The Shadow Company mounted and began a swift encircling action to try and get ahead of the army of the Hag. Perhaps they would find the adversary, Perhaps they would be friendly to their cause. As they rode away from this contingent, one of the war crones who traveled with such military forces caught scent of the Hag-stone and moved to follow. As she did however, a dark shadow crossed her and she lost all memory of what she had felt. She paused as if trying to imagine what it was she was about to do, and then returned to her place in the formation.

The Shadow Company rode fast for some time, until the came to a series of steep hills, the last had too sharp an incline to simply ride over. They dismounted and scrambled up encouraging their horses to follow. They made such a comic scene of awkward fumbling as they took the incline that even the Fore-Crone had to smile at their antic speed.

Tristen stopped them at the top of the rise, found a declivity where the horses could be quieted and stationed in case they needed a quick departure. And quietly he led the other five to the top of the hill and what they saw below was marked by six sudden intakes of breath. Below them a huge valley spread out before them and what they saw shocked them into stunned disbelief. There were thousands of the Hag's troops massing in the valley. The detachment they had seen was nothing compared to what they saw below. A long sea side valley blocked by high hills on two sides opened onto a large plain at the end of which lay a splendid city. Their destination, Tanis, lay like a jewel in the distance. The great port city in which they had hoped to find passage to the Island of the Hag was now locked in a deadly siege and it looked as if the Hag was not going to wait long before she attacked.

A long line of black ships beached on the shore were obviously the source of this multitude, yet they had seen at least one detachment march up from the west along the sea. Perhaps others had come overland to fight as well.

"Set help us," Zu asked. "How many do you think are there?"

"Seventy to Ninety thousand, at least," Tristen whispered.

"That group we saw was merely another part of the encampment coming to join the main body of the Hag's force," Zu said. "What in Set's name could have drawn them here?"

"The wealth of Tanis brought them here, that and Set's Chosen, whose banner now flies over the city, or hadn't you noticed, Hag's Ally," said Tristen looking at Zu in amazement.

"With this many of the enemy in front of us, how many more may be in back of us? How many scouts do they have riding the perimeter to secure the encampment? How long will it be before we are discovered?" he continued. The six slumped back in despair their backs now to the Hag's army.

"We have come so far, it seems hard that the Hag blocks our way to Tanis and safe passage to Crete," Boone said.

"I do not think you have much to worry about," said a seventh voice, unfamiliar and deeper than most. All six turned and saw nothing, except shimmering air.

"Who speaks to the Shadow Company," Tristen shouted with the fire cup potion at the ready. His sword was out; he was ready to fight a pitched battle if necessary.

"The guardian of the Hag-stone speaks child murderer." Whereupon, the Fore-Crone in her Dragon form shimmered into view. Her appearance was startling. She was not the monstrosity Dragons are expected to be. She was not quite petite but she was not enormous either. Her golden scales caught the light and made the red of her eyes and mouth all that more dramatic as she spoke. But it was the Wingspread that announced her power, that and her sudden appearance out of seeming nothing. When all except Zu were shocked at this apparition, Tristen looked with fury at Zu.

"A Dragon was here all the time following us, and you never said anything about it," Tristen challenged drawing his sword and menacing Zu.

"I hoped we would not need her. Obviously, the guardian thinks the stone is in danger or she would not have revealed herself to us." Zu offered trying to calm Tristen.

"The stone can fend for itself quite nicely. It has for thousands of years, thank you. It is the stone bearer that I defend, and his companions. There is a certain war crone who has your scent, Stone bearer; I would wrap yourself again in the dampening cloth if I were you. I have twice now stolen her purpose in searching for you. I won't do it a third time."

Zu eased himself down from his perch and made for his horse and pack. Once he had retrieved the dampening cloth, it was not long before he returned to the discussion.

"It is done, Fore-Crone," Zu reported.

"What is done you traitor?" Tristen demanded.

"The Stone bearer has a bag in which the Mace of Ra was housed when I found him. The bag has special properties which conceal the signature of this power as it moves across the land. In effect it blinds the stone. And so conceals it from those who are tuned to its powers. He mourned the loss of the Eytties who properly would have honored the stone bearer had they known he was before them and so removed it from his body. Why do you think your recent travels have been so pleasant? The Oceaniads have been guarding you and providing for you because the Stone bearer had made himself known. Now it is dangerous to do so, since the armies of the Golden One have massed before us and it would be so confusing for us to explain ourselves to them. It is easier this way," the Fore-Crone managed to explain with her dragon's tongue and teeth.

Tristen was not much soothed by this speech, but he at least understood, and so ceased his menacing gestures and contented himself with glares.

"If you will listen to me, I think there is something important going on here that we may turn to our advantage," the Fore-Crone grunted in her deep sarcophagal voice.

"And what might that be, Guardian?" Zu asked.

"As you see there are many ships massed below on the sea beach. They are provisioning this ravenous hoard before they attack Tanis."

"But the high walls of Tanis should keep this lot at bay, said Boone.

"Tanis is just beyond the valley. Tomorrow it will be rubble. Tanis is guarded by a chariot army of 2,000 chariots and fifty thousand infantry. It is a great city. But they are too proud. They have challenged the Hag to a set battle before the city walls. They have no idea how outnumbered they are. They will be obliterated by the Hag's army. That die was cast when Gallendra was lost," The Guardian observed quietly.

"Wait, you mean that this army without chariots can defeat a chariot army and infantry combined?" Dormor said incredulously.

"Absolutely." Show him the sword the temple guardian gave you, Zu, before you left."

Zu drew out his sword and for the first time the Shadow Company stared at the new design, the slicing sword. Tristen brought his out and compared the two.

"Brilliant, just brilliant." Tristen said in bitter admiration. "Look at that edge, sharp as glass. And the blood runnel. Look how it runs the length of the blade. And what balance it has. Meteor metal too." He grasped the sword and tested its heft and feel. "An army quipped as I am would have no chance at all against warriors wielding these. But how will they defeat the chariots? Not even good swords will turn those proud beauties!"

"Simple," Zu said, "They kill the horses and over run the chariots."

"Kill the horses? That's monstrous! They're priceless.

Why would you kill such valuable animals? They should be war trophies," Levit protested. "You're telling me that those beautiful horses will be carrion at battle's end."

"Isn't it a marvelous surprise?" the Guardian answered in a coarse whisper. Perhaps, I will feed most heartily on their carcasses myself tomorrow evening."

"Enough of this speculation. It could just as easily be that this army before us will be the carrion," Tristen complained as he grew in respect for the Guardian and her knowledge of coming events.

"What of your idea, Guardian."

"Well as I said, there are ships down there, ships ripe for the taking by a well armed small force. If we are patient and if you let me make you shadowclad for the evening to erase any hint of your presence, then during the battle when this valley empties its troops into the plain before Tanis to slaughter Set's troops, we should be able to commandeer a ship and be gone. That is, if you do plan to confront Isis in her high place, on Crete," counseled the Fore-Crone.

"Is there no way to warn Tanis and the troops there," Zu asked. "My brother may be there."

"Your brother is indeed there, and he already knows what is coming, after all he was defeated at Thebes I believe by this same strategy," the guardian reminded Zu.

"My brother is in Tanis? Are you sure?" Zu asked incredulously.

"Yes Isis is particularly interested in finding him on the battle field. She has several major scores to settle with him. Tomorrow will be very interesting, and you shall have a very good seat for the show," the Fore-Crone laughed quietly.

"I'll be damned if I sit here and watch thousands of Set's men die without me at their side," Tristen vowed.

"I know how much you'd like to be down there hacking away, but really Prince of Sorrows; you are needed in the high places with Zu here. I cannot allow you to get yourself killed. I would be quite remiss if I did, yes I would," she added trying to calm him down.

"What did you call me, 'Prince of Sorrows." Tristen asked.

"Oh sorry, thought you knew. It's nothing really, just what they will call you, if they don't already. It really fits, don't you think child murderer," the Fore-Crone apologized.

"It this prescience thing I have. I know the future and the past and they all get jumbled up in the present.

"So you know what will happen on Crete," Zu said.

"Certainly, it has already happened, it will happen, it always happens. Time is like that.

"Then tell us who wins tomorrow," Dormor said.

"And spoil your fun? Not me, not me, no sir." She laughed a wicked laugh.

"She's already said Tanis will be rubble." Dormor said. "She knows Tanis loses."

A trumped bugled nearby as a contingent of the Hag's forces swept the perimeter. The six jumped as if they'd been slapped.

"Tell us about this shadowclad business," Zu asked in haste.

"It's just that I wrap you in a spell that makes you invisible and puts you to sleep until the right moment. That way you will not be detected, and you won't get in any trouble either. The future will be honored, and the past will be intact."

"You don't make any sense, Guardian," said Boone, but I don't think we have any choice," hearing the heavy report of armed men approaching.

"I don't like it," Tristen said.

"Settled it is then," smiled Quinn. "Enshadow us Dark one."

As they fell beneath her powerful enchantment, Tristen screamed his defiance. Zu, however, was not affected.

"What's this, Fore-Crone?"

The great Dragon was transformed into the golden woman of the pool. "It should be obvious that I cannot comfort you if you are asleep. There is a pool near here. Let me bathe you and give you solace. Tomorrow will come soon enough." She swept him into her arms and he yielded whatever he had left of manly domination. Zu smiled and welcomed her touch, as she led him sky clad down the steep hill to a hidden spring she had known about for centuries.

In the bright morning, the six awakened quite refreshed by the side of the hidden pool. They had been bathed, their clothes had been cleaned, their horses fed and brushed, their weapons polished brightly as for battle. They were more than a little surprised, Zu saw. He himself was still in the pool, where he had gone to bathe after his night of amour with the Fore-Crone.

They were impatient to be gone, but Zu calmed them.

"Look, the army has not left the valley yet; they are massing and will soon be filling the plain before Tanis. The Guardian took me to see my brother last night. He was astounded to see me riding the dragon but he welcomed the opportunity to plan our attack on Crete. This attack was unexpected. He had hoped to launch his attack on Crete from Tanis, but somehow the Hag out marched him. I know he is well aware of the difficulties that beset him. He knows defeat is a possibility, so he has some surprises for the Hag's army. But he realizes that the best he can probably expect is to inflict great damage on the Hag's army, perhaps to capture as many swords as possible so his smiths can copy them. I left my own with him to ward him as best I could.

"Be patient, there is food on the table over there. Break your fast and let us be gone as the Guardian leads us."

Zu rose up out of the water blithe about his sky clad body. None of the Shadow Company could take their eyes off him. The morning sun caught his the fine hairs on his chest and belly, turning him into a blaze of gold. The heavy thatch of his groin blazed as a sun. The Hag-stone had so charged his radiant body that his very skin was aglow. He dressed as casually as if he had been entirely alone, while the others ate fruit and bread, which they washed down with water cool from the spring. As they finished, the Fore-Crone shimmered into form again, and greeted them with a prayer. This time she appeared in guise of the huge battle hardened giantess as Zu had first seen her. Tristen was shocked but gladdened. This was a warrior and just now they could use an able sword arm.

"Well she said," finishing her prayer of greeting, "are you ready to steal a ship?"

"Indeed we are" said Dormor looking at their new ally. Will you fight along side us?"

"I doubt you can sail a ship alone, small one. I am a trained navigator and I know these waters well. No one will prevent us from sailing once I am on board."

Tristen was still angry from being prevented from joining Set's army, but remembering what the Guardian had said, comforted him and made his peace for the first time with Zu.

The Fore-Crone gestured and the table of food vanished. Evidence of their visit had been erased. As the others mounted she began to walk faster than they could ride. They circled the base of the hills until they found the road into the valley.

When she was sure the troops were well advanced to the other end of the valley, she led them out onto the road.

"The first ship is a leaker, but the second ship is a new fast double masted beauty. That's our goal," the Fore-Crone led them into a quick time advance on the ships.

As they closed on the ship at a fast gallop, four sailors came out to meet them, thinking they were more of the Hag's troops late for the battle. Thinking the Fore-Crone was a War crone; they relaxed their guard and prepared to greet her as ally. It was a mistake they made only once, as the sailors were slaughtered where they stood.

"What about the horses, Tristen? We can't take them on board. We'll have no need of them on the island," Levit asked.

"Leave them, they'll find their own or new masters soon," the Fore-Crone directed.

As they scrambled on board, they surprised the captain and navigator at breakfast. Tristen dumped them unceremoniously overboard and secured the ship while the Fore-Crone, Dormor, Quinn and Zu shoved the ship into deeper water. It didn't take much and as they scrambled up the ropes to the deck, they were surprised to find Tristen searching the ship's stores for supplies. The Fore-Crone took over as a one woman crew. She seemed to be everywhere at once, and it was not long before the sails billowed out sending them quickly seaward. Their departure was noted by the other ships and one gave chase. But at a glance, The Fore-Crone saw its sales slacken as it fell behind, becalmed in a dead sea. Soon they were alone on the sea, flying with the wind further away from land with every breeze.

"Unbind the stone, Stone bearer. When the Oceaniads know you are on board, we will have fair sailing and good winds." Tristen was amazed at this exchange and shook his head as he sat on a coil of rope watching the huge woman with breasts like river stones steer the ship.

"I know what you are thinking, Child Killer, and you should have a care. These thews would crush your manhood like grapes in a wine press."

Tristen blushed, crimson red, smiled and went to the stern to relieve himself.

Sea Voyage

As the Fore-Crone had predicted with the Hag-stone unbound, fair winds, mild seas met them. Zu had never really been at sea before, and was mildly agitated when they left the sight of land. From horizon to horizon was nothing but the deepest blue imaginable. Great clouds like high piled foam sailed overhead, an argosy of dream. Zephyrs played in the sails, perfumed winds laden with the odors of the desert or of the great fields of mustard which grew wild along the coast of Syria. Zu was happy, indeed most of the Shadow Company was happy to be at sea. All save Tristen.

"Where is Set, Zu? Why is it when we needed assistance back there at Tanis that it came from this Fore-Crone person rather than Divine Set? Don't you worry about that?"

Zu sat quietly for a moment, considering what Tristen said.

"You don't understand Set, Tristen. I am not Set's Chosen. Rau is. He possesses me when HE chooses. I have never been able to charm him into coming at my command. When I have been possessed, it has always been to protect the life of Set's chosen, or to confront the Hag directly, as happened back at the temple we just left."

"I did not know you had been possessed recently," said Tristen.

Zu told Tristen as much as he could about the battle with the Hag, and the multiple possessions which had thwarted her contamination of the Temple. It was still pretty foggy in his head.

"But what I don't get is why didn't Set possess you back there at Tanis," Tristen said. "Have you been possessed since the Fore-Crone embedded the Mace of Ra in your body?"

"No. Set has been nowhere near. And that is amazing too since the Hag-stone has so charged my radiant body that I would have thought he'd be drawn to me like flies to honey."

"What do you mean Radiant body?" Tristen asked puzzled.

"Well, I just mean the body of energy that surrounds the visible body. Its part of the secret lore of Set, I can't tell you much about it, unless you want to be shorn of your hair, lose your warrior's cap, and take the initiation," Zu laughed.

"You don't seem to be missing either hair or cap, Zu," Tristen asked seriously. "Why should I?"

"Good point. But you'd have to take the Assassin's training and really, you lose more than hair and cap in that process. Anyway," Zu said thoughtfully, "it is something to be considered. If Set does not arrive when we really get into the thick of battle with the Hag I shall be very much surprised."

"I wonder if we should wait for that? I mean, what if this Fore-Crone has somehow blocked Set's access to you by embedding this hangstone in you? Isn't that something to consider," Tristen continued. "She seems to be a titanic presence. I've never seen her like. Couldn't she be doing something like that?"

"I…well…I had never considered it," Zu confessed.

"If you were to consider it, how would you prove it?" Tristen persisted.

"Let me think about it. It is possible, I admit."

"Just don't take too long," Tristen whispered with a new urgency, "we may be sailing with the Hag herself seduced by a willing ally."

Zu was now confronted by a problem he had not considered.

He began to search his memory for clues to the problem. He remembered that Rau himself had commanded he secure the Mace of Ra. He remembered that he had not seen the Fore-Crone actually embed the Hag-stone in his body, only that she had told him what she'd done, and indeed as he searched his memory, he had every symptom that something was different, tremendously different about him. And there was that third stone in his sac. No, he realized, he had the Hag-stone. But was this Hag-stone, the "Quell-me-not" of the Mace of Ra? Surely it was. Nemesis had named it directly, honored it. Had not the Oceaniads honored it and him as its bearer? Zu was confused mightily, but so far things seemed to be as the Fore-Crone had said. And did she not owe him her freedom. Well she said so. But could she have simply tracked the Hag-stone itself and pretended to have been liberated by his assassination of the traders? Then he remembered the bag and its effect on the Hag-stone.

Things seem to be as the Fore-Crone indicated. Why should she try to deceive him, did she not know the future and the past together? But if she knew the future and the past, then why did she not know where the Hag-stone was? Ah, thought Zu, a chink in the armor of the Fore-Crone. Something did seem to be amiss. What else was there?

His mind now went into overdrive trying to remember to reason out the consequences of his actions and their present predicament. A test, he needed a test. That should do the trick.

But what kind of test. Silently, he reached into his pack and retrieved the cloth which hid the Hag-stone's presence. Quickly he wrapped the Hag-stone and waited for the results. That nothing happened immediately did not surprise Zu.

Most of the elementals in the area knew of his presences as Stone bearer, they might not need the constant presence to reinforce their attentiveness to the ship. But when they encountered some new elemental that would begin the test. Zu realized he was playing with fire here, but so be it, he thought.

About midnight Zu sat up in his berth. Something was wrong. He felt it. What? The ship was not moving. That was it. The sea was becalmed, utterly. Zu dressed hurriedly making sure the Hag-stone was draped properly, and quietly began to prowl the passenger compartment. What was it? Something else was here.

Something else was wrong. He opened the sliding door that led to the deck and listened for a long moment. Nothing. Then he looked high overhead and saw to his amazement a second dragon, battling the golden one. More to the point, the golden one seemed to be in trouble. What can this be about? Dragons are sacred to the Hag; they protect her and secure her lines of energy. Why would two of them fight? Perhaps he thought, the second one has not detected the Hag-stone and fights the Golden One for the possession of the Shadow Company. He watched for a long while, then by way of experiment, he removed the cloth from the Hag-stone. Immediately, the second Dragon made a mad dive for the ship, followed by the golden one who was tearing after it. Zu hid behind the passenger cabin watching their descent to the ocean surface.

"Where is it? I know I felt it here? I will have it, or I will have your scaly hide, Fore-Crone. Ahh." silence.

Quickly, Zu covered the Hag-stone again. And waited.

"Where did it go?" Came the voice. I must have that stone. It will enable me to put an end once and for all to that nest of gods who destroy our temples."

"No. Sister. It is not yours. Foretime demands you yield your demand. Isis may deliver it to you. But for now it and its bearer are under my protection."

"May?" thought Zu. Doesn't she know? Perhaps she is not what she pretends to be, after all."

Zu decided the time had come to test his fate. If he was the bearer, then Set would have to come to his aid. He opened himself to Set, he put the chant in motion and he shed his robe. Then he stepped out onto the deck in full sight of the two dragon's sky clad. Had Cain been alert he would have seen Zu step out on the deck like a walking flame, so bright did his radiant body blaze into the moonless night. Both dragons were taken by surprise.

"What is this who walks towards us like burnished bronze?" asked the stranger.

"He who marks the end of time. He who walks under my protection. Now go before you completely ruin foretime," the Fore-Crone whispered.

"Going is not what I had in mind quite," said the stranger. The red dragon moved toward Zu, wings open, back arched, its great tail searching for position from which to support its strike. Zu continued to walk like a man in a dream, when Set took him like a thunderstorm takes a desert valley.

"So the god comes to me," hissed the red one. "Excellent, I will not have to wait to possess the stone; I will finish this business here."

Then Set struck, Zu-Set was suddenly in the company of all the gods, Osiris included. Power coiled through Zu amplified many times by the Mace of Ra, and hurled itself from the mace at the Red one who menaced Zu. She was caught in a corrusicating fire, lifted free of the deck entirely. As she struggled against the lightning fed flame, the golden one screamed at Zu.

"Stop this, Stop this. Beloved. Don't destroy her. She only has to be taught a lesson."

"You do not know me, do you Fore-Crone?" Zu spoke with the voice of multitudes.

The golden one turned from the terrible cascade of burning in which her colleague was caught and looked at Zu more closely. She scrambled towards him turning her head first one way and then another looking at him alternatively from each great eye.

"Peace gentle gods. We are not your enemies. Spare my friend; she will trouble you no more. That I swear."

"For that one it is too late, Fore-Crone."

The golden one had only time to look upward before she saw the cascade of ash begin to fall as the enveloping radiance mixed with the power of all the gods completely incinerated the Red Dragon.

"We will now deal with you golden one," Set-Zu whispered. But when Set-Zu turned to wrap her in the same consuming fire, she had vanished entirely. The deck was suddenly alive with the other five members of the shadow company, who had been watching through the louvered door. They knelt before Set-Zu unable to take their eyes off the walking flame, Zu had become. Then Zu was alone, dark, himself again. As he crumpled to the wooden deck, Quinn caught him in her arms.

"Man of fire, I did not know your identity. Songs we sing of you. Come to my arms now." She said as she cradled his head and shoulders in her lap.

"What can we do for him?" Dormor asked. "I've never seen anything like him."

"He'll be alright," came the gravelly reply as the Fore-Crone reappeared. The Hag-stone will supply what formerly the fourteen were required to deliver.

"Where did you come from, Fore-Crone," Tristen challenged drawing his sword.

"Do you really think that puny pocket knife worries me, Prince of Sorrows? Put that away. Most of this is your fault anyway. You doubted me and my loyalty to Zu, so the Red Dragon had to pay for the test with her life. She was a great force in the land. This was not well done. Thousands will die because she is gone." Tears could be seen in the Fore-Crone's eyes as she picked Zu up and cradled him against her giant's breast and moved to return him to his berth.

Tristen stood as if pole axed. When she returned, he asked." What did you mean when you said thousands will die?"

"We who assume the form of Dragons are ancient beings. We have been here since the founding of the planet. We guard the goddess's lines of force and vitality. The Red Dragon was guardian of the life force that flowed through the southern side of the great sea. With her gone, drought and famine will strike.

Entire areas that are now lush with vegetation and animal life will become dessert. What the gods have done is to impoverish an entire subcontinent. Pretty good for a day's work, wouldn't you say, Prince of Sorrows? Do you imagine that what we are about here is merely about a battle between princes? Are we just challenging one elite with another? You will one day hold in your hands the fate of all men, and you will be judged for your decisions. Have a care, Prince of Sorrows that your Sorrows do not include mourning for the absence of all life." The Fore-Crone vanished again and was gone.

While the five sat in solid depression for several hours, the ship itself seemed to seek its own way. Its sales caught new wind; the sea itself added new speed with a sudden current which sped it away from the scene of the great battle they had witnessed. When Zu stepped out on the deck, they saw he was still sky clad, but that his hair was now flame red and his skin a milky white. Against this new colorless flesh, his ritual blazes stood our as if in high relief. A large thick lapis line now outlined each eye, where he had normally worn coal. Zu was beginning to look more like an apparition than the extraordinarily handsome youth who had joined them in the tavern. Moreover, he seemed to be walking in a trance.

"Zu?" Tristen asked. "Are you alright?"

"We are better than alright, Prince of Sorrows. We are here with you."

Tristen realized he was not talking to Zu anymore; he was in the presence of Set-Zu.

"How is it possible, Divine One, that Zu has been replaced by a god?"

"The Hag-stone is a fountain of radiance. Now that Zu wears it in his body, we can draw on its glory to come and go when we please. We may never leave him."

"We?" asked Tristen.

"I am Anubis, and Set is here as well. The others have left us for the moment, but they will return when they are needed.

All five except Quinn were overcome with this news and did not know how to behave. Quinn stood her ground.

Anubis-Set-Zu turned to her questioningly. "Do you know us, little one?"

"Yes, I know you. You were supposed to be our defenders against the Hag. And you abandoned us to our fate. Now I am the last of my tribe. Why should I bow to you, you who destroyed us?"

"That is a very good question. Perhaps you should have chosen better allies." Set-Zu turned on his heal and strode to the bow of the ship searching for some index that the ship was under control.

That Which had Never Been

The Fore-Crone in her dragon form landed in the courtyard of the Death Mother's Temple on Crete and quickly took her giantess form. Her long legs served her well as she needed speed to find Mira. Obviously, Mira had not expected her, so she was busy directing the business of transforming the booty of the Golden One's Armies into trade goods, so the armies could be provisioned. Ships heavily laden with the gold, silver and treasure from the six cities of Set which Celeste had conquered were docked in her harbor, and the process of unloading them, cataloging the booty was very time consuming.

Equally, difficult was the negotiations with traders who were bringing provisions for the army. Mira's temple had become command central for the expeditions against Set and the armies of his Chosen.

When the Fore-Crone stormed into her reception chamber where scribes were delivering their reports and news of the great contests currently being waged were heard, she threw the well ordered proceedings into chaos. None had ever seen a Fore-Crone; she was a creature of legend.

"Set Comes, Dark One, the end times are coming. You must prepare for that which should not be, or all will be lost, this day."

Stunned by the titanic female presence before her, Mira, hesitated, dismissed all those then in the room and ordered the doors sealed. Then Mira quietly said, "Great One, we are honored by your presence among us. Your tidings are surprising and unexpected. Could you explain yourself?"

"I have lain for centuries prisoner of wizards: I have been the treasure passed from generation to generation of Wizards, the treasure seized by one wizard from another. Now Zu, brother of Set's Chosen has unintentionally liberated me and I have done that which I should not have done creating that which should not be," the Fore-Crone wept as she explained how she had found Zu bearing the Mace of Ra, how she had embedded the stone in his body, how this had produced in Zu a radiance which the gods had seized in order to manifest themselves in the world more potently than ever before. Now instead of being in this world, only on occasion, they had a permanent foothold: A living god walked the earth, he was that which should never have been. Now he was on his way to Crete to destroy Isis once and for all.

Mira took this news quietly. She had had the experience of receiving the news of cataclysm once before so the experience was not new to her. She rose up from her chair, took the arm of the Fore-Crone and asked her to walk with her.

Together they walked out into the sunlight. She ordered one of the watchful priestesses to bring them wine and they settled on a low wall overlooking the bay and the town bring resurrected from the recent destruction. It was a beautiful vision of prosperity and dynamic energy mixed with natural wonder.

"Look below Fore-Crone. You can see we are rebuilding the sanctuary of the goddess, her holy city and her people grow in health and wisdom. You have heard of the success of our armies restoring the rituals of Isis in city after city, defeating the liars wherever they stand before us?"

"All these things I have seen. They are truly wondrous," admitted the Fore-Crone.

"Do you think these things could have been achieved without the active presence of Isis walking among us? We have lost Gallendra. We have lost the Sacred Isle. But we did not lose that which was most important, our love of Isis and her love for us," said Mira patiently.

"Yes, but I have created something not even Isis has anticipated. I have done that which should never have been done. How was I to know that the stone bearer was Set's Chosen? I have opened the doors between the worlds on a permanent basis. I have given away our greatest advantage," the Fore-Crone said in despair.

Finishing their wine Mira said gently to the ancient giantess: "Walk with me to the top of the mountain, we will talk to the Golden One herself about this thing you have done." Together, arm in arm; they began the long walk up the mountain to the lens of power. The way was beginning to take on the look of that in lost Gallendra. Wild flowers bloomed every where. Great patience had been given to collecting these and planting them along the path up the mountain. Standing Stones were being erected by the Stone Mother in places of power. Rites designed to summon their benefits were being created, special drumming pavements were being built. The statue of the first Harvest King was complete and stood in a place of high honor. Great stones had been found and turned so a climber could find rest and beauty all at the same time. The Stone Mother had found natural springs and created catch basins for them and created winding brook beds where the overflow could irrigate gardens on the mountain slopes. Everywhere they looked as they climbed harmony and order were being created by working with the land to bring forth that which already existed but had never been encouraged.

"I am impressed Death Mother, you have made the mountain sacred to her who is life itself, this is where the treasure you have captured from the cities is being spent then?"

"Very little," said the priestess. "Most of this work is done by volunteers as part of their celebration of the return of the goddess to this island. Most of the treasure is being expended on building materials for the city below, for creating a new fleet and for re-supplying our armies in the field."

The two walked in long silence until they came to the lens of power. Mira began the ritual of opening and entered but found that the Fore-Crone was not behind her. Something was wrong; she felt it in her bones. She turned to see what had happened and saw not the Giantess but a sacred Golden Dragon. Why would the Fore-Crone seek entrance into the lens of power as a Dragon, she asked herself."

A gentle hand touched her shoulder, and the voice of her daughter/goddess spoke. "This one is an ancient power, long banished from the sacred places of women because of her service to wizards and mages. She had forgotten her ancient crime. I have reminded her of it and now she demands entrance."

"Demands, Demands? How can any demand of you, goddess?"

"These ancient ones are titanic powers, and they have forgotten their place comparatively. She will have to learn anew what it is to be a Fore-Crone and What she is compared to Isis."

Mira went out of the lens to confront the Golden Dragon, when she saw it swept up in the claw of a dragon so enormous that it seemed as a mouse to an elephant. Looking up to the top of the mountain, she saw the most astonishing sight. An emerald dragon perched atop the lens of power so enormous as to blot out the sun. The light changed altogether beneath her. It was the sacred light of the eclipse she saw, and in it the golden dragon looked small, pitiful and brown. Then both were gone. She searched the sky to see what had become of the two, but of them there was no trace.

Reentering the lens of power, Mira was amazed to see Isis and a beautiful young woman deep in conversation. They turned when they saw Mira re-enter. "There you are, we wondered where you had gone. Won't you come join our conversation; this Fore-Crone has much to tell us."

"I know she has told me most of it, I think."

"What do you make of it Death Mother?" asked Isis of her High Priestess.

"There is so much I do not know."

"Like what?" asked Isis again.

"I do not know for example much about this sacred stone Quell-me-not. I do not know what its powers are and how they might effect you or our mountain home. I do not know what the gods are able to do, how they can project power through the stone bearer into this world? I do not know what they hope to achieve, if they do come here? I cannot understand why they would want to destroy your citadel goddess, except that we have returned to them the favor of what they have done to your priestesses and temples."

"Well let's deal with the first of these. Quell-me-not is one of the four foundation stones of the world. It was stolen from my throne by none other than the Fore-Crone here. It is a source of such radiance that it is the very life force itself. Now she is bringing it back to me, or so she thought. That was her design, you see. She found this group of spies who were attempting to infiltrate the island, and reconnoiter it for an invasion fleet sent by Set's Chosen. But our successful attack on Tanis has sunk this fleet and those plans quite entirely. But the Fore-Crone is not as prescient as she would like to imagine herself to be. She did not know that the one she met was Zu, twin of Set's chosen. Moreover she did not know that the gods had marked him specially to their service.

"So when she hid the Hag-stone in his flesh to preserve it from discovery and theft, she really supplied the gods with the one thing they never had, a permanent source of radiance. The things their priests have had to do to sustain their presence in this world are unimaginable. Their rituals are incredible.

Nevertheless, those are no longer needed since the Fore-Crone here unknowingly gave them the key to heaven.

"Now they come, to answer your second question. They have enormous energy at their disposal. It is quite the opposite of Quell-me-not's. It is possibly the greatest desecration our world can sustain without being utterly destroyed. It is what they used on the first of my ancient temples to break the bonds of the ages and cauterize the life forces forever in that place. And that is what they plan to do here, if we let them. With the Hag-stone in their vessel, they are enormously more powerful than ever they were.

"The one saving grace is they do not know as much about the Hag-stone as I do. The other problem is that they possess my stone of reckoning. This stone is a stone of judgment. It was created when the first cities were created. It gives the bearer the authority to judge rather than be judged. Together with Quell-me-not it is an awesome force that comes towards us. I think we can defeat it, but even for me, it is no sure thing. The best we may hope to do is bring it to its knees in a stalemate. But there is another possibility. This is what I want you to do, Death Mother." Together Isis and her High Priestess talked while the Fore-Crone sat apart weeping. When they finished, Isis said:

"You have much to do, much is to be done. Send the Stone Mother to me as you descend to the temple, I have some special tasks for her. And send me the Chief of my Noble Men. We will be ready for he who comes."

Mira nearly flew down the mountainside to begin her preparations. Two things happened on the way down. First she saw the Golden Dragon explode head over heels from the lens of power as if she had been expelled with tremendous force. It was with greatest difficulty that she was able to right herself in mid fall and assume controlled flight. Secondly, she noticed the Stone Mother carving with her bare hands in a huge standing stone, the likeness of Isis. When she informed the Stone Mother that the goddess had urgent work for her, that huge woman's speed betrayed her large form. Back in her own temple she called her priestesses to her and sent a message to the Chief of the Noble men that he too was urgently required by Isis. So began the preparations for the cataclysm that would be.

The Ship

Zu walked the deck of the ship now in perpetual motion, or so it seemed to the Shadow Company. They avoided him as much as possible, never quite sure what he would do next. They had been amazed when he seized the great rudder and reoriented the ship so that it would reach Crete. They could not quite believe the speed they were moving at. The ship seemed to strain at every seam, it groaned now as if unimaginable pressures were being applied to surfaces never intended to sustain such an assault.

Yet it all held. They stood at the rails of the ship watching the sea move passed them unlike any sea they had ever seen. It was as if the hull were a luminous knife which sliced through the body of the sea goddess in an orgy of blood. They had not been prepared for the arrival of their old ally the Fore-Crone. Or the image in which she appeared.

"Who's that?" Tristen said, rubbing himself obscenely when he saw the golden beauty that was the other form of the Fore-Crone.

"I don't know, but the way things have been happening around here, I believe I'd play it very cautiously with her," Dormor warned.

"Ahh, She's a woman isn't she. All women like the same thing. She'll find Tristen's sword just the thing for her sheath," laughed wickedly.

"Have a care Tristen; we are going to need you in the coming battle." But Tristen shoved Dormor away and marched off to confront this stranger.

"Well, are we lost? Does the young woman need directions?" The look Tristen gave her left nothing to the imagination, and her response was both quick and savage.

"Listen to me this once, Child Killer, there is nothing you have I am interested in and if you touch me I will rend you into so many uneven parts that not even the fish will know it is a man they devour."

Stunned in his tracks, Tristen quickly backed away. Then his eyes lit up. "I know you in another form. You are that ugly dragon, tall bitch with the big hands. What is the Fore-Crone doing here? I thought you'd had enough." Those were has last words as the Fore-Crone pressed him into shadowclad silence and moved off in search of Zu. It was not long before she caught sight of him, and from no where produced a beautiful lyre and began to play the most haunting and intoxicating music that could be imagined. Zu immediately came towards it and was pleased to find his ally.

"I thought we'd lost you, lady."

"No my beloved, you were never far from me. But you look tired, have you slept?"

"Not in days, it seems. I've lost track." Zu offered.

"Why not come with me then, the island it not far from here, and we could bathe in one of the many sacred springs and I could refresh you," she offered.

"Did I not carry you to see Rau in Tanis before the battle? Am I not in your debt entirely?'

When Zu and the Fore-Crone left the ship it slowed to a near dead stop in the water, as if its propulsive force had suddenly been snatched away. Levit, however, was no novice around ships and soon had her underway again. But of Zu there was no sign, and the Fore-Crone too was gone.

They made landfall at night on the southern edge of the island, beaching the ship on a small strand quite hidden from the rest of the island by tall cliffs. They were now five and without Zu they felt alone, isolated but more in control of their destiny. Quickly abandoning the ship they made for the rocks and began to climb inland. When they reached the top of the cliffs they began to travel west, in the direction of the city by the bay they had been told held the great temple. By night fall they were on the perimeter of cultivated fields and were beginning to see dwellings of those who maintained the land. They were beginning to look for a concealed place to camp for the night, when they heard the sounds of a terrific fight in front of them. Edging closer they saw a pitched fight between a troop of Set's soldiers and the island home guard. In the offing ships of an invasion fleet could be seen. Set's advance guard was clearing the beach of opposition for the invasion. And Set's troops were in difficulty.

When the five waded into the fracas in a rear attack, the home guard were taken by surprise and in that moment Set's swords drew enough blood to turn the battle into a rout. When the body count began, the Shadow Company discovered Rau giving orders. It did not take long to be required to explain how it was that Zu was not among them. Rau was taken off guard, entirely. He had expected Zu would have beaten him to the island, but he had not expected Zu to confront Isis alone. Rau joined the Shadow Company, left orders for the invasion to begin, and raced for the temple high above the city. Tristen was the first to reach the temple area but Levit and Dormor were not long in joining him. What amazed them was that the Central temple of the Hag was completely deserted. There were no defenders, no temple guard, and no high priestess to demand they return to the sea. It was entirely unexpected. Rau arrived with Boone and Quinn and charged into the temple itself. The great doors were standing wide open, the night winds blew through the halls whipping the flames in the great sconces on the walls into brilliance. The temple was bare. It had been stripped of all ritual gear. Nothing which could be taken as booty and nothing which could be ritually desecrated. In the central hall the highly polished stones were like mirrors against which the shadows of the wind whipped flames danced. The silence was unnerving. Behind this was a throne room and in the throne room a throne, and on the throne, Mira.

When the shadow company entered they were astonished again since the room was completely paved in gold. Its walls were gold plated; its ceiling was filled with golden tracery. Mira herself seemed to be a golden statue that is until she moved.

"Does Set's Chosen crave an audience with the power of this island? Has he come as a tourist or as a man interested in trade goods. Perhaps he thinks to come as a conqueror? Let Set's Chosen speak."

Rau was completely taken aback by the calmness of the Priestess when confronted by such powerful intruders. Surely she knew who he was and of what he was capable.

"I have come to conquer this island and destroy the temples of Isis and her accursed rituals forever. I will not sleep until the world is swept of her brood of haglings and men are free to rule as they see fit," Rau spoke loud enough that echo's could be heard through out the temple.

"Why would you destroy she who gives us life? Why would you defile the sacred places of she who freshens your wives and brings your children to term? Why would you pollute the sacred places of the force who fertilizes the crops and brings rain and sun and all good things to men and women? Why would you do this terrible thing?"

"She does none of these things you allege she does. Isis is a fraud; she is the power hungry woman who would trick men with knowledge of herbs and earthly forces. Any man can match her trickery if he is given the time to consider the workings of it."

"I see, so a man can bleed each month with the goddess's blessing, a man's belly can swell with new life, a man's breasts can produce milk, from a man's loins new life can be drawn? You are being comic, sir. Rau be serious. These are serious times."

"I am in deadly earnest; I bear the stone of Reckoning and the sacred blazes of Set. I am come to confront your goddess and pull down her high places," as he said this, Rau removed his armor and tunic and stood sky clad before Mira. He did not know how this was going to end, but he knew it was Set's time to act. From behind Mira's throne a second identical woman strode. Tristen knew who she was immediately, it was Elizabeth. He rushed toward her, but was stopped when she rebuked him.

"Husband, what are you doing in this sacred place? Why have you come to the sacred earth of the goddess? Do you not know that here lies the heel stone of all life and healing? Think what you do." Elizabeth stepped toward Rau, a penumbra of energy building around her unlike anything he had ever seen. Still Set did not manifest himself.

"From behind the throne a third being with the identical face stepped, it was Zu. He was walking as in a trance, energy poured off him as when a mountain stream hurls itself off a high ridge to become a waterfall. His sky clad form shocked Rau, since he seemed to be a man on fire. His radiant body was in flames. He was clearly possessed by Set.

Rau ran to him only to see him freeze as if in a paralytic fit. Around his neck a strange collar bore a huge gem stone.

"What have you done to my brother, Hag?" Free him and let the fight commence."

"I see, a fair fight, is that what you are after. You are a greater fool than I would have imagined you could be. Even now my fleet of 200 ships from all across the sea are bearing down on this island. By morning the burning hulks of ships and the cries of drowning men and women will fill the sea with terror. I have trapped your invasion fleet and your invasion force. Every able body man and woman on this island waits my call to attack you.

In their hands are the newest weapons Isis can devise.

They all are made of meteor metal, Set's Chosen. Not brass. The black metal of their swords will drink an ocean of blood tomorrow, and Set's rituals will be obliterated forever. The goddess does not fight by your rules, she fights to survive, and survive she will.

"What holds my brother?"

"Oh that. That is Queller, the counter weight to Quell-me-not. In the Great throne of the worlds founding it balanced Quell-me-not and cancelled its force. It has an amazing effect on the stone bearer don't you think. I gave it to him as a gift

When he arrived. He thought it so powerful he put it on without question."

When Set heard this news, he abandoned Zu and shifted his force to Rau. Rau felt the odor of Set curl around him and as he assumed the position, realized that without the fourteen he was probably not going to survive. Perhaps some of his priests would make it to the Temple before it was too late. They would know what to do, he thought as he fell into Set's abyss. Set took Rau as did Anubis, Horus, Ra, Min, and even Osiris. All the goods poured into Rau's form. As they did so his body seemed to swell, the ritual blazes burst into brilliant color and began to writhe. His warrior took armor until it was like brass. Zu collapsed without the support of Set in a resounding crash. As Set-Anubis-Ra-Horus-Min-Osiris-Rau stepped forward the Fore-Crone stepped out from behind the throne in her giantess form.

"The gods have no place in this sacred ground. Your presence here is foul and a desecration. It will no longer be tolerated. It is my task to remove you from this place if you do not leave of your own accord."

Set-Anubis-Ra-Horus-Min-Osiris-Rau laughed horribly. "You confront the entire pantheon of the gods yourself Fore-Crone. We know you are an ancient and titanic power, but really you are nothing here." A bolt of lightning shot from Set-Anubis-Ra-Horus-Min-Osiris-Rau which the Fore-Crone side-stepped easily. As he was beginning to mount a second attack, the Fore-Crone moved to the fallen Zu, turned him over on his back and pulled from his body the Mace of Ra. Where maleness had been was now femaleness, and in her hand the Fore-Crone held the true Mace. Set-Anubis-Ra-Horus-Min-Osiris-Rau was shocked to see the stone he had thought to wield stripped from him so easily. In the hands of the Fore-crone it was a terrifying weapon as it magnified her own power a thousand times over, and would not allow itself to be quenched. An arc of god's fire shot from Rau and struck the mace full on the Quell-me-not stone. The response was deafening and blinding. When the shadow company came to their senses, Mira was gone, Zu was gone, and the Fore-Crone and Elizabeth were gone. Rau was blackened, but unhurt, thanks to his infestation of gods. He was up and moving trying to discover where his adversary had gone. A quick survey of the temple, determined that the battle had moved onto the mountain. Bright lights were seen high on the mountain-top, and Rau and the shadow company began to climb as never before. Drums were heard on the mountain a strange tempo, order and yet chaos emerged from the sound which seemed to envelop the mountain top. As they raced upward, the very stones seemed to come alive.

Dormor was crushed beneath a huge megalith which seemed to clutch at him just outside the temple. Quinn stumbled and fell when one of the steps gave way. She was tumbling away to safety as only a trained thief might when she too was seen being trapped beneath another great stone. Levit was snatched by the Stone Mother as he paused to catch is breath. He had mistaken her for a statue. But it was not a statue that crushed his skull beneath her huge hands. Tristen and Boone followed the crazed Set-Anubis-Ra-Horus-Min-Osiris-Rau who seemed more to fly up the steps than run. At the summit, he paused confronting the lens of power for the first time. But he did not have to enter it, as the Fore-Crone attacked him with a plume of molten rock geysering from the Mace of Ra. Surprised, Rau was encased in the liquid rock, Boone was sure he had been incinerated and in his rage attacked the Fore-Crone himself. She buried him under tons of stone as he moved towards her in Berserker rage. Tristen was all who remained. With a mighty blow he struck the stone pillar where Set-Anubis-Ra-Horus-Min-Osiris-Rau had been. It shattered revealing Rau none the worse for wear. Tristen charged into the lens of power with Rau close on his back, only to confront four identical women and a golden beauty, Rau took to be Isis herself. Consequently his first attack was directly on her, gouts of coursicating fire poured from him enveloping her in withering incineration. But as she held Quell-me-not she was unharmed.

One of the women held up her arms. "Enough of this insanity." Her voice rocked the mountain top. Tristen and Rau came to a sudden and unexpected halt mid step. If you continue this I will obliterate the gods entirely from this earth. I will seal them up forever behind a wall of timid flesh. If you stop this battle, now there may be a way for us to live together in peace."

Rau screamed obscenities at the speaker and hurled himself at her bodily, his radiant form bursting to incandescence. Zu stepped into his path and said. "Brother, peace. Is there not a place for all of us here?" Set-Anubis-Ra-Horus-Min-Osiris-Rau incinerated Zu before the last word left his mouth. And in the split instant the unthinking incineration revealed itself to the Rau possessed by the gods. He recoiled in horror and tried to regain control of himself, but it was too late. Zu was gone.

Tristen launched his own attack against Isis, and Elizabeth stepped into his path, their young son in her arms. Tristen slaughtered them both in the Cup's madness. Mira blocked Tristen's path with her own body, bringing her ring of sundering up to encircle him. But he side stepped her and struck her down as well. Two remained. The Fore-Crone and the other identical woman. When Rau struck the Fore-Crone she opened her arms to receive the blow and enveloped Set-Anubis-Ra-Horus-Min-Osiris-Rau in her arms and carried him down to the floor and into the stone itself. Only Tristen remained. He turned on Isis herself and as he struck at her, she took her promised revenge. She enveloped Tristen with an enormous flow of power, and in him, she also enveloped every living human man. She sealed up the doors. Possession she made demonic and terrifying. Incarnation she stoppered altogether as a single event occurring only in myth. Dreams she blocked as insignificant. At the door of the magic plant she stationed two raging demons who would slaughter any who passed that way who was unprepared or unwilling to surrender. The Door of the sacred song she sealed with amnesia. The door of sexuality she sealed with Rape. The door of visions she sealed with insanity. One door only she left ajar, that of voices. The whispers of the gods would be enough, she thought to drive the gods insane with frustration, and to be so subtle men would never understand what it really was. The goddess stepped beyond the lens see the dark sky ablaze with the burning ships of the battle between her own fleet and those of Sets. As she moved back towards the lens of power, a wall of ivory blocked her way. She recognized it immediately, the tooth of Anubis. Behind her a stone collapsed upon her. The stone of reckoning. In a last attack the gods succeeded in sealing her away from her lens of power, her throne of domination. A dark cloud of unknowing swept across human civilization and the days of horror began. The gods were absent. The goddess blocked. In the silence men and women went silently quietly insane.

Alone among men, Tristen knew what had happened. He knew everything. He alone was not mad. His curse was that he knew what he'd done. He knew he'd slaughtered his own son and heir and the Beautiful Elizabeth as well. He knew the gods were gone, and Isis blocked. He knew that Civilization had to proceed as if there were gods and goddesses, but without access to any of them in the way human kind had known them. He became king of Crete, and the Prince of Sorrows. He became prince of sorrows because he alone knew the awful isolation of a godless world.

978-0-595-67608-8
0-595-67608-1